MW01251403

Beyond Revenge

Beyond Revenge

Godfrey Wray

First printing July 2005

This is a work of fiction. Names, characters, places and incidents either are the product of the author's imagination or are used fictitiously, and any resemblance to any actual persons, living or dead, events, or locales is entirely coincidental.

This book was printed in Georgetown, Guyana.

CONTENTS

GODFREY WRAY

To my Mother—Edna (Barbara) Wray

A child is nothing
A mother is everything
It's never too late
To appreciate

and

Also to my courageous sister-in-law,
Marcia, whosc petite body warmed
a huge heart.

Acknowledgments

This book should have had twenty-eight chapters instead of the twenty-seven you're about to read. However, my experienced editor advised—nay, admonished—me about the wisdom of having eight pages of names of persons I wanted to acknowledge. And I bowed to his superior judgment.

But I insisted on a few.

Special thanks to my wife Leslyn, my six children and their mothers, my patient relatives, my inexhaustible supply of friends, especially from the Albouystown YMCA, and an indomitable spirit named Sandra.

As always, my dearly departed mother, Edna (Barbara), took pride of place on earth; and now in heaven, she jostles with the Creator to fully open the door of opportunity that had been left ajar so long.

Thanks to a real friend, Kester Alves, with whose death I have yet to come to grips. He and another brilliant journalist, Carl Blackman, always felt I had more to offer and exercised infinite patience, urging my coming of age.

My buddy, Oliver Hinckson, read the first part of this manuscript, and his copyediting scalpel set the stage for the final effort. Another associate, Handel Andrews, a brilliant historian, performed corrective surgery, then stamped the seal of approval.

My youngest son Jason, Vincent Small, Mrs. Yvonne Holder (who ofttimes challenged my cavalier use of the Queen's language), Rannie Johnson, Dennis Nelson, and my brother, Estwick Northe, must also stand out for special mention.
Without them and countless others, this effort would have been futile.
I had cause to consult scores of books and Web sites while preparing this work, far too many to name individually So too the many other

persons I shamelessly bothered in my attempt to check facts and details.

It is not easy to turn unstructured and disparate thoughts into a novel.

I truly thank all those who helped me along the way.

Prologue

Even in her terror, she could only think of the white man as "Lucifer" as his hands squeezed her breasts and cruelly pinched her nipples after having violently ripped the blouse from her bosom.

He was trying desperately to get aroused, but the alcohol in his system served more as a depressant than as an aphrodisiac. She vaguely remembered Shakespeare or some other poet writing, "Alcohol increases the desire, but lessens the performance."

He must have read her uncomplimentary thoughts, for suddenly, without fanfare, he viciously spread her legs and forcibly entered her, effecting a grinding assault of her body and senses.

"Oh God, please let them stop," she screamed silently, but Lucifer's eventual, gasping climax was the only answer to her prayer.

Then it was the smooth-talking black man's turn. He was somewhat merciful, wanting, it seemed, only to mark his name in the night's deed book.

She couldn't decide whether to catalog him as "Slick" or "Quick."

And then followed "Don Juan."

He had been "Master of the Game," engineering, prompting, and directing. He now unbuttoned the fly of his Calvin Klein slacks, knelt, and unceremoniously mounted her, his vacuous eyes riveted on her tortured green orbs.

Despite her misery, Ruth's sixth sense made her look searchingly at her Spanish-speaking tormentor. What she saw sparked a feeling of dread: violence and sadism roiling behind a patina of indifference.

She stopped struggling, countering violation with impassivity. And very soon, a shudder signaled an end to her ordeal.

She lay there insensate as Don Juan gathered his cronies and made a strategic exit from the scene. But not before the leader plucked a hundred-dollar bill from her ripped shirt pocket, the first such note she had earned in her life.

She was not likely to forget that day, when she was raped and robbed in the United States of America—the democratic capital of the world, where every person was guaranteed the protection of the law.

Bruised and hurting, Ruth Elizabeth Ferreira, whose call name was Lizzie, remembered how Lucifer had challenged her to a winner-take-all third game of pool after she had won the first and allowed him to take the second. She had protested, but his male ego would not let him settle for a draw.

She had then pocketed the ultimate black ball with a textbook cross-cushion shot of geometric precision that defied explanation. It was not the toughest shot she had ever played, but Catholic priest Father Clement O'Hara would have been proud. After all, it was he who had taught her, his accuracy and acumen products of many an Irish pool hall.

Lucifer was a bad loser, calling her a cheap hustler. Don Juan and Slick made him apologize, and it was under the umbrella of peace and goodwill that she had accepted their offer of a drink after politely declining an invitation to "do the town."

She was almost sure it was somewhere between the first and second margaritas when she had been slipped either a Mickey Finn or Spanish Fly, and this had made her drowsy and nauseous.

She had rushed to the ladies' room and, with the aid of a finger, induced regurgitation of all she had in her stomach.

Dizzy and faint, she hesitantly accepted the offer of a ride to the Flatbush YMCA in Brooklyn, New York, where she was staying.

All three gentlemen volunteered to ensure her safety, and she felt secure as they addressed one another in strict military parlance— private this, corporal that, and sergeant the other.

She fell asleep along the way, only to be rudely awakened when her panties were being ripped from her body in the dank loneliness of a heavily forested area.

She was a devout Catholic, an Amerindian whose grandmother had descended from the ultra-aggressive Carib tribe of the West Indies and South America and whose grandfather was a progeny of the black English middle class, sometimes mockingly called Afro-Saxon. She had been painstakingly tutored by an Irish priest stationed in her river village, had progressed to become a commissioned officer in the Guyana Defence Force, and had been sent to New York on an international mission.

She could not believe what had happened to her. She felt rather than saw the darkness of midnight creeping up on her. She was very tired.

Tired from thinking and from trying to dredge up pleasant memories. Scenes flashed before her eyes; a montage of incidents without meaning or coherence. She kept seeing a Catholic priest, a beautiful long-haired woman, and a precocious little girl with close-cropped hair. Those persons came superimposed on scenery that signified rural pasturing and communal living.

She couldn't remember having ever been in such a state—so uncertain of herself. Her mother Margaret and Father O'Hara had always been her bookends, her life supports—she was in the center, buttressed by two slices of love and adoration.

They were always there for her, but now on her first North American mission, she lay spread-eagled, bruised, and violated.

Unbidden, Psalm 23:6 came into her mind:

Surely goodness and mercy shall follow me
All the days of my life
And I will dwell in the house of the Lord
Forever.

I kept my part of the bargain. I was good, the best I could be, and where was the mercy I should have received? she asked herself bitterly.

As for dwelling in the house of the Lord, that wasn't going to happen again. She had been betrayed by Father O'Hara, the whole Catholic Church, and the God she had come to love so much, talking to Him daily.

Where were they when three despicable predators had drugged her and despoiled her body, rendering asunder the membrane of everything she considered inviolate? How could the same God who had consistently answered her prayers, albeit in His own time, turn His back on her in her most desperate moment? Was this Almighty asleep in his heaven while she was being desecrated?

Unholy thoughts and a dark fury clouded clear thinking as the battle with doubt raged in her head.

But one thing was very clear to her. In this bastion of democracy where she had had absolutely no say in her humiliation, she now had the democratic right to dispense her own justice. She had been taught that courage and patience were keys to moral fiber.
She was now going to draw heavily on both.

Fortuitously, she had glimpsed the license plate of Lucifer's

Ford Explorer, and the three letters and four numbers had been etched in her brain.

A faint smile pushed past the grimace on her face as she straightened herself From a recumbent position to get her beatings. Her mind-set precluded clear thinking, but as a church bell somewhere signaled midnight, ironically a Father O'Hara mantra entered her head: "Yesterday is history. Tomorrow is a mystery. Today is a gift."

A new day was dawning.

Three simple lessons would be taught in New York and a big score settled back home in Guyana.

She silently vowed to accomplish them without help from any source.

> *To everything there is a season,*
> *A time for every purpose under heaven:*
> *A time to love*
> * And a time to hate*
> *A time of war*
> * And a time of peace*

Chapter 1

Georgetown, Guyana

At five minutes to noon on Good Friday, the holiest day on the Catholic calendar, Father Clement O'Hara was in fine fettle, softly humming a racy ditty he had composed for the church's enthusiastic youth band.

The priest was Irish by birth, but since taking up duties in Guyana, the former English colony of British Guiana on the tip of South America, he had been ensnared by the infectious music of the wider Caribbean, especially the tantalizing lyrics of Trinidad and Tobago's calypso and the pulsating rhythm of Jamaica's reggae.

And so the tune he was quietly working in his head was influenced by the famous Jamaican Bob Marley's "Rivers of Babylon"— an adaptation of the popular Psalm 137. That rendition was one of the finest pieces of soul- inspired music he had ever heard, and throughout the years, he hummed it incessantly.

He adjusted his soutane and walked out the presbytery, which was across the way from the magnificently ornate Cathedral of the Immaculate Conception, standing like a divine reproach over Georgetown, the capital city.

More than half the Christian population of Guyana was Catholic, but few bothered with the church's official appellation, opting instead for "Brickdam Cathedral," which was easier on their tongues.

Although there was no pedestrian crossing, traffic yielded silently, and the priest and his ten bedecked altar boys crossed the road.

The hot asphalt underfoot hastened their pace as the clergyman took amused notice of the galaxy of vehicles parked bumper-to-bumper around the perimeter of the church's compound, along busy Brickdam Drive and on the parallel side streets.

Father O'Hara's benign grin blossomed into a full smile as he surveyed the mass of humanity in their Sunday best, for he knew that all those who could not find the time to enter the portals of places of worship throughout the year made sure they did so on that particular day.

Good Friday was not only a must-go day, it was the day to make a fashion statement, what with such a captive audience.

Unnoticed, he shook his head as he thought how sad it was that over the years, the charade had become more manifest—church- going habits dictated by clothing rather than conviction.

The priest genuflected and ascended the marble altar that was tastefully adorned with red roses, orchids, crimson peonies, bougainvillea, and the common daisies.

Father O'Hara was a consummate innovator and refused to be hamstrung by age-old boundaries and shaky beliefs. Some of his fellow priests sometimes thought he sailed too close to the proverbial wind, but his unorthodox approach kept the cathedral full, and the bishop seemed unperturbed.

The mass had reached its liveliest point when Father O'Hara, with exaggerated panache and ceremony, announced that the spanking new band would use biblical text to intone the deep feelings of slave descendants, some of whom were right there in the audience.

The sultry voice of the lead singer had only to utter the opening stanza of "Rivers of Babylon" and the mass choir of eight hundred congregants joined in. .

It was a contest between lusty vocalizing and unbridled enthusiasm.

But above the holy cacophony, there rose an overriding operatic contralto. Heads turned surreptitiously to seek out this welcome intrusion, and the chorus of discordant contributions quietly suffered a natural death.

The priest felt a chill up his spine. The last time he had heard such a melodious voice was some seventeen years ago in a small village up the mighty Essequibo River. It was a haunting reminder of the halcyon days when he was a rookie at his first rural posting. There, he had helped inflate flat, uninspiring vocal delivery into powerful arias and ballads on a scale that equaled the one he was now hearing.

He let his Irish brogue take over and, as conductor, signaled the enthusiastic players to expend less energy. An allegro duet ensued as Zion became Africa and Babylon took the form of the New World to which African men and women had been dragged in chains.

He descended the altar as if directed by some magnetic force over which he had no control.

Down the aisle, twenty pews from the front, there she stood, beating a silent tattoo in the palm of a hand with a Chinese fan, voice unwavering.

The Essequibo River, the river of Babylon, and the river of emotion that coursed through his veins—all suddenly coalesced into a confluence that threatened to engulf him in time. The song ended, the rivers stopped flowing, and the beginning of light applause soon became a pleading encore.

Never had this venerable edifice, accustomed to requiems and dirges, been transformed by such operatic entertainment.

The liturgy was always the same as centuries before, the hymns no different. But that day, the high dome, which enhanced the acoustics, seemed to resonate with new life.

Father O'Hara had to raise his voice for an end to the applause and a return to the accustomed pious ambience.

The rest of the two-hour mass went in a blur, the priest handing over control to his patently appreciative assistant, though this overt gesture was not motivated by altruistic urging, but by an urgent desire to control his ragged, inconsistent breathing.

It was indeed Margaret, whom everyone called Maggie.

He had first seen her when she was sixteen—a brash upstart on the verge of becoming a recluse. By eighteen, he had engineered a total transformation, and she became an ebullient young woman—bright, outgoing and quick to laugh.

He never openly admitted it, but she was always his crutch when his spirits flagged.

Here, Father O'Hara's mind went into reverse like a cassette being rewound, and he remembered all too clearly the two most pivotal points of his life—crossroads in the shifting sands of time.

Thirty years ago, in the United Kingdom, he had been teetering precariously at the edge of an emotional and spiritual abyss, and he had opted to save souls instead of saving lives as the doctor he could have become.

Two years later, in the equatorial climate of Guyana's interior, he had struggled with serious theological doubts. But Maggie's challenge had made him hold on to his faith as his body and mind had been sorely tested time and again.

Maggie had gone on to win scholarship after scholarship—academic, sports, music and drama—until she decided she really wanted to be a teacher. Training College was followed by several stints at premiere grammar schools and she quickly rose to the prestigious position of senior mistress at a very early age.

Now Maggie was here in his church, taking control as usual in her unassuming manner.

It wasn't easy for him. In fact, it had taken him a considerable time to recover his emotional balance, and he covered his discomfiture by taking her hand and leading her to the first pew, empty except for two lonely Bibles.

Her lips, so fragile and vulnerable without the ostentation of lipstick mesmerized Father O'Hara. Her eyes, as always, were like pools of mystery and playful mischief, and he did not like the queasy feeling in his stomach.

He was scared of Maggie, more than he would admit. She stirred feelings in him that lay dormant for a very long time. Her openness and expressive nature added to the allure.

It had always been that way.

She reminded him so much of his Patricia, an exquisite Irish creature he wanted to marry in his youth. Her drunken stepfather had battered her senseless when she threatened to expose his unwanted advances to the entire village in Northern Ireland.

She had lain comatose for one week before succumbing.

Father O'Hara, then Clement O'Hara, a robust twenty-four-year-old university student, had lost all control, stripping the criminal stepfather and whipping him with a leather bullwhip along the entire length of the community's main street. The fact that it was three o'clock in the afternoon, the time when schools released their students for the day, served more as an incentive than a mitigating factor.

All the villagers knew about the incident, but when the police came to investigate, none corroborated the miscreant's story.

Meantime, the village elders hurriedly packed O'Hara off to a London seminary for immediate posting overseas.

They were now in a small private room next to the vestry and behind the main altar. The lambent flames of hanging candles cast dancing shadows on the walls and ceilings. He was suddenly jarred out of his reverie. Margaret was saying something, already into her second sentence.

"You took control of her life, like your own daughter. I never objected because you were the only person capable of bringing out the best in her. But you shaped her life and steered her into the army, fashioning her into some kind of female Rambo. You knew my concerns, but you never took my side. Now, you have to take some of the blame because I dreamt last night that something happened to her."

The evidence offered in that tirade was a little unfair, he thought, especially since he did not know what she was talking about.

"Father, something has happened to Lizzie. Do something. Call the army. I just know. The spirits of my ancestors have spoken to me."

Her only child's name was Ruth Elizabeth Ferreira, and she almost always used either of the two Christian names. When he heard her say "Lizzie," he knew for sure that she was not her normal self.

"Maggie, calm yourself Only yesterday, I received a postcard from Lizzie, and she said she was okay."

"I got one too. But it was posted two weeks ago. Since then, something has happened. You should know I've never been wrong when I get visitations."

The priest was a man of exceptional learning, a graduate of the university of life—and street smart. Also, he had abiding respect for the native beliefs and traditions of the Amerindians.

There were nine tribes in Guyana, and although each had variations, as a whole, they all strongly believed in the spirit world. According to folklore, this animism placed good and evil spirits in the heavens, lands, trees, animals, rocks, water and people; and for hundreds of years, they have held firmly to the belief of spirit communication.

An uneasy feeling took control of the priest; the mere idea of anything happening to the daughter he had adopted in the sight of the Lord was disturbing. It took all he had to keep a tight lid on the thought of the possibility of a debilitating vacuum in his life.

"Father, what if God didn't protect her from something terrible? Why would He let something happen to her?" she asked. "I feel it in my bones. This is not just intuition. What are we going to do?" she demanded.

Father O'Hara pretended not to hear the searching questions, boldly blunting their sharpness with a thrusting query of his own.

"With all that you've been taught, why do you fly in the face of the Lord without cause?" he countered.

"I'm sorry, Father, but I can't think right. But let me ask you a question. We are the two people she loves the most, and in the past, we connected on what you call the astral plane at some time or the other. Haven't you felt anything funny?"

"Not really" he replied, his laconic response intended to be a mendacious evasion, as some diplomats explain away minor shifts from the truth.

Maggie discerned the slight hesitation in his response and unceremoniously rushed to him, gripping his neck and sobbing uncontrollably.

"Father, you are not telling me the truth. I can tell. I know you well enough."

Father O'Hara wanted to remind her that prevarication was a luxury priests could not afford. But no words came. His pulse was racing. The contact with a woman's body, one as sensuous and voluptuous as Maggie's, was all so sudden, like a flash fire. Self-control almost flew out of the church's stained glass windows.

Outwardly serene and lightly patting her shoulders, he was burning inside. How could he tell her he had had bad dreams, seeing his Patricia at first, then Lizzie after, being relentlessly pursued by demons? How could he speak of other dreams in which she always appeared naked?

He hugged Maggie and prayed fervently for her and Lizzie and for his own body and soul. He wondered if self-flagellation would lessen his guilt.

She untangled her sinewy arms, looked at him straight in the eyes; and blurted, "Father, please don't let us down. You are her godfather, the only father she knows and the only father she wants. She wrote me a letter, and it was all about you and how all you taught her was now manifesting itself. You're her Father no matter what. Don't let her down, Father," she implored.

He watched her with concern and a little trepidation. Speech was still beyond him. All he could do was try to breathe normally, think rationally, and act calmly. He was at his wit's end, attempting to comprehend the thrusting of accountability for Lizzie on his shoulders as if he somehow bore the responsibility of paternity.

Why was she doing this? Why was the father she kept secret from Lizzie not brought into the picture at this crucial time?

He never fully understood Maggie when she was a leggy teenager enjoying life to its fullest, and now, as a matured single-minded parent, he felt more out of depth.

He wished he could go for a long swim in rough waters to let the tide wash away the mistakes, doubts, and now immoral thoughts and dreams that had lifelike qualities. He felt he was a danger to himself and the church.

And he knew the root of it all—the doubt, which would always exist, after one fateful night when a dream seemed so real, and the embarrassing evidence next morning added to the perplexity.

Chapter 2

Brooklyn, New York

Noon was sixty seconds away, and the Brooklyn park was serenely peaceful on this Good Friday—just another ordinary working day in the commerce-driven Big Apple. The New York midday sun struggled to penetrate heavy, opaque clouds enwrapping the area like a shroud. A bell tolled discordantly in the distance as if the ringer was in a hurry to dash off to lunch.

For Lizzie, it was the signal she had been waiting for. She knew that the next few minutes could determine the rest of her life. She had to see a certain man up close, see if he had a deep gouge on the left side of his face, the only real damage she had managed to inflict in her moments of terror.

A shrill whistle sounded, and almost immediately, the massive front door of the corporate complex across the square burst open, disgorging a teeming mass of white-collared workers scattering in various directions.

Elizabeth, for that is what she preferred to be called, stretched her neck like a periscope atop a submarine, searching for a tall, petulant, red-headed white male with blotched, pallid skin. She shuddered as she remembered another vital piece of information, the fact that he was abnormally hirsute and had large clumps of black hair on his hands.

She nervously looked at her watch. Two minutes had passed and there was no sign of the brute she had named Lucifer.

She was close to panic.

For four days, she had observed him from a distance, and his lunchtime routine was a virtual ritual.

It was always a leisurely stroll across the park, a seat on the third corrugated iron bench, followed by the unzipping of a sturdy canvas food container. Sounds of mastication would be followed by generous gulps from a giant bottle of diet soda, all the while, his Adam's apple moving like a slow-speed piston in a well-oiled cylinder.

Today, she had planned to get close enough to make the final confirmation, and then she would force-feed him a dose of his own medicine. Never again would he join with others to take advantage of vulnerable women.

However, she was getting ahead of herself. For to impart a lesson, a teacher needed the presence of a pupil, and it looked like today, Lucifer was going to be absent.

At last, there he was, a wild mop of auburn hair, scything through the crowd, heading for his rendezvous with nature.

She was relieved, and the exhilaration she suddenly felt was not unlike the excitement she had experienced years ago when she was awarded her black belt in kara-do, a bastard combination of conventional karate and judo. She was the first female to achieve this feat in Guyana, a mineral-rich country in South America, which is culturally linked to the Caribbean.

She sat down quickly, adjusted her sunglasses, and leaned on her derelict shopping cart—just another bag lady with no place to go.

He passed her with a glance full of disdain, cataloging her presence as part of the social flotsam and jetsam that upright, hardworking people like him had to endure in the immigrant-populated city. And he instinctively turned up his nose at the sight of thick rows of dreadlocks cascading past her shoulders, almost to her waist.

Impatience gnawed at her, but she willed herself to stay put. There was no rush. Time was on her side.

Then he turned his head, and she saw the six-inch welt on his cheek.

The tumblers in her head fell into place, and she sprang into motion after his second bite into what looked like a homemade burger.

Her movements were normally characterized by subtlety, grace, or poise. There were none of those now. One minute, they were a world apart, and the next, she was in his face, whipping off the dingy-looking New York Jets cap and the sunglasses with such sleight-of-hand movement that, in less confrontational circumstances, an encore might have been in order.

A casual question broke the silence: "Do you remember me?"

Their eyes met and locked; his narrowed in bewilderment and hers belligerent and focused.

It was the color of her eyes that provided the catalyst for immediate recognition. and the shock that followed, and it was as if he had been struck by a bolt of lightning.

The last time he had been so close to those piercing Irish green eyes was about a week before, across a pool table, after she had whipped him for a hundred-dollar bet.

"I'm the girl you and your two friends had fun with the other night," she said calmly, as if making an inconsequential remark about the weather.

Confusion contorted his countenance into a mask of indecision. His face mirrored the perplexity of a child caught between lights at the famous bewildering junction of Nostrand and Flatbush avenues in Brooklyn.

For several seconds, he could neither move nor utter a sound. His trademark Adam's apple bobbed irregularly, like a canoe adrift in an angry sea.

Too much time had passed. She could not allow him any respite to gather his thoughts. She hit his windpipe with a deft karate chop and felt gratification as bread, meat, and salad flew in different directions.

It was a devastating blow, meant not to disable, but to disorient.

He gasped for air and found he couldn't muster a coherent thought.

His mind wandered uncertainly, meandering through a labyrinth of confusion.

How was it possible, he thought raggedly, that a mere wisp of a girl weighing at most 140 pounds could incapacitate an ex-United States soldier who, only last week, had tipped the company doctor's scale at 164 pounds?

The answer came with a resounding kick to the groin. One minute, he was getting up from a sitting position; the next, he was flat on his back, both hands locked in protective embrace of his private parts. A split second of flight—up and down in the blink of an eye.

Another well-aimed kick, embossed in steel-tipped Timberland boots added to his pain. However, this excruciating blow, although crippling in intent, served to galvanize him into some sort of action.

He felt rage, hot and searing, as he jumped up from a kneeling posture. But what should have been a second's worth of motion seemed like an eternity.

He was now like a bemused creature scuttling in crablike manner, vainly attempting to regain equilibrium, but achieving little success.

And pain had now become a close friend, clinging with unwanted intensity.

In his military glory days, he had been a bruising middleweight boxing contender and had also put in many hours on the wrestling mat. But for all of that, it had not prepared him for a rumble in the jungle or, more aptly, an object lesson in the park.

His assailant's hands and legs were like windmills, coming from all directions, and he was powerless and certainly in no shape to weather this obvious storm of revenge. She had the stage to herself, alternating as actor and producer, and he was an unwilling participant in the one-dimensional pantomime.

Never in his life did he pray so fervently. As a staunch Catholic, the words of the Lord's Prayer came readily to him, but for some strange reason, his thoughts were being translated in Latin.

Why was he thinking in a foreign language when a mad woman was delivering terribly devastating blows while making unflattering references to his manhood and muttering blasphemous epithets in standard English? he wondered.

Hands outstretched in supplication, he stuttered, "Oh my God! Why are you doing this to me?"

The invocation and rhetorical question brought an appreciated halt to the pummeling for a brief while.

A mockingly melliferous voice answered his question with queries of its own.

"Why? Don't you know why? Have you lost your memory? Have a good look at me. I am going to be your worst nightmare. I want you to remember me always."

With those words, chilling in their intensity, she pulled a long zip on her black cat suit, and the garment slipped past her hips and lay in a bundle at her feet. She was stark naked.

A perfect body carved by a master sculptor, made imperfect by the many welts and bruises he had helped to put there.

Involuntarily, his mouth opened wide as if he were in a dentist's chair; and despite his precarious position, he was assailed by a curious amalgam of desire and regret.

But there was no more time for sightseeing. The cat suit was back in place, and abject hatred was replaced with utter contempt.

More blows rained down on him, immediately spurring a flashback to the chatty patron behind him in the cinema not so long ago, who, amidst a one-man kung fu demolition of a dozen bad guys, kept shouting in some sort of Caribbean lingua, "Blows like old clothes."

It sounded trite then, but now, in this milieu, it was realistic.

She was now tired, spent, and very disappointed.

She had expected some form of opposition, some resistance, some aggression. Instead, she had faced an enemy who obviously could only rise to the challenge when imbued with bottled spirits and bolstered by the presence of co-conspirators.

She had vowed to track down the three culprits who had raped her and do them serious bodily harm. This first foray was seen as the litmus test of her "get even" commitment, but somehow, she seemed unable or unwilling to deliver the *coup de grace*.

Meanwhile, Lucifer had taken advantage of her introspection to crawl a few yards, but she was not done with him.

Covering the distance in a few strides, she grabbed him by the lapels of his spring coat, sat astride him, and looked unblinkingly at him. He could feel the heat radiating from her blazing eyes as she effortlessly raised him into a sitting position

"Remember me always," she commanded and kissed him lightly.

He blinked.

And in that fleeting second, she rocked back and sent him into a state of oblivion with a crunching head butt, the sound of which seemed to reverberate throughout the park.

She ripped a leather wallet from his pocket, extracted all the bills, and then threw the still-bulging, credit card-saturated billfold onto the ground beside him.

*   *   *

Tears most often exorcise emotions. And right there, Lizzie's exorcism was enacted, undignified and unnoticed. .

Hugging the dilapidated shopping cart, she cried for an interminable period, hoping to wash away the stain of hurt and cleanse her mind of further revengeful thoughts for the moment.

And her tears were indeed cathartic, instilling a calm she had not felt for a long time.

She had shut certain passages of the Good Book out of her mind, especially the part, which says, "Don't repay evil for evil. Wait for the Lord to handle thy matter." And also another, which advises, "Love your enemies! Do good to them! It was times like these when Christians challenged the word of God and became atheists and nihilists, she thought. How could you love a beast that has no respect for humanity? Wait how long? she wondered.

Lizzie had a phenomenal memory, but some bits of information were more indelibly inscribed than others. One such was from Father O'Hara, her spiritual mentor, who had jocularly told of himself as an errant youth embracing the mantra "Revenge is sweeter when the other person would have forgotten."

Lizzie wiped her eyes with her fingers, removed the dreadlocked wig from her head and placed it in her borrowed cartful of trash, then walked across the park to a police car idling by the entrance. "Officer, a man was just mugged in the park over there."

With barely a glance at her, the lawman slammed the car into gear and sped off in the direction of the pointing finger.

Lizzie felt somewhat relieved after that bit of benevolence. Somehow, she felt less guilty.

In the meantime, the dark clouds had disappeared, giving way to brilliant sunshine.

Unconsciously, she turned right and then left, and before she realized it, she was standing in front of a Gothic-styled cathedral whose towers dominated the landscape in that part of Brooklyn.

Unhesitatingly, she mounted the church steps and walked inside. She dipped her index finger in the font and then made the sign of the cross before genuflecting in the aisle and kneeling in the front pew under the penetrating glare of several stone saints.

It was no time for confession. It was time to have a long conversation with the Man Above, He who controlled destiny.

She was not going to remonstrate with Him for allowing that dreadful thing to happen. He had puzzling ways of doing things. Maybe it was a test, however horrible.

But what about that oft-repeated psalm, "He keeps you from all evil and preserves your life. He keeps his eyes upon you as you come and go, and always guards you."

She began in earnest, "In nomine patris, et fillu, et spiritus sancti." Then followed her prayers, tumbling out in staccato fashion, in that age-old language that Catholics were trying so hard to keep alive.

" Latin will never die, " Father O'Hara had one day replied with certainty to a brash youngster who had queried its relevance in modern times. The priest had not elaborated, aware that elucidation would only fall on deaf ears.

Lizzie recited twenty Hail Marys, then walked to the rail of the main altar to beseech God through the imposing alabaster statue that dwarfed all others. She begged forgiveness for forgetting Matthew's word: "Your heavenly Father will forgive you if you forgive those who sin against you."

Lizzie was a practical person, aware that she did not have the time to wait for divine forgiveness. She knew from praying for mundane things, that her God took His own time to answer.

Disconsolate and dissatisfied, she headed for the door, unsure of the next move. The midday sun shone with intensity, breaching the shade of the domed skylight and stained-glass windows, casting myriad moving shadow amidst the pews and along the aisles.

She threw up her hand to protect her eyes. Just then, a priest, who the spitting image of Father O'Hara, touched her shoulder lightly and said without inflection or irony, "My child, I can see the worry on your face. Throw off your problems. God will look after you. Just do what you have to do. Don't linger over it."

Lizzie did not break stride. Had she heard correctly? she wondered. Was it a message from Father O'Hara? Was it a mirage?

Never a procrastinator and being an army officer, she knew that indecision in the wink of an eye could mean life or death for those expecting guidance.

In a flash, she was out of the door, out of the gate, heading away from the park, which was awash with police cars and an ambulance paying noisy attention to Lucifer.

Though the sun was still at its zenith, she felt oddly cold, an unfamiliar chord vibrating in her spine like a badly tuned guitar in the hands of novice.

But there was no turning back.

The strident voice in her head said, "One down, two to go."

A voice from afar intoned, "Dominus vobiscum."

Chapter 3

Army Compound, Guyana

Colonel Roger Benson, a military icon in the Guyana Defence Force, was in no mood to be trifled with. His world was in danger of being torn apart, a world he had patiently constructed.

In his previous job as a prison warden, he had come face to face with the country's degenerate underclass, and he had fought many battles, mentally and physically, with the underworld's worst. When he joined the army, he had to deal with another rough breed of unsophisticated recruits .

But his current problem involved a different kind of battle. The opposition was formidable—a supremely confident young female officer, who, although being a single unit in a prestigious army of over twenty thousand, was indeed a formidable army of one.

And the disturbing news had come at an extremely inopportune time.

Amid a particularly satisfying early morning sexual encounter with a new female officer recruit, he had been interrupted by the ringing of a telephone. A call on the regular phone would be swiftly handled by his answering machine. But this was the red phone, whose number only a handful of people possessed. Regretfully, he disengaged his body from the sinuous bundle under him and padded to an alcove in a far corner.

"Hello." A long pause.

"What?" A longer pause.

"When?"

He had a gift for succinctness, easily bored with extended sentences and long speeches—a misologist of sorts.

In the meantime, the young female was listening carefully to the monologue. She felt sure the next word would be "where."

She lost her silent bet, for the next word was harshly expelled.

"How?"

This handsome, debonair man never failed to amaze her. She had been warned that he was a consummate philanderer with no serious intention. But she was going to prove those doubters wrong and further her career in the process, she thought confidently.

Her reflections were rudely interrupted by a brutal, authoritative command.

"I don't care how. Find the subject and isolate. Spare no expenses. Good. Call me on my cell anytime. Thanks, pal."

"What's wrong, Colonel?" she asked peevishly. Even in bed, she addressed him as a senior officer—a not dissimilar habit with the long string of bed warmers. It was his bearing, his quiet authority that did the trick.

"Sorry, got to go. Big emergency."

"Please, don't leave me halfway."

"Halfway is better than no way. Don't you remember chapter 3 in your manual, the part about making the best of any situation? C'mon, soldier, time for a different kind of action."

He moved around the bedroom with silent purpose. Anger was in his deportment and impatience in his stride.

He was trying hard to be civil, but lines of worry furrowed his brow. It was the first time she had seen him so unsure of himself. In the two months she had known him, she had not imagined this seemingly fearless man could possibly be prone to worry.

But worried he was, and though he was working hard to disguise his concern, whatever was the matter at hand, it seemed to be woefully unsettling.

And so Colonel Benson had no time for "BS" at the first meeting of the day.

He acknowledged Lieutenant John Gibson's salutations and grunted, "Proceed."

Gibson eschewed scholarship. His diction was immaculate, but he was a boring speaker. His affectations, mostly comical, were synchronized with his delivery, almost as if he had extensive theatrical training.

Asking him to use restrictive or less-effusive terminology was a big no-no with him. So when the colonel told him to "get on with it" and present his report without ambiguity, the young subaltern took umbrage.

"Do you want precise details as is customary in the civil service, or do you want an unstructured discourse?" This was all said in a supercilious disdainful manner.

The officer consulted his wrinkled palms as if seeking the answer, unconsciously rising from his chair in the first movement towards crushing the little tadpole in front of him. But the slight pressure on his rigid wrist from a delicate hand quelled the riot in his head, and he regained control immediately.

"My son, tell it anyhow you want."

Everyone in the room was circumspect, knowing that the "my son" admonition was the ultimate red flag, clearly stating that the boss was at the end of his tether; and from that point, those who were tiptoeing would be doing so on hot coals, very hot coals indeed.

Everyone knew except Mr. "Prim and Proper" Gibson, whose idea of winning a battle was getting in the last word.

"I object vehemently to being addressed as your child, since we obviously don't share the same genes, I am definitely not a progeny of yours, nor am I your ward."

The gentle pressure on the colonel's hand had tightened with every word delivered, and by the end of Gibson's delivery, it was like a prisoner's restraining strap. But the laws of physics say that a red-hot iron cannot be completely cooled with a single immersion into water.

"Get on with it, you little punk. If your joke report wasn't absolutely necessary, I would kick your ass all the way to Kaieteur Falls."

As the crow flies, that would be a distance of hundreds of miles, and everyone in the assembly, except Gibson, chuckled.

The colonel whispered to the woman officer, Yolande Belgrave, of the firm restraining hand, "Sorry about the bad language."

A soft pat on his hand told him that he was excused, but it would cost him something, sometime in the future.

If looks could kill, Gibson would have died, been buried, and his body waiting to rise on the third day. He could literally feel the contempt hovering like a dark cloud over his head while blue skies and sunlight brightened other parts of the universe. He knew genuine fear. Not for his physical well-being, but for his future, which he was sure would be littered with choice words like "little shit," "my child," and "kick your ass."

Every time he heard those words and that of the majestic world wonder Kaieteur, they would evoke memories of that day when he had earned the scorn of a seasoned cadre of professionals.

Colonel Benson heard not a word.

He only realized that Gibson had uncharacteristically cut short his dissertation when the room's silence became increasingly deafening. He peered at the people in the room through the gaps between the ten digits that covered his face. He was miles away in Brooklyn, New York, on the ground organizing a reconnaissance to pinpoint the enemy. "Colonel?" his second in command worriedly enquired.

There was a slight pause. Then the senior officer said, "Take over, Major Livingstone. I've got an emergency."

This was neither the time for semantics nor empty debate. He did not have the patience for otiose people like Gibson, whom he put in the same category as those rude reporters who continued to pester him daily with inane queries and ridiculous suggestions.

He remembered his early days in the nascent Guyana National Service before transferring to the defence force, where he had taken up arms in defence of his country and other third world nations aligned with it, then followed his meteoric rise through drive and ambition.

He was also there at Jonestown in 1978, though it was more of a mop-up operation—an eminently successful one for him.

He was not a toy soldier brandishing a ream of O and A levels. He was an action soldier. The executive codgers were the ones to sit and talk all day while getting soft and fat. Some couldn't even fit their tunics, their only exercise amounting to running around trying to keep track of their soldier-mistresses, who often played foot-and-loose with the younger brigade. He reflected cynically on the quote from psychiatrist/novelist Walter Percy: "You can get straight A's but still flunk life."

Lizzie had disappeared over a week ago in New York before his CIA buddy had called him. They had found the tiny transponder, which had been secretly inserted in the identification bracelets of all course participants. Hers was among the gruesome remains of four persons killed in a highway accident, and the authorities were still checking for final details, but they could not do DNA tests because the bodies had all been claimed and relatives were screaming for privacy. Cremation was likely in all four cases.

Colonel Benson was not comforted by those inconclusive details. He wanted proof ostensibly for official reasons, but secretly to put to rest fears that anything could surface concerning his personal involvement in a dangerous experimental CIA exercise.

At first, he had erected an emotional wall between Ruth Elizabeth and himself, but without knowing it, she had found the chink where the heart's putty had fallen away. Her honesty and lack of complication penetrated his armor, and he had really fallen for her.

She was the most interesting woman he had ever known—strong, determined, passionate, and humorous. She knew her direction and was incapable of being intimidated. When he had learned that she was a virgin at twenty-six, he was not surprised. Her first lover would be the man she chose. And he, Roger Benson, had that distinction. As to her being unfaithful, he put that in the realm of high improbability.

But a wisp of smoke had the potential to grow into a raging fire, and he knew he could afford no such diversion as falling in love at that point in his life. He had his eyes set on marrying the daughter of a senior politician, and though she was a plain Jane, she could enhance his upward mobility, a situation he sought with morbid intensity.

Lizzie was a danger to his plans, and he had to act condignly. For him, a diplomat was a person who could tell you to go to hell in such a nice way that you actually looked forward to the trip. So he thought long and hard about his approach to solving his problem and, as usual, came up heads.

A few weeks ago, his friend at CIA headquarters in Washington had sent him an email offering the army a course in new experimentation called SMET (selective memory evaluation theory).

Stanford Charles had jokingly hinted that the E could also stand for "eradication."

It was made to order for him since he was the one to select the three candidates.

The colonel was a firm believer in fortuitism, a doctrine that had propelled his career. And though not overtly a practicing Christian, Proverbs 25 sprang to mind:

> As cold water to a weary soul
> So is good news from a far country

A pang of guilt hit the officer right in the gut, but his features remained inscrutable as he mentally discarded the emotional twinge.

Chapter 4

Payback Time

The woman walked into the pool hall. There were at least three d, men there, some locked in combat on the felt swards, some urging on their favorites and others hugging the long bar, sipping drinks and trading stories.

All heads turned to look at her, immediately assessing her availability letting their imaginations run riot—a stunningly beautiful woman, ignoring the gender code with haughty indifference.

She could feel the eyes on her ass, her tits, her legs; but she resisted the overpowering urge to get the hell out of there. She had to play cool.

Men stepped aside as the chocolate beauty glided to the bar and ordered a rum punch with a sliver of pineapple, a telltale sign of Caribbean heritage or association.

The young woman's features bespoke a mixture of races. For the not discerning, she could be classified as a Boviander, a copper colored product, of a union between an Amerindian woman and a West Indian Negro. To the more knowledgeable, her hair texture told of an Asian or European connection. But it was her melanian complexion that cast doubts.

She was tastefully dressed in a daringly short black mini-dress, with white buttons tantalizingly placed to expose just enough bosom and still considered decent. A Gucci pocketbook, matching long boots, and a single strand gold chain completed the ensemble. This was the third consecutive night that she had stopped in at Al's Pool Hall and Lounge, a trendy work hangout a short distance from the Atlantic Avenue subway maze. Still, she hadn't laid eyes on the man she was so anxious to meet.

She looked around the establishment, hoping that there would not be a fourth night. Time was running out, and there was still a third lesson to teach. And too, it had cost her quite a few dollars while sitting at the bar, engaging the bartender in what he must have thought was idle conversation about three patrons.

She sensed rather than saw when the nattily dressed Mr. Slick arrived.

There was a definite change in the pace of the evening. The cool ambience suddenly became livelier. High fives, hugs, and soul handshakes dominated, and the barman was now honestly earning his wages.

She watched all of this even though she had her back to the bar. Her powder compact, opened and placed at a strategic angle, captured everything.

She saw when one of the guys at the bar drew Slick's attention to the fact that an attractive single woman might be in lonely distress. And she observed how Slick gathered himself, patted his hair, and sauntered over to her table. King Pimp in action. All s:ations alerted.   .

"Good evening, beautiful lady. My name is Clarence. I'm the owner's friend. When he's not here, I am the joint's ambassador."

She ground her teeth silently. Words formed in her head. *Hello, Mr. Ambassador. Hello, Mr. Slick. Hello, Mr. Clarence Slick.*

But instead, she took off a pair of dark glasses and said, "Hi, my name is Michelle. Good to see that somebody has balls in the right place. Forgive the pun. I was about to leave. I heard so much about New York, and here I am, an out-of-town girl among so many men, and I have to buy my own drinks. Guess you can't believe everything the news services write about the Big Apple."

A click of the fingers and the barman appeared. "Jones, this young lady is without a drink, what are you doing about it?"

"Correcting the situation right away, Mr. Hudson," replied Jones on cue.

So Clarence has an attachment-Mr. Slick Clarence Hudson. *Wonder if he had anything to do with naming the famous river that separated Brooklyn and Manhattan*, she reflected sarcastically.

The bartender continued to bring drinks without signals. And during the social interaction, Slick talked nonstop, mostly about himself. He boasted elliptically, "I don't believe in any Holy Book, I believe in the gospel according to me... Life is what you make it...Uncertainty will never characterize my life...I know where I am going ...The sky is not even my limit."

Two trips to the bathroom had not derailed Slick, and by that time, the young woman, though smiling, was constrained to suppress her anger, which had been building like a storm.

She picked up her purse and moved to get up, saying, "Thank you for everything, but I have to go."

Slick would have nothing of the sort. "The night is but a pup. Let me show you the town. Let's take in the Village. You must go there, or else you haven't seen New York." '

These were almost the same words that she had heard on the fateful night almost two weeks ago. But this time, she was fully prepared.

"Okay, but you'll have to recommend a nice hotel for me afterward. My aunt is old-fashioned, and I wouldn't want to wake her after midnight."

"Leave that to me," Slick said, adding, "no problem," as if to instill confidence.

It was déja vu. Only this time, he was driving a Lexus SUV—a moving disco, complete with TV and bar. "This car is a beauty," she said in a coy, girlish voice, purring with admiration. "What kind of work do you do, if you don't mind me asking?"

Slick replied offhandedly, "I deal in commodities. People want something at a particular time or place and I'm the man to shake it and make it happen. It's all about logistics."

Profound bull! *Pimping dressed up and labeled under commodities market,* she thought.

She was chagrined, but she ploughed on.

"Must be fun moving around meeting new people all the time?"

"I love it. I won't give it up for anything in the world. It has all kinds of unexpected rewards. "

"Are you married or seriously attached?" she asked.

Prevarication invariably comes with gestures: an involuntary tic of the eye, excessive blinking, licking of the lips, little movements of the fingers, hands, or feet. Slick's lie came via his fingers, drumming the steering wheel and staring straight ahead.

"I'm divorced and in between relationships. What about you?"

"I left my live-in boyfriend in Florida to check out the Apple." .

Slick just couldn't control his enthusiasm. What unbelievably good luck. A prospect right here in his lap, in his vehicle.

"If you put your faith in me, I can easily find a gig for you, and soon you will have your own pad. NY is the place for a chick of your class."

"Okay, let's enjoy tonight, and then we'll see what tomorrow brings."

The rest of the night went in a whirl—the Village, 42nd Street, Tribeca and Staten Island. Slick marveled at her ability to handle alcohol, unaware that she could drink most men under the table, not by choice, but because of a strange phenomenon. The Amerindian tribes in the Caribbean existed on a daily diet of cassava and other indigenous proteins. Either a single protein or a combination produced an alkaline that absorbed alcohol, keeping it out of the bloodstream, and so it took hours of hard drinking to put a native away.

"Time to go," she prodded Slick, whose speech was beginning to slur slightly.

He offered no objection.

On their way back to Brooklyn, via the Manhattan Bridge, Michelle startled Slick with a question out of nowhere: "What about kids?"

Slick grew pensive. This line was getting too personal. He, Slick, was letting her dictate the conversation when he was "the Man." He should be grilling her.

"Enough about me. Tell me more about yourself."

"I'm Spanish-American," she lied uneasily.

But as she spun her unlikely tale, uneasiness gave way to amusement. Slick was hanging on to every word and storing the ones for which he might have use in the future.

"Don't forget the hotel," she reminded him.

"Nah, got that covered. And I'll handle the bill."

"Thanks, but I'm not in an impecunious state."

"Impecunious. I like that. You are one classy lady. Wish you didn't have to go back to Florida. We could do a lot together. I could set you up. Get you a nice pad. You got poise."

The obsequious admirer was unleashing a barrage of solecisms, garrulous in his pimp language. Thrust, parry, and riposte. It was a fencing match. He as sparring for an opening to deliver the death lunge, and unwittingly, she seemed to be providing it in gratification.

Out of the blue, she blurted, "Can you spend the night with me?"

Slick smiled. He didn't have to delve too deep to dredge up false placebos. This babe was as good as gone. He had timed it perfectly, lunging and scoring. Touché.

As if on cue, Slick pulled into a parking lot, eerily lit by a revolving neon sign proclaiming "Cherry Pink." It looked exactly as it was meant to be—a den of profitable iniquity, a venue for hurried, snatched sex.

To the right was a topless bar, and outside, a dozen or more whores draped languidly around phallic-shaped uprights. It seemed like a convenient arrangement. While the dancers inside teased and promised, the professionals outside were there to deliver the seasoned goods.

Slick commanded, "Stay in the car until I look after the room."

On his way, he stopped to rermonstrate with some of the ladies of the night, his irritation underlined by spirited gesticulations.

But tonight, he wasn't going to let work get in the way of play. He was recruiting. And he had to handle this out-of-town babe with kid's gloves. She was a godsend. He knew some big ones who wanted to graze in green pastures, wanted to smell fresh roses.

Shortly after, he returned, juggling a large brass key in his bejeweled hand.

He was in command of the situation. "Let's go. If you need anything, we can call room service."

Beneath her sangfroid, she seethed. But she had to continue playing the game.

*　　*　　*

The room was a monster, a kaleidoscopic aberration. It was painted in bright, jarring colors. She felt like puking, but she rode the bucking bronco in her stomach.

Pink walls—on which animals and humans copulated; ornate brass-railed bed with pink polka-dotted sheets and frilly purple pillow cases; a stuffed pink pussycat in the center of the bed, legs appealing to the ceiling, a red bow festooning its neck. Brass flowerpots with cactus plants, and on a side table, a closed Bible.

All this she saw in a quick sweep of the surroundings.

The only thing missing was a pink cherry. Maybe that was difficult to find in such promiscuous times.

Michelle spotted a door and darted for it. Vertigo and strabismus seemed to be the offending disorders, and it took a full minute of cold water applied to the head and eyes before she completely regained her poise. Then she removed contact lenses and re-entered the main room.

"Wow, looks like I had too much to drink!" she said airily.

"Come, let daddy look after you. Soft strokes wil.l soothe a sweet sister."

Such crude attempts at alliteration do not sit well with some people especially when they are somewhat disoriented. Her mood change perceptibly. *What the hell was he babbling about?* she wondered.

She ground her teeth again and forced herself to say "nice words."

"Just a little bit of Shakespeare," he uttered, stretching out his arms to embrace her.

That was it. She knew she couldn't indulge this naked, unlettered pretender any longer.

Without any attempt at finesse, she straddled him, her short dress conveniently riding up to her hips. Underneath, she was naked, her clean-shaven vagina glistening with promise. Slick couldn't take his eyes off the mound of Venus, and his hands involuntarily matched towards the promised land.

Michelle grasped both hands and guided them back behind his head.

Slick was aghast. What was she doing? Didn't she understand that he was the leader and she the follower?

He tried to wrest his hands away, but those delicate fingers were like clamps.

Oh! She wanted to play rough. *Good*, he thought.

He struggled to unseat her, and all the time, she just stared into his eyes. Eyes that had been brown at Al's were now reflections of green fire trapped in a shimmering pool of light.

Green eyes, green eyes, green—but they were brown only moments ago.

Then he remembered there was such a thing as contacts.

"Shit," he exploded, a scatological outburst more commonplace among West Indians, no matter what color or creed. This one-word epitaph is categorized in the same idiom as the ubiquitous F word and a peculiar Guyanese coinage, beginning with S and rhyming with "punt."

"Not a very complimentary greeting. Anyhow, I'm glad you remember me," said Michelle in a teasing and mocking tone.

He was shaking. All of a sudden, sweat began pouring from his lanky frame and spittle appeared like unwelcome visitors at the corners of his mouth.

Fear works with lightning speed.

"Payback time, Mr. Hudson."

At those words, Slick began to buck and heave, but his intrepid rider easily mastered the gyrations the same way she had done while riding recalcitrant horses in her village for so many years. Slick was now on his belly, thrashing about without benefit of his hands, which were still locked in a vice-like grip.

Now, Michelle went to work with clinical detachment. She had learnt a few things about every part of the human anatomy and a lot about certain central parts, especially the nervous system.

Slick's head was pushed forward and down into the pillow, exposing the back of the neck encasing the first seven vertebrae forming the cervical region. Bunched knuckles descended precisely on the right spot and the naked lover was immobilized. She climbed off his back with nary a glance at him, and from her bag took two pairs of handcuffs to secure his hands and feet to the bedposts.

Then, from the same bag, she produced a bottle of honey and a feather six inches long.

For days, she had let her imagination run riot plotting vengeance. Slick was no match for her physically, so she had decided to settle for long-term humiliation.

Michelle slapped Slick hard, and he jumped out of oblivion like a startled rabbit, eyes riveted with increasing suspicion as the honey was expertly dispensed with the feather over his writhing body, on his penis and scrotum, and on the rim of his rectum. "

"What are you doing, bitch?"

"My nickname for you was Slick, but that sobriquet is inadequate. You are hereby christened Snake, and I want you to meet one of your own species."

With that, she unzipped the inner part of her bag. Out shot a tiny head with two enlarged eyes, and she lifted the foot-long creature and set it reverently on Slick's belly.

"Let me explain something quickly to you. This is a rare South American snake. It will lick all the honey off your body; then it will search all the orifices. 'Shakespeare Man,' you know what that means—your ass, your ears, your mouth, and your penis. Ta-ta. Remember me always."

"Bitch! Bitch! I am sorry for what happened. I had too much to drink the other night. I didn't know what was going on. Don't do this to me, please."

Michelle refused to be sidetracked. Halfway to the door, she turned, as if remembering something of utmost importance. "Oh, it's only poisonous when it gets excited. Enjoy the rest of the night."

Slick was unmindful of her advice, shouting incoherently at the top of his voice.

The wisp of a snake slithered joyfully; flicking its tongue with amazing regularity, tickling and sending shivers throughout his body.

Slick should have known that all pet snakes behaved the same way; but he was so terrified that objectivity could find no place in his confusion.

Instead, he held his breath like a deep-sea diver as the snake made its way1 between his legs, and then he felt a penetrating flick at the tip of his anus. Slick lost all control. The anal sphincter controlling the passage of wastes from the body opened its gates and a nauseous excretion spread, quickly ruining the pink sheet.

Incontinence, always a jealous cousin, followed soon after, forming a creek around the island of feces.

Michelle walked over to one of the women idly bracing against a wall, gave her a twenty-dollar bill from the wad she had taken from Slick's wallet and told her to take a whisky and soda to her pimp.

She hailed a cab, got in, and instructed the Haitian driver to keep the meter running.

In five minutes, the area was transformed into bedlam, motel guests quickly evacuating their love nests, propelled by the shouts of "Snake, snake!"

The management was berating Slick for his stinking habits while the topless dancers peered from a safe distance. His own girls had already deserted him, knowing with certainty that from that night onward, he could have no hold over them.

Slick had no money, no clothes, no jewelry, and no car keys. Michelle had removed everything. And all, except the wad of money, would be donated to one of the homeless men who limed outside the armory at Atlantic and Bedford avenues in Brooklyn.

A cop car and an emergency services vehicle came in response to management's insistence, and Slick was whisked away, draped in a borrowed sheet.

He would never be "the Man" again.

"Where to, lady?" the driver asked impatiently.

"Downtown Brooklyn. The Marriott Hotel."

When she arrived there, she walked away in another direction, boarded the subway at the Nevins stop, and headed back to her sanctuary at the YMCA.

On the train, she made a mental note: *Two down, one to go.*

Chapter 5

A Lover's Duplicity

She lay in the darkness of the room, her eyes bright with the anticipation of seeing her loved ones in the very near future. She did not think it possible, but for days, she had done the improbable to completely blank out one person and a series of connected events out of her mind.

Thoughts of the one and only man she had fallen in Love with and his subsequent betrayal would have affected her current modus operandi, so she had shut the door on her emotions.

She had implicitly trusted Roger Benson and had given him all that was precious to her. Then he had sold her out.

He had contrived to send her on an overseas mission fraught with danger, after realizing that mutual feelings were becoming too strong. To think he would sink to the level of offering her as a candidate for an experiment in memory tampering. All he had to do was call off the affair. It would have hurt her, but she would have gotten over the disappointment.

She and Roger had made love countless times, but the first time remained emblazoned in her mind as if it were put there by a red-hot branding iron.

They had gone to the Timehri ranges, twenty miles outside Georgetown, for handgun shooting. As usual, she had easily overshadowed the other female officers and gave the men a run for their money. Roger, who was then a lieutenant colonel, offered her a ride back to the city, and she gladly accepted. They had been seeing each other secretly for a while and had gone on many dates, but a silent agreement precluded sexual entanglement.

On that particular day, they had stopped off at his home in Lamaha Gardens ostensibly for him to get a bath and a change of clothing.

An offer of a drink was followed by coy acceptance. An

invitation to relax a bit saw acquiescence. The drinks flowed, the mood changed.

Inhibition and military discipline flew out of the jalousie windows, and within minutes, they were giggling and caressing.

Shortly afterwards, they were stripping in tandem, and then there was nothing between them—neither physical nor doubtful. Intoxicated with the heightened passion of the moment, she forgot everything except what was happening to her. She just wanted to be one with him—he inside her, she enveloping him.

His tongue traced her body, explored the velvety mound and entered the cave of hidden pleasure. He kissed a taut nipple, teased it between his teeth, then drew circles around the areola.

He kissed her everywhere. Nothing was inviolate. He inhaled the scent of her, tasted her body moisture, and drank in her sparkling sight.

It was the first time for her, but an onlooker would have doubted. For even as an eager learner, she was matching him passionately, gesture for gesture.

Her heart beat an unsteady rhythm, her head was spinning. Then she heard herself moaning softly as his male hardness became the counterpoint for her yearning acceptance.

Guttural sounds and heavy breathing combined to ignite a passion that neither realized existed.

A wave of ecstasy was building to tsunamic proportions, and it was only his expert control that kept the dam from breaking.

He was lost in a cloud of contentment. She was exerting her own authority and liking the new role.

Neither wanted an end.

It was an exquisite roller-coaster ride, the feelings spiraling higher and higher until time became frozen.

Her eyes pleaded her readiness to surrender, but he expertly prolonged the moment.

Then with a final thrust, their bodies collided and exploded like fireworks on a starry night.

After they had done their fullest, they lay spent, satisfied and smiling smugly, definitely on cloud nine.

"Is there more where that came from?" he asked softly as his fingers plaited the strands of her being.

"Want to find out?" she asked teasingly.

They made love three times that Saturday night, a trilogy of immense proportions-an orgy of orgasms, each more spectacular than the other.

Later, as she came back to earth, a voice from afar penetrated her reverie: *Sex is an instrument of marriage.* It was Father O'Hara's pontifical admonition, but her heart was telling her head a different story.

In the morning, she awoke, quickly reliving the night before, pleased as punch. Her first sexual experience had been dynamite, and she let her mind luxuriate in the memory.

Roger, her lover, was fifteen years older. Just past forty, hair slowly acquiring the salt-and-pepper look. He had the dean-cut features of a pampered socialite still clutching the memories of yesterday. His demeanor was pleasant, warm, and engaging, and he embraced life with an artful blend of bonhomie and insouciance. The big differences in age meant nothing to her. She loved him. That was all that mattered.

Lizzie lay in the bed and wondered how a person could always remember the smallest details of the first and last liaisons and have little or no recollection of the in-betweens.

And so her mind drifted to the last occasion when their bodies had been joined in sweet surrender during the last hours before she departed for America.

The farewell party the night before for the three selectees and a group leader on the SMET course had been memorable, she thought, as a composite portrait of the evening's highlights flashed before her.

The officers' dub was aglow with immaculately tailored suits and gorgeous evening gowns exposing just enough cleavage and flashing encouraging glimpses of legs and thighs through tantalizing splits. Brilliant speeches and colorful presentations were followed by a whole lot of champagne. And afterwards, there was the incredible love-making.

Early next morning, Lizzie had slowly opened her eyes. She was lying on her back, but she did not have to turn either side to get her bearings. The mirrors in the ceiling did it for her, reflecting a king-size bed in the wake of a tornado. One pillow on the floor, another stuck between the headboard and the wall, sheet crumpled.

And lying contentedly amid the carnage was the love of her life. To everyone else, he was Colonel Roger Orville Benson. But for her, he was "Rog" —the man who had taught her to be proud of her God-given talents in an army tailor-made for men. The man who had unlocked her reservoir of love and made her feel like a real woman-the man for whom she was willing to die.

The air was redolent of supercharged sex, and the perfumed scent wafted languidly all around.

She leaned on one elbow, lithe body hanging possessively over the sturdy torso with the extra large appendix scar stretching from the middle of his tummy.

Basking in the aftermath of post-coital bliss, she surveyed the scene again, gratified and satiated.

If this were not eloquent testimony to the measure of love, then she would probably never know.

She had reached the peak of passion, orbited the earth, played among the stars, and landed on the moon all in one night. She had lost count and almost lost consciousness after her fourth orgasm, but suffused with joy and aware that her man was also caught up in the same throes, the hurricane had continued unabated.

Then a new day had dawned with sun filtering through shuttered Demerara windows, fowl-cocks crowing, and families getting ready to tackle the burdens of another day in the slow-paced Caribbean republic.

Roger stirred, stopped moving, then sat upright in one fluid movement, eyes alert.

"Morning," he crooned huskily, reaching to stroke Lizzie's curly hair. "Morning," she replied, smiling.

Before she could add anything else, he asked jokingly, "What did you do to me last night?"

"What did you do to me? Or better still, what did we drink last night?" The light banter continued until there was nothing more to be said. Lizzie was the first to move. She glided across the sheets and into the arms of her lover. Roger wrapped his long, strong arms around her taut body and stroked her back at a point just above the buttocks. It was her area of lowest resistance, and they both knew it.

In response, she bent her head and bit his right nipple. She heard the catch in his breath and nibbled faster.

Two pairs of hands moved in unison, searching, seeking, and finding familiar tender territory.

Here, the god of love might easily have looked at the entangled limbs and thought he was seeing an octopus; a choreographer would have applauded the subtle, orchestrated movements.

In a flash, Roger had covered Lizzie's body with his own; the piston-like rhythm was gaining momentum, and both had adjusted to precise coordination.

And why not?

It was teacher and pupil combining.

They had gone this route countless times, each answering the other's call, each knowing when to shift gears and positions. The missionary position was always the first. Next, she took over at control tower, high above and dictating the pace. Then on to what they playfully called the switch around, the elevator, the spread eagle, and, finally; the dismount.

It was during the gradual alighting that the maid chose to arrive for work, ringing the doorbell impatiently. Without a break in stride, Roger shouted to her, 'I'm coming,' and indeed he was not telling a lie, for Lizzie felt him shudder and then release a jet spray of his manhood into her soft, safe haven that greedily engulfed its warmth.

*   *   *

Ruth Elizabeth remembered every bit of the tearful farewell at his doorway. She wanted him to accompany her to the airport, but they both knew it would be a breach of protocol.

She heard her last words to him reverberating in her head, but as she lay in the lonely and cheerless YMCA room, she repeated them for emphasis: "I love you, Rog. Please wait for me."

His reply, dripping with feigned sincerity, had been "I will always love you. When you return, we will do the right thing."

Later, she sat daydreaming on the aircraft, trying to unravel the enigmatic "right thing," and before the plane had landed at JFK airport, she had happily come to the conclusion that those words could only mean marriage, and ultimately; kids and life happily ever after.

Throughout the five-hour flight, Roger had floated in and out of her mind, taking over all other thoughts. She had to fight the urge to use the aircraft's new telephone technology to call him, formulating some trivial question to ask.

Now, in retrospect, as she stared at the room's ceiling, she felt used and betrayed. She had the overpowering urge to talk to someone, but who was there? She had an uncle in New Jersey, but she figured his phone might be tapped. She would put nothing beyond Roger and his pals.

She grimaced in distaste.

The swine—he had meant nothing of what he had said. It was all play acting, a big hoax. And she had been too besotted to see beyond the scrim, the veneer of pretence.

She fingered the ring he had given her for her birthday a few weeks before, debating whether to throw it as far away as possible or give it to someone she would never see again.

She did neither, opting to continue wearing it, to be a constant reminder of her lover's duplicity.

Chapter 6

In the Beginning

S he had her Walkman tuned to a local radio station, and it was waxing the O'Jays' Family Reunion. A disc jockey with a coarse, sexy voice told her she was listening to KISS FM.

Tears came to her eyes as she remembered the togetherness of her villagers, people who were taught to embrace the concept of unequivocal sharing from birth. Father O'Hara had added his Irish openness to the culture, and the village of Mora Mission, close to the Venezuelan border, continued to be one big community center.

She knew, without a doubt, that she would never have reached the heights she had already attained if it were not for the paternal devotion of her godfather. She wished he were a relative. He was so knowledgeable, so perfect.

She had never seen her father. Her mother avoided any mention of him. According to her, he was a non-factor as was evidenced by the vacant line, where father's name should have been, on her birth certificate.

Over the years, she had learned that biological parents were responsible for birth; however, those who fostered one's personal growth were the real mothers and fathers. She was a case in point.

Father O'Hara had taught her everything in simple and uncomplicated form, and her mother had gratefully abdicated her responsibilities. It was Father O'Hara who had explained the female biological changes to her.

It is said that it takes a village to educate a child. Lizzie knew this to be true, for she got more than her share of edification, becoming the darling of several village communities in her neck of the woods.

She was an inveterate reader, greedy for knowledge, especially of the outside world, as she constantly referred to matters non-Guyanese.

She was naturally bright, and with Father O'Hara's daily dose of spiritual and worldly teachings, she became the most erudite villager at age ten.

Brightness turned into excellence, then brilliance. Many saw it as genetic since her mother had an IQ that had astounded teachers throughout her school life.

She was no "child of the forest." Neither was she a "buck" girl, as some Guyanese disparagingly refer to the Amerindians.
She was born to be a scholar. And her priestly father made her believe in herself more and more each day.

Her peers called her tomboy. But she didn't mind. Her mentor had convinced her that this moniker was more an honor than a tease. However, he warned her not to be too ostentatious in her exploits since some boys could not handle being bettered by girls.

Arm-wrestling with two adopted cousins, Manuel and George, gave her a strength not usually associated with girls of her age. Isometrics was what the priest called the exercise, explaining with infinite patience that in the beginning, the boys' hands would seem like immovable objects, but gradually, she would be rewarded with a slight budge. He explained that muscles manufactured in a gym could never equal God-given strength, which could be finely honed to produce maximum leverage whenever required.

For the first two weeks, Lizzie questioned Father O'Hara's optimism, then ever so slowly, she gained a slight advantage, and soon, she had completely conquered both boys.
She never went searching for challenges, but whenever they came, she did not flinch. According to the villagers, her indomitable will definitely came from her mother.

Lizzie was the pied piper of her village. She loved all kinds of music—steel band and string band, contemporary and classical. All the kids followed her around as she sang lustily and played air guitar in their imaginary band, at times accompanied by her "singing dog," Ginger.

No one bothered Lizzie. She was an "untouchable."

Several warp-minded ones eyed her with lascivious intent, but they tried nothing. They knew they would suffer extreme bodily harm, and therefore, smothered their unhealthy thoughts.

By the time she had enlisted in the army, she needed no protection. She was primed and prepared for the real world.

*　　*　　*

Her thoughts returned to Brooklyn.

It was time to prepare for her third and final vengeful act in New York. But first, she willed herself to relive the barbarity that had irreparably damaged her life. She wanted to be in the right frame of mind to face the toughest of the three rapists-one who camouflaged violence and terror behind a mask of benevolence and corporate courtesy.

She was cognizant of the priest's sage advice that the element of surprise was almost always the key to victory, that "no man expects a woman, especially one smaller in physique, to attack first. In that split second of macho hesitation is the window of opportunity. Grab it and use it to full advantage."

This was first imparted to her after a brief, but brutal, altercation with Mook, the village idiot. He was a slow, unimaginative boy, unkempt and with a face only a mother could love. But his heart made up for his looks.

A group of boys liming under a tree in the schoolyard had promised him a quarter if he pinched Lizzie's behind.

Mook, whose nickname meant someone who was gullible and easily fooled, did exactly as he was told, but his reward was more than monetary.

Without warning, he received a stinging slap, followed by all eighty pounds of Lizzie's fury. With no particular strategy, she battered and humiliated him before he could offer resistance.

Father O'Hara witnessed the confrontation and Later likened her to the American welterweight boxer Aaron Pryor, who had used the same windmill strategy to overpower Guyana's Lennox Blackmoore in a world-tide fight.

After that unorthodox, but spirited display, the priest made his gym available and taught her the finer points of boxing. She quickly and quietly became an expert.

Father O'Hara taught her everything he knew. And it was a lot.

She once asked him how one man could possibly be so adept at so many things, and he had smilingly answered, "So that I could pass them on to you."

As she later learnt, every boy in that part of Northern Ireland, where the priest was born, had to enlist in the youth. army from age ten. There, they were taught the rudiments of physical combat, including the one aspect she never liked-head-butting without causing damage to one's own head.

The priest made teaching easy and exciting. He would erect a cardboard caricature of a man with all the vital organs highlighted. Then she would have to perfect the art of throwing darts by scoring on the body parts he randomly selected. Fun and anatomy combined to forge her into an accurate and lethal opponent.

Later, he would test her hearing, daring her to listen beyond the susurration of wind and leaves.

At first, she would hear nothing else but the rush of the wind and the rustling of the leaves; then he would ask, ""What about the frogs, the birds, the crickets, the drone of the motorboat laboring upstream?"

And behold, her ears would pick up all the sounds of dissonance where none had been, simply because the auricular senses had now been attuned.

She loved to watch the sun go down as well as see it gradually emerge on the horizon in the early-morning mist. She would lie in the hammock strung up under her mother's house and count the stars, positioning her body to fully enjoy the cool, refreshing breeze whipping across the wide expanse of the Essequibo River, remarkably pure after its long journey across the Atlantic Ocean.

While she gazed skyward, Ginger would crave attention, vigorously wagging his tail, cocking his head, and pretending he was sniffing out an advancing enemy. With his acute canine intuition, he knew that a dog's sense of smell was his most endearing feature, and he took advantage of this whenever Lizzie's attention wavered.

Other dogs were man's best friends. He somehow knew he had to fill the role of the sibling Lizzie did not have.

Lizzie always talked to Ginger, and he proved to be a good listener, answering queries and making statements with a movement of his tail or a quick ear twitch. Communication became normal, and their rapport developed into a special understanding of each other's true feelings.

As if by telepathy, the dog would look up at her, and she would bend down to ruffle the shaggy coat of the loveable dachshund, mouthing the words "I love you, Ginger."

Woof, woof, woof, followed by three twitches of the ear, was Ginger's way of expressing the same sentiment.

She instantly remembered how their lives became enjoined.

Father O'Hara had taken her by boat to a small village upriver, and one pup from a litter of twelve kept following her around. When it was time to be separated, the exuberant puppy alerted the entire community to the inhuman act about to be perpetrated.

His wailing and vocal pyrotechnics were so dramatic that the owner, a Venezuelan diamond trader, was happy to pass over ownership to the appreciative young lady.

From that day, they became inseparable as Lizzie depended more and more on his sharp senses of smell, hearing, and sight. And for a creature with such short legs, his alacrity was a sight to behold.

Early on, the villagers had come to believe that the dog was an incarnation of the spirit of one of her grandparents, sent from the netherworld to guide and protect her. Both grandparents had drowned in the Essequibo River when their boat capsized on the way home from church.

Chapter 7

Growing Up in Albouystown

Lizzie was still ensconced in her room, her thoughts drifting and meandering. It was a soporific flight down memory lane, and it was taking her soaring to many places. But despite the course changes, it was to the South Georgetown ward of Albouystown that she kept returning.

*Albouystown—with its puzzling mix of ethnicities, each distinct
in skin tone, hair texture, and cuisine.
Albouystown—an epicenter of social deprivation that has its parallel
in every capital of the world.
Albouystown—a tough neighborhood where one had to have an
overpowering reason to pay an unscheduled visit.*

At age eleven, she had passed the common entrance examination with flying colors and had earned the right to pick the school of her choice. Her mother encouraged her to select Queen's College, considered the country's premiere grammar school, but Father O'Hara's influence, as usual, silently won out, and she enrolled at St. Stanislaus College.

He argued that it was the highest-ranked Catholic school, and because of its location in the heart of the city, he could keep an eye on her. There were additional benefits of free school clothing from societies like St. Vincent de Paul.

Lizzie now had to live with her cousins and others—the Rodrigues family of ten in Albouys Street, next yard to the famous Albouystown YMCA that kept churning out a stream of top-class boxers. She had seen many world-ranked fighters there and actually had the opportunity of sparring with a few of the national pugilists.

At first, Lizzie was terrified when she saw where she had to live—a three-room structure in a massive tenement yard with a standpipe in the center, where world news and much more private exploits were discussed in lurid details.

Terror turned to respect and acceptance, and within days, she had bonded with kids of every ethnic concoction and faith, envying their carefree attitude, their ragged clothes and mostly their wholesome dignity.

She soon learned that children in the area spent a lot of time playing in the yards, streets and gutters. It was like a release, a sanctuary on the outside, well rid of the feeling of claustrophobia. Those "pickneys" embraced this freedom, so aware that cramped conditions were fraught with volatility. A persistent cough could earn a serious reproof; a suck-teeth, an immediate censure; and God forbid, a fart.

In those days, every senior female was addressed as "auntie," and those adopted relatives had the right to administer punishment, if necessary. Parents never queried.

But the person to fear was the grandmother. Granny or Mama was always the indomitable matriarch, instilling discipline with quick hands, a fiery tongue and cutting looks. And if you thought belts were made to hold up pants and squeeze in waists then you were a moron. At an early age, errant children learned that those leather belts had a more practical use—to whip all parts of their bodies.

It would be safe to say that nobody in Albouystown had ever heard of corporal punishment and its legal hoopla. There existed a simple credo—Do something wrong in the eyes of the elders and you got whipped. And don't entertain the thought of seeking a cop's help. He might add a few lashes of his own.

Many persons admit that they are better citizens because of the tough, homemade discipline.

And somehow, every grandmother seemed to have a sonar system more accurate than anything science has so far produced. One penetrating look would reveal what one was up to or had already done.

The nine years Lizzie lived in Albouystown would have crushed or maimed the spirits of a lesser being. However, the seeds of Father O'Hara's tutelage germinated rapidly and made her blossom into an outstanding scholar and athlete.

But it wasn't an easy ride.

She had to earn the respect of her peers and elders who first saw her as an underprivileged "Lil' buck girl from Essequibo."

By the time she was thirteen, she was teaching children her age and earning bowls of fruit and slabs of chocolate for the good deeds.

She won the grueling annual YMCA cross-country race (the under-thirteen section for boys). She was a champion swimmer and an expert fish catcher; the small edible kakabeli from the Sussex Street trench providing many meals for the Rodrigues family.

Although the YMCA was a boys' club, the indefatigable secretary, Mr. Cedric Barrow, turned a blind eye. He was heard to say, "All of you refer to her as a tomboy. That is enough qualification."

However, it was in the boxing ring that she made her biggest leap to earn the respect of the entire neighborhood, where nothing was a secret for long.

Her coeval cousin Joaquin was a timid soul, a natural magnet for bullies. His fight record proclaimed three fights, three losses. A trilogy of futile fistic frustration. And one didn't have to be a boxing pundit to know that the arena of pugilistic endeavor would never be littered with his victims.

Every day, an *enfant terrible* named Bully Jack, relieved Joaquin of his lunch and whatever coins he had stashed in his fob. The day Lizzie discovered the aberration, she confronted the advantage-taker and instructed him to "cease the unlawful activity at once or face the consequences."

The bully laughed in her face, dismissing her with a deprecatory flick of the wrist.

Lizzie knew she should be cautious, but she felt a wave of animosity sweep over her like a physical assault. "I challenge you to do battle under the Marquis of Queensbury rules." This was Father O'Hara talking, not her.

The bully and his cohorts held their bellies and roared with laughter at her absurd invitation.

That was the moment to quit, but something Father O'Hara had told her about honor and respect kept intruding. "I'll fight you in the ring at the YM, and if I win, you will stop bullying my cousin."

Jack was quick on his feet, his shoulders hunched. He enquired smugly, "And when you lose, what will I get?"

Lizzie was stunned. What had she gotten herself into? "What do you want?" she asked innocently.

Jack pretended to study the heavens, then in a conspiratorial tone, whispered, "When you lose, you have to be my girl. If you don't turn up in the ring, it's the same thing."

If she hadn't known before, she knew then that there were many more reasons she had to perform a miracle. And as usual, Father O'Hara would have to provide the ingredients, she mused.

She looked at the teen tyrant's face. It was like a road map of disaster. An old wound that must have required a dozen stitches dominated his forehead. Another, obviously inflicted not long ago, adorned his left cheek. And a bulbous nose also displayed scattered marks of violence.

His eyes swam in suppressed anger, and he showed all the mannerisms of a thug, the "bad boy" visage accentuated by an exaggerated swagger. Lizzie could only think of him as "forced ripe"— stranded on the brink of manhood.

Father O'Hara did not hide his annoyance. His cheeks got ruddy red as he remonstrated with her for failing her first big test. He had coached her in the art of diplomacy, and he had particularly warned her about openly challenging boys. Many couldn't handle the embarrassment of being bettered by the "weaker sex." The majority considered it emasculating.

It took a lot of pleading with Mr. Barrow to sanction the boy-girl encounter since the omnipresent secretary was aware of Bully Jack's character. Only when Father O'Hara guaranteed his presence for the bout did Mr. Barrow capitulate.

The YM was filled to capacity. Those tardy boys who hadn't paid their subscriptions desperately tried to get the secretary's attention, others pleaded for consideration.

Bully Jack had bet all his savings—62¢—that the "buck" girl would not turn up, and when he saw her protector, Father "Something," glancing surreptitiously at his watch again and again, he could almost feel the extra coins in his pocket.

If he had done his homework, he would not have been so cocky. He might have guessed that it was a ploy to sap his nervous energy.

So when the shouts of her peers preceded her entry into the ring, she had already won part of the first round.

Damn it. She actually turned up. I wonder if this delay was planned. I'd better just walk up to her and finish it with a hard right cross, he thought.

Analysis was not his strong point, so he opted for concentration. In the meantime, Lizzie had read the indecision in her opponent's eyes, and she drew strength from that.

Mr. Barrow, who was the referee, said, "Touch gloves and do your thing. When I say stop, do so immediately."

Bully Jack threw four successive roundhouse rights, but only succeeded in destroying the errant air. A jab and left cross hit the same airy enemy while his female nemesis circled without throwing a punch.

The priest was muttering something like "Obfuscate, exasperate." Then he was switching to "Stay and pray, move and groove."

Looks like they have done this before. I'd better be careful, Jack said to himself.

He was very careful, so much so he clearly heard the instruction "Might is right." But he was powerless to avoid the snaking right hand to his left eye. Three stinging left jabs peppered the same eye, then another painful blow instructed the auditory nerve to cease carrying impulses to the hearing area.

Eyes unfocused and bereft of hearing, he plodded around the ring like an automaton, and Mr. Barrow, a true diplomat, quickly stepped in to call a no-contest.

Father O'Hara gave an unholy Irish yell and hugged Lizzie in a manner that raised eyebrows of those unaware of his influence in her life.

"Father, you told Mr. Barrow what to do. I can see your hand in this."

The priest could only shrug an assent as her friends and senior YMCA members inundated her with congratulations.

"Have you ever fought in a ring before?"

"Many times!"

"Have you ever fought a boy before?"

"Many times!"

"Have you ever lost a fight?"

"Not yet!"

Father rescued her after what seemed like a hundred other questions, and together, they wended their way to nearby Billy's Parlor, where she was rewarded with an enormous glass of a combination of mauby and pineapple drink, commonly called a "mixture."

"I hope you have learnt your lesson. It won't be so easy next time. Whenever you challenge anyone, you must have all the advantages-surprise, training, surroundings, and motive."

"Father, how do I deal with Jack after today?"

"You know the answer-Don't procrastinate, originate." Another mantra.

"I'll find him by himself and call a truce. Let him brag that I came to him and asked for peace."

"Good girl, attaboy. Right on the spot."

And as if by local decree, she was never again referred to as the "little buck girl."

Chapter 8

A Change of Pace

Two days prior to her departure to the United States, she had gone back to Albouystown to say farewell to her adopted aunts, uncles, and cousins. And the unwelcome transformation of the environs deeply disturbed her.

The ward had always presented a contrasting, two-dimensional picture of a community of enormous will and fading hopes. One could always see the older people clinging obstinately to dignity while the younger generation seemed caught up in a cyclone of hopelessness.

In the past, the area had produced countless scholars and leaders, but the paucity of children in school uniforms was testimony that education, as a symbol of hope, was no longer an imperative.

Many ambitious persons had risen from humble roots to heights of power and wealth. Many found success through a relentless work ethic. And many, first in their families to go to college, led the way out of the quagmire that tenuously clung to those without ambition.

Whereas poverty previously welded neighbors, the prevailing ostentation spawned by illicit endeavors, fractured relationships and provided the catalyst for the unending saga of violence pervading the southern province.

While she was having a few words with Paula, a former schoolmate, she noticed the aura of hopelessness. Already a mother of four, her friend sat astride a bright red Honda scooter, both arms encircled with bangles and other bands of gold, her neck festooned with countless chains.

Yet it seemed she would be in a constant state of impecuniosity, waiting for her children's father to make the big score. Invariably, he would be caught and jailed, and she would have to share her favors with some young stud waiting in the wings.

Lizzie was perplexed as she watched both males and females liming at corners, idiotic mumbo jumbo passing for conversation. There was an unmistakable feeling that the present generation was just marking time, waiting for a tidal wave to engulf it. She dearly remembered the sermons about a generation problem unlikely to be solved during her lifetime.

"Girl, ah hear you going away to the States. Put me in yuh suitcase, nuh," Paula said in a matter-of-fact tone.

"Mommy, you would go away and leave me?" chimed in a precocious, half-naked girl whose distended belly was capped with a bung navel.

"Nah, ah only joking. But by the way, who's talking to you? This is big people conversation."

"Sorry, Mommy," the child said, skipping off, delightfully sucking away on her comforting right thumb.

Lizzie joined in, "Yes, girl, I'm going on a highly classified course. I don't know how long it will last."

"Eh, eh, what kind of thing is that? They ain't telling you how long? What happen, you ain't got family and boyfriend?"

Lizzie was amused at the street logic, and she responded casually, "That's the army for you, girl. I swore to serve my country and follow orders."

A red Corvette convertible with black top down cruised by; and Paula cut short the debate to shout, "What's up, bro, let me get a raise, nuh."

One of America's most expensive cars stopped, a hand with a gold band that only a weightlifter could comfortably tote, snaked out, and a bundle of notes were proffered.

Amidst the degradation and abject poverty, there were those who lived the lives of sybarites, indulgent and voluptuous.

The deportee stepped on the gas, and the juggernaut disappeared up the road.

"Badass ride, eh. Cost the overseas 'Banna' over $90,000 U.S. to buy, ship, and pay customs. I see the papers myself," Paula boasted, a vicarious thrill evident in her voice.

She wasn't finished: "In Guyana currency; that is nearly 14 million bucks. Wow. And he is a good man, you know."

Lizzie wondered how she could conveniently forget to mention that the good man kept on making his living off the misery of his own people by means of little rolled cigarettes, vials, and rocks.

She was so disgusted by this tacit acceptance of skewed logic that she blurted, "How can you respect a man like that, selling drugs to his own people and showing off with all that money?"

"Better to be a king in hell than a slave in heaven" was the laconic reply. Lizzie's face reddened with anger. Something was wrong with these people. Surely, they could see that through the largesse of the drug lords, they, the puppets, would remain forever in the unending cycle of poverty, eking out a minimal existence, watching life go by.

"Wake up, girl. You can't squander your life away in this place," Lizzie remonstrated.

"Don't forget, you used to live here too," Paula reminded her.

Lizzie rejoined, "There is a world beyond this hopelessness. You didn't dictate where you wanted to be born, but you sure as hell can move in the direction you want to go. It's not where you come from, it's who you are."

All of this seemed lost on her friend. To her, Albouystown was her world, and she felt safe in the jungle she knew—not somewhere out there in unfamiliar territory.

To the north crowded the urban life of the city where the middle class jostled for material things. To the south were the thriving mega businesses, with their corporate intrigue.

"What to do, girl. I can't get no job. All I have is a school-leaving certificate. And you know my temper. I ain't going to work in nobody's kitchen. Not this girl."

This intransigence irritated Lizzie, and she was getting angrier by the minute, but a warning bell rang in her head a la Father O'Hara— Anger is one letter short of danger.

It was time to leave this breeding ground of despair. Poverty was indeed ingrained, having become part of the natural fabric. Proud and happy men and women she had looked up to now seemed old and sad, no longer strangers to hunger, drifting aimlessly about the fog of existence like restless ghosts.

During the time she lived there, she had felt a close kinship to poor, yet proud people. Now, seeing so many young ones squandering their lives in the ghetto fuelled a fear of what would most likely happen in the future. The youngsters preened and strutted, eyeing their jewel-adorned seniors and hoping to be like them someday. Gang rankings and turf power were the aims of the game.

Albouystown was now a simmering cauldron ready to blow.

New dons had taken control, and one in particular had bludgeoned his way to the top with fists, guns and dope. Showing him disrespect in his scary world was a life-or-death decision.

This was no boardroom with a CEO. This was the king all the way from another county, the Boss man with a fiercely loyal militia, which included a coven of loose women living in communal concubinage.

The narrow streets accustomed to dray carts and pedal cycles now accommodated the most expensive scooters, cars and SUVs—a parking lot of depreciating metal.

On the other hand, the neighborhood stank of urine, garbage, and dilapidation—everything horrible about the rot and decay of generations of accepted poverty.

From all appearances, it seemed better to be a king in hell than a slave in heaven.

And while a sociology professor might have labeled the specter of Albouystown "a kind of shifting social environment with no start or end," the bald, blunt truth was that the once-proud neighborhood had been broadsided by official neglect, and the resultant carnage was now seen in the lost generation that continued to prance and parade in flagrant ignorance.

However, Lizzie was too emotionally drained to dredge up any further rational thoughts. She bowed her head, climbed into the waiting army vehicle, and said goodbye.

Her other friend, Bernadette, would hear of her visit and intended departure and feel aggrieved, but she was in no mood to venture into the one-block section of upper Albouystown called "Hell's Kitchen," a realistic twin to the socially deprived "Tiger Bay" and "Warlock" in other parts of the city.

The vehicle passed the now-notorious landmark called "Taps," previously Mr. "Gussie" Chin's shop at Barr and James streets, where countless old-timers swore the best mauby in the country was sold.

Across the road another "Taps" acquisition, formerly Mr. Green's drugstore, famous for the owner's stentorian voice and a purgative that always brought instant results. If one were brave enough to down the potent "bilious wash," one had to embrace the wisdom of staying close to toilet facilities. To do otherwise would be to invite a catastrophe.

The famous Joe Louis shop, with its slanted bridges, loomed ahead at the intersection of Hunter and James streets.

Seemingly stacked by a contortionist, this precariously perched, unpainted structure held more items than many established supermarkets in the better-off sections of Queenstown and Central Georgetown during the '60s and the '70s.

In those days, it seemed the shop's Portuguese owner never slept, since a coded rap on a particular window in the wee hours of the morning brought instant service.

Lizzie's eyes took in the changes and the differences. She still felt a close kinship to the area and its curious history, but she knew she could never live in that environment again.

"Let's push it, soldier. It's getting late," she said authoritatively. The corporal needed no further urging.

Chapter 9

The Memory Game

L izzie awoke with a start in her Brooklyn room.

She had dozed. off after reflecting on her last visit to Albouystown. And not long after, a frightful dream had intruded her subconscious, one in which she saw a crazy-looking man in a white coat hovering over her with an electric drill. What was even more worrying was the fact that her head was held firmly in place by two iron clamps.

She jerked upright, quickly examined her surroundings, and was relieved to see she was still in her room. Perspiration had already settled on her forehead.

In a minute, her mind rewound to the last night of the course.

The farewell get-together at the Staten Island Marriott had gone well, and she had enjoyed talking with the therapists, analysts and psychiatrists associated with the mnemonics project.

The seemingly implausible end results of the memory-enhancing program had been explained in graphic, mundane terms, and all the participants had been given awards for contributing to such a noteworthy world cause.

Selective memory evaluation theory (SMET) was a genetic breakthrough for the free world, and the White House administration was gung ho about it.

The idea was to isolate the gene that controlled memory. Experiences imprinted on the brain cells as memories could then be transferred on a minute chip from one person to another, could be downloaded, erased, and also duplicated.

Professor Jefferson, an eccentric-looking expert with wild electric hair, was unstoppable in his unfettered optimism. His hopeful vision focused on a world where terrorists, criminals and evildoers could be made wholesome and into perfect citizens with the simple switch of a mneme.

Lizzie had enquired openly about man's right to change God's creation and to tamper with a person's personality. She asserted that the brain controlled everything, and when it was compromised, lots of unexpected problems could arise.

The professor looked slightly hurt by the challenge to his prognosis, but quickly moved on, encouraging his captive audience to open their minds to the wonders of science. Obviously a patent agnostic, he launched a tirade against Catholicism and anti-science mud-heads. He pointed out that man only used 10 percent of his brain cells and if there was a way to extend usage, who in heaven's name should stand in the way?

He talked fluently about transitory memory loss, prefrontal lobes, enhanced and eradication transplants. It all sounded so simple.

However, Lizzie was concerned when, during the course, she had observed persons walking beyond their fenced area, just repeating multiple numbers and equations in a monotone.

Later, she was acutely dismayed when she attempted to initiate a conversation with an English girl who had a pronounced Cockney accent, and the latter indicated that she only spoke Spanish.

Only two days before, Lizzie and the young woman, who said her name was Mary Beth, had a pleasant twenty-minute debate on the merits and demerits of sex before marriage. Now, she showed no sign of recognition, and her thoughts were being rerouted in another language.

Lizzie had also paid special attention to the exercise where a crew-cut American teenager was correctly answering questions about Russian geography. And she could not help being amused as a middle-aged Jew spoke unerringly in the Jamaican dialect—an incongruous amalgamation, but nevertheless, a hugely successful experiment.

This brain-tampering might be interesting futuristic work, Lizzie mused.

But was it moral?

She moved to reengage the garrulous scientist, but she was deliberately cut off.

Officer Yolande Belgrave, the head of the Guyana team, was the intruder, effusively hugging her and saying loudly, "Time for me to go. I have to rise and shine early tomorrow."

But she casually cupped her right palm and whispered in Lizzie's ear, "Urgent. Meet me in the ladies' room in two minutes."

Lizzie's countenance did not change. She kept a smile on her face as the danger bells tolled ominously in her head. Thanks to Father O'Hara again. The priest had taught her every conceivable card game, but her favorite was poker, which demanded more than card skills. It called for perception, sagacity, and complete control of the facial and optic muscles.

She was startled by the urgency of the instruction, yet the official paying dose attention to the brief embrace would later write in his report that the encounter was without incident.

Lizzie's mind was not on what the professor was saying. She was counting off 120 seconds, and with a quick "Back in a minute," she was off to the hastily scheduled rendezvous.

As soon as she pushed the door, Yolande grabbed her and rushed to the last stall, hurriedly flushing the toilet and whispering, "Ruth Elizabeth, something is very wrong. You are earmarked, along with six other 'guinea-pigs' from other countries, to go with a CrA group to another location way up in Arizona. The new project is hush-hush, but it definitely is to remove stuff from your brain ... nothing to do with evaluation or analysis."

"What are you saying? Where did you get this from?" Lizzie asked in shock.

"Did you see me talking with the disheveled-looking man with the battered Panama hat?

"Yes, why?"

"He was in charge of the entire project until yesterday when he queried your inclusion in the eradication project. His evaluation of you is, quote-unquote, 'Superior, with a perfect score.'"

"Why me? What does all this mean? I'm beginning to be frightened." "The doctor guy, I don't remember his name, was so pissed off that he breached protocol in pointedly asking me why the Guyana administration would volunteer you for the memory loss aspect of this operation. He smelled something fishy and wanted no further part in the operation."

Officer Belgrave flushed the toilet for the umpteenth time, leaning forward to commiserate with Lizzie, painfully aware that she, in turn, was staring in space, wavering between disbelief and perplexity.

Yolande hissed urgently, "You've got to get away tonight. After tomorrow, it could be too Late. You'll probably leave here in a comatose state, and your mind might never be the same again. It's inhuman, and when I get back home, I'll do my own digging. The shit will hit the fan, and somebody's going to pay. In the meantime, they might be watching your every move, so be careful."

She paused briefly, ruminating, then with a confidence she didn't feel, said, "But why am I worrying? If anyone can do the impossible it's you. Get out of the hotel at all costs."

The shock of the urgent message was like a hammer blow. Lizzie bent over, consciously attempting to slow her erratic breathing. And after she did, she eased herself into an upright position, reflecting on what her fellow officer had just disclosed.

She understood the significance of every word. There was no mistake. This was Roger in his most devious mode. The master manipulator going to the extreme to wipe out memories and suppress feelings. Ugh!

She fought the urge to vomit, clutching Yolande's arm for support, and soon the debilitation subsided. Her head was now clear, repugnance giving way to determination.

It was a macabre story with elements of underhand doings and a fair degree of complicity. But somehow, she was not terror-stricken. Father O'Hara had told her that the many disparate fragments she had gathered along life's path would one day conflate into a single unit of unbounded power. She could almost feel the surge in her veins.

She hugged Yolande and said confidently, "Thanks for everything. I know I took your place in Roger's lineup, but you never showed me a bad face. You're okay."

"What! You mean you knew about Roger and me?"

"The army is not the best place to keep secrets. Yes, I know. He told me it was a brief fling, but others have suggested otherwise."

"No time for girl talk. Get moving."

Lizzie shook her hand, and Yolande could feel the rush of adrenaline flowing through the young officer's body, supercharging at maximum speed. This was the champion girl—ebullient, dynamic, and dangerous. There was nothing sedentary about this soldier, and some people were about to find out. She knew exactly what she had to do and what course she had to take.

Lizzie walked back to the voluble, enthusiastic professor who had the floor, waxing excitedly about a world minus lawbreakers and full of do-gooders. His face shone with sweat; spittle flew in every direction. He was a man on a mission of breathtaking scientific breakthrough.

Lizzie waved goodbye and sauntered over to Stanford Charles,

Roger's CIA friend who had made frequent trips to Guyana for God knows what.

The American was a perfect clone of his Guyanese counterpart. Both were ambitious and ruthless, aware of their imposing bearing and good looks. Both were just past the forty-year mark.

"Can someone give me a lift to the hotel?" Lizzie asked. Then she added, "I understand we're leaving for another location early tomorrow morning."

Although he knew her real name, on this exercise, he always addressed her by her code name. Each of the three participants had been assigned a nom de guerre. Hers was Lovely Lass or Double L. The others were Torpedo Mike and Brazen Lady.

In his husky "Soul Train" voice, he replied, "Why, yes, Double L, that someone is I," bowing playfully.

"But first, I must congratulate you. Your evaluation puts you right at the top of the heap, and we're sending you to a higher level of participation under the supervision of United Nations' top scientists. It's a global effort, and you will put your country on the map. The two other participants will stay at this local facility to undergo less-rigorous exercises."

Lizzie ground her teeth and kept smiling. She asked simply, "How many of us are going on to this facility, and where is it?"

"Just a few of you who qualify as the most adaptive—one girl from Brazil, one from Venezuela, and an Arab boy. I don't remember the others. The evaluation center is in Washington, and you're going to be extremely busy over the next six weeks, so maybe you ought to write a letter to your mother and I'll make sure it's posted tomorrow."

"Are you going with us?"

"Sorry, I wish I could, but I have top-level meetings from as early as nine o'clock tomorrow. But I'll be keeping in touch. I don't want Roger to think me negligent," he said with a knowing smile.

Lizzie fought hard not to choke on the platter of lies being served. She coughed politely behind a tight fist.

"Thanks for everything ... Colonel, I'm ready to go." The slight hesitation was because she had only just noticed the addition of another star on his epaulet. He and his bosom buddy were ascending the military ladders simultaneously.

Birds of a feather climb together, she surmised.

Lizzie knew that time was not on her side. She had a few calls to make, some necessary double-checking.

The colonel not only dropped her at the hotel, he accompanied her to the elevator, effusively urging her a good night's rest and reminding her to take the two tablets he had given her in the car.

Lizzie thanked him again and rode the elevator to the fifth floor, but she didn't enter her room. Instead, she sprinted down the stairs.

She was just in time to see Colonel Charles giving instructions to a tall black man dressed like the regular concierge. She recognized the imposter. Half an hour ago, he was attired in full African garb—dashiki, sandals and embroidered headgear. She kept bumping into him at the party, and once, jocularly asked him if he was stalking her.

Intuition, her strong suit, was at work, but she had paid no attention. She felt a chill, and it was not because she was standing close to an air-conditioning unit, it was the inner feeling of dread and cold certainty that evil was in the air.

She retraced her steps to her room and used a phone card to call the twenty-four-hour number the American colonel had given her in case of emergency.

The charade began.

"Hello, may I speak to Colonel Charles?" "May I ask who is calling?"

"Colonel Benson's secretary from the Guyana Defence Force."

"Hey, girl, your voice sounds different, like if you have a cold."

"Yes, I do, plus it's this archaic switchboard. It's older than Methuselah." "That bad, eh? What can I do for you?"

"My boss might pass through New York tomorrow. He just wanted to know if the colonel was free for lunch."

"Jeez, girl. Your boss is out of luck. The colonel leaves early tomorrow to take a scientific team to Arizona and won't be back for two days. Some business he has to oversee himself. I heard him muttering about 'the things you do for friends.' By the way, one of your people will be going on to Arizona for advanced participation. It's all top secret CIA stuff, so I don't know the details. You Guyanese seem to dominate whenever you come on these courses. What's so special with you guys?"

"Nothing special, maybe it's our British background or just our resolve to do our best at all times."

"I envy you guys. I met your four representatives the other night at a function, and they stood out among the crowd, especially the young captain. She has the potential to become a diplomat, and

BEYOND REVENGE

her diction is so perfect. I'm sure she's the one who topped the course. Congrats to her."

The irony of the gratulant compliment was not lost on Lizzie as she replied, "I know who you're talking about. Anyhow, thanks again. Talk to you soon."

"Bye. Do something about that cold."

The phone went dead. The room suddenly became funereal. An overpowering lugubrious feeling took control.

She now fully understood the depth of deception, the shaky underpinnings of her love, and the brazen scope of international intrigue.

Lizzie sprang off the bed as if stung by a wasp. She found the pair of soft gel tablets after ripping open the packaged pharmaceutical. The colonel had given her maximum strength sleeping pills, guaranteed to keep her in bed until they came for her the next morning. She flushed them down the toilet.

Challenge was an aphrodisiac to her. Once a question was asked, there must be an answer. "The answer is always there," said Father O'Hara. "You just have to find it."

He had preached to her again and again, underlining the value of the mind, which he likened to a sifter, a collator, and a host of other things.

She knew she had to travel lightly and move quickly while pedestrian traffic was still hectic. A woman traveling solo at night with an overnight bag was a target and could also attract the unwanted attention of the police.

She donned her dirty, but comfortable sneakers and the brand-new dark blue tracksuit she had bought at Macy's one-day sale the day before. She debated whether to discard the headpiece, which she saw more as hindrance than help, but the consistent shifts in weather patterns over the past few days influenced the retention.

She placed her passport into a zipped interior pocket along with her return plane ticket and remaining allowance of $243.

She regretted having to leave behind some of her best clothes, shoes, perfumes and makeup, but what good would those be to a zombie whose brain had been altered.

She stuffed selected items into a small wheeled pull-along handpiece, then removed the silver bracelet, which was said to be

71

an identification band, but she knew was a kind of transistor to electronically keep track of a person's movements. She thought of leaving it on the bed, but decided against it. Into her pocket it went.

She had picked the tiny lock the first night it had gone on her left wrist, and the nightly exercise always took forty seconds.

She used the exit stairs to the basement garage and let herself out on Compensation Drive, perpendicular to Lincoln Place, where traffic was in full flow.

She hailed a taxi and headed for the Staten Island ferry to take her to the Bowling Green subway station in Manhattan. From there, she would board the no. 2 train and travel to the end of the line in Brooklyn. She would then walk to the Flatbush YMCA, where she would rent a room under an assumed name. If they insisted on identification, she would ask for the requisite twenty¬four hours to provide a driver's licence.

All she needed was a trip to an office supplies store and it would be a cinch. The intelligence branch of the army had taught her well. Disguises and fake IDs were par for the course.

On the way to the ferry, the taxi had to slow to a crawl as uniformed police tried to control traffic and disperse curious bystanders swarming the scene of a major traffic accident. As the cab slowly crept past the wreckage, Lizzie rolled down the window and threw the transponder into the tangled heap.

She leaned back in the plush comfort of black upholstery, symbolically washing her hands on a potentially destructive chapter of her life.

There was absolutely no uncertainty in Lizzie's mind. Even though she had only once traveled to Brooklyn from Staten Island, the directions were imprinted like a map in her head as if intuition had somehow known she would one day need them.

She knew she could not use her passport. In a few hours, they would know which part of the world she had presented it.

However, if push came to shove and a night's accommodation was a problem, she would climb into one of those junkyards she had seen on Utica Avenue and cool out among the remains of once-expensive cars, discarded chassis, and other scattered vehicular viscera.

She was totally focused and beyond fear.

A few days later, she strolled around Fulton Mall and then wandered onto Flatbush Avenue, where she spotted Al's, sandwiched between a real estate office and a 99 Cents Only store. She chose a pool table in a far corner and played eight games all by herself. The next afternoon, she returned and was into her tenth rack when Lucifer congratulated her on her skill and invited her to engage in a "friendly" game.

She didn't know it then, but her life was to change dramatically.

Chapter 10

Setting the Final Stage

Dominic Chavez was not yet thirty, but he was already a millionaire, owning a series of computer and electronics stores

All his establishments looked alike, like McDonalds any part of the world. The logo with the interlocking italicized Letters *D* and *C* proclaimed that Dominic was in the neighborhood.

The baby-faced magnate, who was always well dressed, was looked upon as an easy-going, laid-back guy, always twirling a toothpick in his mouth. But those dose to him knew the kind of animal he really was.

After an absence of just over a week, he had returned to Al's, where he held the reputation of being one of the hardest hitters of the ivory balls.

Since the army had cured him of his quick temper and predilection to lash out with his fists at the drop of a hat, he had confined his overt aggression to the pool tables.

And it was at Al's that he learned of his buddies' recent calamities.

He listened intently as the barman related how Clarence had high-tailed it out of town after the distasteful hotel episode and how Mike had to spend a few days in the hospital. Both men had been undone by the same woman—one time dressed as a Bag Lady, and on the other occasion, in the guise of a glamorous out-of-town chick looking for Big Apple fun.

Dominic thanked the bartender for the news as he sipped his vodka and cranberry juice, reasoning that the triangle would not be complete without an encounter with him.

The next day, he strengthened security at all six businesses in New York and put his two bodyguards on extra alert—Sanchez, his lifelong partner, and Zapata, a former top-ranked boxer turned street fighter.

He knew he could take care of himself, but he agreed with whoever had said it was "better to be safe than sorry."

He did not believe any one woman could have taken down Sergeant Mike Rogers, who was a fire-eater against the Afghanistan rebels, earning a breastplate of ribbons for bravery.

As for Specialist First Class Clarence Hudson, he was no slouch either, able to hold his own in any conflict. After the war, he could have become a tough and successful businessman, but he chose the flesh trade instead .

Dominic was nervous and on the lookout for that green-eyed fox they had "fixed" the other night, and every female who approached his office had to be given what he humorously called the "eye test."

So that when the attractive young nun walked into DC on Flatbush Avenue, and with a British accent, asked to speak with the manager, the two bodyguards glanced briefly at the brown eyes and hastened to tell the boss that a beautiful "sister" had come to brighten his day.

They were running interference for the boss man in the same way others had done during the wars while Dominic used his cunning to exploit all kinds of situations.

The more things change, the more they remain the same.

Church had always had a peculiar fascination for Dominic. His parents were dirt poor, but believed it their destiny. They also believed what the church preached against contraception and abortion.

And so he and his eight brothers and sisters were caught in the middle.

The family lived in a dusty Puerto Rican village perched on the side of a craggy mountain. Dust was everywhere, garbage was omnipresent, and disorder was way at the top in the pecking order.

But there was no dust in Dominic's life. He was fastidious to the hilt.

In a sea of chaos and untidiness, he was a conspicuous buoy of neatness and perfection and turned his back on that community the first chance he got, enlisting in the United States Army to which he had been accepted on his eighteenth birthday. In fact, he had not yet reached that milestone, but artful duplication on his birth certificate had helped.

Now, all his stores were kept scrupulously clean with two

employees called sanitation technicians on duty all day, each equipped with a small vacuum to gobble up any stray bits of paper or dust that dared defile the pristine surroundings, inside and outside.

It might have been excessive obsession with cleanliness and order, but observing the strict rule was a sure way to guarantee continued employment.

As the well-shaped body dad in nun's habit glided further into his store, Dominic's experienced eyes peeled off the somber garments Layer by Layer. His x-ray eyes could see a body that the fashion DJs would tremulously describe as svelte, willowy and seductive.

He considered himself a connoisseur of feminine pulchritude, adept at separating natural beauty from the enhanced variety, heavily dependent on the opulence of Lipstick, rouge and powder.

He was immediately drawn to this holy presence, possibly because since Good Friday; he had not gone back to church.

Come to think of it, he mused, he hadn't followed his established weekly routine. And this was obviously because of that night when he had done the unthinkable to a green-eyed devil.

That night—and he could only think of it as that—he and his army buddies had taken advantage of a drugged young woman. It started out as teaching her a lesson, but it had ended in outright rape.

Rape—one of the most heinous crimes known to humanity, and frowned upon by society. He could face up to life imprisonment, and that was a no-no with him. He hated confinement and detested following orders.

The memory of the dastardly act tormented him, and he tried desperately to exorcise his guilt.

All his adolescent and adult years, women had come willingly into his life, his handsome mien and superbly fit body attracting them like moths to the flame. He had a lovely wife, three children attending expensive Catholic schools and a string of readily available mistresses.

He had seen the face of death in Desert Storm and Afghanistan. He had overpowered so many challenges in his entire Life.

What had led him to join in such a despicable act? He could not find an answer.

But this was no time to do a psychiatrist's job on himself The nun looked like she needed help, and he was there to provide answers.

Wearing a phlegmatic expression, he sauntered across the floor.

"Can 1 help you, Sister?" he asked in his most reverent voice.

"I was wondering if I could have a quick word with the manager," she said, a little breathlessly, as if she had traveled a long distance.

"Today is your lucky day. Not only am I the manager, 1 am also the owner of this corporate chain," he replied proudly.

The nun took off her dark glasses, and he immediately noticed light brown pupils superimposed on a background of color he could not identify between the quick flicks of her eyelashes.

Dominic's offer of a seat was accepted, and as the nun sat and crossed her legs, his eyes increased in wattage.

She introduced herself. "My name is Sister Ruth."

His hand lingered as they exchanges greetings. "I'm Dominic Chavez." Like a camera, his eyes recorded bountiful breasts, a serenely beautiful face, and magnetic eyes. There was no makeup and no discernible hairstyle, but neither her vocation nor her attire could hide natural beauty.

Imperceptibly he sniffed, and was rewarded with the scent of Timeless perfume and Imari skin cream. He knew those Avon scents well.

His sister had been a representative for that company when she arrived in America, and many times she had e-mail fights with the salespersons for not sending certain ordered items, unaware that he, Dominic, had pinched them to sell in the projects he frequented.

The nun coughed politely to attract Dominic's attention and when he turned to look at her, she said, "The orphanage where I work needs a computer and I'm shopping around for an inexpensive one."

"For the orphanage I'll give you a 50 percent discount on the latest Compaq, 256 megabyte DDR RAM, 40 gigabyte hard drive, plus combination DVD/CD-RW drive. I'll also throw in an Epson printer free."

He spoke animatedly, his eyes never still, moving all over her body, darting to the doorway when someone entered, and zeroing on the cashier as she completed a transaction. Amid the inconsequential chitchat, he continued to catalog, decipher and make snap judgments.

Lizzie traced his movements unerringly, and her early diagnosis told her clearly that despite the calm eyes shaded by expensive peepers, the Italian suit, the Rolex watch and the diamond studs in both ears, she was indeed observing a dangerous predator.

Then, like an undertaker unctuously consoling the bereaved with a constant flow of plaintive incantations, he took her elbow to guide her to the half-price giveaway bargains.

"Don't worry, Sister, I'm a Catholic. I'm going to give you a deal you can't refuse," he told his customer, taking pains to underline his allegiance to the church.

If that ploy was meant to put the nun at ease, it had the opposite effect and it took a major effort not to wrench her elbow away. His continued deference was far from making her comfortable. It had the converse effect—increasing the menace.

She put on a brave face as alarm bells went off in her head and her bowels constricted just a little.

Watch out girl, this one is lethal, an inner voice screamed.

Suddenly, Dominic seemed to make an on-the-spot decision. He turned to the nun, snapped his fingers excitedly and said, "You know something, Sister. I have a computer I can donate. The only thing, it's out at my country house near Westchester. Would you have time to come out and check it out this weekend? I can get one of my drivers to pick you up, and if you're pleased with it, it's yours."

"Wow, do you really mean that? The orphanage would really appreciate your kind gesture," said Lizzie in an equally excited voice.

"While you decide whether you're coming on Saturday or Sunday, let me print you a route map from Map Quest on the Internet."

The nun appeared to be consulting a diary when Dominic returned with the directions.

"You know what? After mass on Sunday morning, I have the rest of the day for myself. I can drive out there. What about one o'clock?"

"That's a good time, Sister. I'll probably have a few friends over, so you'll be able to relax and enjoy yourself for a change."

It was Sunday, and Dominic could not conceal his excitement.

Since Wednesday, when the nun had chosen the day to pick up the computer, he had had to fight to suppress his feelings.

His head kept on telling him that it was impossible even to get to first base with a nun, much less make a score. But conceit and an unblemished record of conquests told him nothing was beyond his reach.

If only he could break through the shield of chastity, he would be elevated to a plane where only the Creator could challenge him. And while he was unlocking the padlocks of bondage, he would make her absolve him of the evil deed he had performed with his friends not so long ago.

His stores were open every day. At noon, he told Sanchez to

"hold the fort" while he took care of some business.

The slow wink that accompanied this command told Sanchez everything.

Sunday was play day. He smiled knowingly, wondering how old or how slim the business was. However, he said easily, "Leave everything to me."

He was glad. Since Wednesday, after the departure of that attractive young nun, the boss had been preoccupied, drifting off with thoughts he didn't want to share. This was unusual because they shared a bond far beyond the mixing of their blood one midnight when they were twelve years old in Puerto Rico.

"Go for it, Dom. Pity it couldn't be that nun who has taken over your mind the last few days."

Dominic spun around, his face an expression of mock seriousness. "O ye evil beast, what wicked thoughts thou harvests."

With that admonition, he pirouetted the other 180 degrees and hastened away lest his face betray his intentions.

The county's records listed Dominic's hideaway as Emerald Nest, but after his first few outings, he had renamed it Surrender Point. He had found that on every occasion, some aspect of surrendering would be involved, whether voluntarily or involuntarily.

He would surrender large sums of money, and in exchange, one lass would give up her virginity, another would discard her vanity, and the uninitiated would free themselves of inhibitions. It was not always a smooth exchange, but Dominic had never been displeased on the long drive back to his favorite Brooklyn.

He was surprised to see a blue Volkswagen Jetta idling in the parking lot of Surrender Point. In it was Sister Ruth, and when she saw him pull alongside, she turned off her engine and climbed out of the car, apologizing for the early arrival.

Dominic was pleased. He told himself he had been right all along. The vibrations were there. They were on the same wavelength. This nun was a woman first and foremost, and it was obvious that his charm had penetrated the facade of piety.

He was in awe of himself and the impending conquest. He would soon be elevated to great heights with a banner that screamed, "Hail the Man! He is in a class by himself"

How many men could lay claim to seducing a nun? He knew

of none. Sister Ruth interrupted his thoughts. "I brought a change of clothing because I figured your friends might be uncomfortable with my habit. In point of fact, it might be altogether better if you didn't mention my ecclesiastic devotions."

Dominic showed her to the guest room and he entered another bedroom to remove his Armani suit and Bally shoes, putting on Pierre Cardin shorts, polo shirt and loafers. He took off his heavy gold chain but kept the diamond on his little finger. It was big enough to substitute if ever his yacht lost its anchor.

Minutes later, when Sister Ruth emerged, she was a complete secular being, dad in colorful cotton blouse, clinging short pants and cute open-toed moccasins. He could see no telltale signs of underclothes. What he could see were nipples, proud and protuberant.

He crossed his legs to hide the bulge in his pants.

She sat beside him on the sofa and he inhaled her scent as she chatted animatedly about a range of subjects. Then after what seemed like hours, she suddenly jumped up.

"Where is the computer?" she asked, seemingly unaware of Dominic's wide-open mouth and lustful expression.

"It's in that bedroom," he stammered, heading towards a dome-shaped pair of doors.

There it was—a fully Loaded computer with a four-in-one printer/scanner/copier/fax.

"It's all yours if you like it." His voice was matter-of-fact. It was as if he gave away a computer every day.

"Oh, my gosh, it's a miracle. The Lord has answered my prayers. He guided me to you."

Sister Ruth rushed to plant a kiss on the cheek of the very generous Mr. Chavez, but the aroused magnate had another destination for her fresh, unpainted lips. He grabbed her arms and crushed his lips on hers.

He felt her resist at first; then she ceased to struggle, seemingly resigned to the inevitable.

She put up only token resistance when he guided her to the king-sized bed. Then she let him loosen the buttons on her blouse, releasing a pair of pert, prominent breasts, which somehow reminded him of a matching set of stalagmites he had seen in a Disneyland cave.

She stopped him for a moment and murmured something about pills, Leaving him to collect her purse, which had been left in the guest room.

She had been gone for almost three minutes when a lightning bolt slammed into his erotic membrane. He wondered what kind of nun would be walking around with birth control pills in her handbag.

The door opened slowly, and he had his wordless answer. He saw a woman dressed in battle fatigues and light army boots, no longer a nun. And he knew even before he lifted his eyes to hers that he would see green eyes flashing mockingly at him.

As soon as the confirmation was made, the door shut with a loud thud.

Lizzie was off to set the perfect stage since she was sure the enemy would be enraged by the elaborate deception in his own backyard.

Chapter 11

Third and Final Lesson

Her wariness of the man came from a gut feeling-and raw instinct. He was an animal. A beast dressed in silk and cashmere.

And more frighteningly, when she looked past the charm, he came across as a puzzle with more than one piece missing.

Although her confidence was high, she was very aware of his ruthlessness, and she underwent a sequence of changes: fear to revulsion, consternation to single-mindedness, and then rage to caution.

As soon as she slammed the bedroom door, she raced to the back porch, whose glass sliding door she had earlier disengaged. Down a short flight of stairs and across perfectly mown lawns she loped, before vaulting a chest-high wooden fence and pausing momentarily to allow the pursuer to see in which direction the pursued was fleeing.

She didn't have long to wait.

Dominic burst through the open porch door clad only in his polka-dot boxer shorts, and minus footwear. He looked every bit an angry bear.

A cheery wave from Lizzie seemed to further infuriate him, and she could hear the answering growl despite the distance between them.

She ran on among scattered pine trees and thick saplings, deep into a forested area. Dominic followed at breakneck speed, wanting only to catch the conniving bitch and really teach her a thing or two.

He swore he would give her the mother of all lessons and never again would she be so presumptuous to provoke and challenge a real man.

Did she think he was in the same mold as Mike, whom she had hospitalized, or Clarence, who had run off to Chicago in shame? Nol He was the controller, the boss man, and she was soon going to :find out. No mercy for the imposter nun.

"Cha, man," he spat out, resorting to the vernacular of his Jamaican friend, who owned a restaurant near his main store.

Lizzie stood waiting in the darkness of the forest, but her mind was a bonfire of emotions. One ember burned brightest, the one that highlighted the fact that she did not dare engage the war veteran in any prolonged physical contest. She had felt the hardness of his muscles and seen up dose the broad, hairy chest.

A rustle of leaves and a solid landing on both feet brought Dominic into a small clearing, and he stared stoically at her across ten yards of foggy space.

He was confused, but he felt an intimacy with fate.

Intuition told him that this encounter could have disastrous consequences, and he had to come good. He could not con his way out. Neither could he bribe the opponent. And he had nothing to blackmail her with.

The weapons he had consistently used in the past were useless now.

The violence-ridden culture of the poor Spanish made intimidation easy for men like Dominic, and thus, he decided to lean heavily on that fact.

'I'm going to crush you slowly. No woman can get the better of me. You think the other night was bad, wait until I'm finished with you today. You'll never fool with a man again."

She was getting restless.

She had read in a book recently that restrained kinetic energy could have a corrosive effect on thinking. The same chapter had claimed that the secret of optimal performance was to keep the mind focused, but the body completely relaxed. From her present state of mind, she doubted that the author had ever tried the exercise of which he spoke so knowingly.

It was her turn, and she shouted back, "From nothing, nothing is made."

This was done to confuse Dominic.

And in fact, it did.

"You calling me nothing? I'm going to show you something," he bellowed at her.

But before he could move, she spoke again, this time in measured tones, calmly and dogmatically, and in Spanish: "No cojones. Un maricon."

Although he realized he was in the slipstream of combat that warranted reliance on his army training, he saw red with the taunts about his manhood and had advanced three paces before he caught himself He could hear his Sunday school teacher reading aloud a passage from Proverbs that all the Confirmation candidates had to memorize: "A wise man restrains his anger and overlooks insults. This is to his credit."

She was no fool, he thought. She was deliberately goading him, trying to disorient and distract him from any type of coordinated game plan.

His eyes bored into hers, and the monologue began again.

"Think you so smart. It is bitches like you who push a man to the limit. You've bitten off more than you can chew."

He stopped in mid-sentence to glance left and right in stunned disbelief. One minute she was right there listening to him, then she had disappeared into thin air.

He bolted between two imposing jacaranda trees, frantically scanning the misty surroundings, looking every which way and all at once.

Where was she? he wondered.

The mocking silence grew loud and spurred his fear. Another intruding thought penetrated: The bitch is playing with my mind.

Suddenly, something cold and solid hit the nape of his neck, and with astounding reflexes, his right hand moved like a shot out of a gun's barrel to grab the object.

A quick glance told him it was his gold chain with the twenty-four-carat crucifix, which he had earlier left on the dining table.

He stared numbly at the piece of expensive ornamentation; his feet like sacks of cement. He looked up in the trees, beyond them, and around them. But no one was there.

Then, as if by magic, she was back, signaling her return with a severe and crippling blow to the tendons behind his right knee.

He was forced to drop into a crouch before pivoting to face the angry enemy, her green eyes penetrating and steady between the branches and vines that separated them.

Gone was his haughtiness of the previous minutes. He scrambled to regain his dignity, and his lips were in motion before his brains had clicked into gear.

He was surprised to hear himself say, "Why don't you stand up and fight like a man?"

A disdaining chuckle from Lizzie underlined the irony and stupidity of the hastily blurted taunt, and salt was added to the wound when she replied, "Then it would still be uneven—a man against a faggot. I should know from your performance the other night."

The ultimate insult was too much for Dominic. The former long-jump champion leapt across the intervening space and could almost feel his hands around her neck. But Lizzie had anticipated the rush of adrenaline the jibe might engender, and she sidestepped adroitly before delivering a crippling "toe punch" to the exposed ribs, even before his body had touched the hard-packed earth.

He was quick to react despite the instant throbbing in his side. He rolled to his right, and through the penumbra of his blurred vision, saw the woman he knew as Sister Ruth come rushing towards him.

He lashed out instinctively and viciously, catching her right ankle and sweeping the pivoting leg from under her, sending her crashing to the ground.

He lunged full length, linebacker style, and a desperate wrestling match ensued.

Dominic used fury as his propellant while Lizzie relied on craftiness to keep her competitive.

Ever so slowly, Dominic's superior bodyweight was tipping the scale in his favor when, without warning, Lizzie grabbed his scrotum and tugged violently.

A strangled cry burst past his lips and he let go of his slippery nemesis. She was up and running, troubled by the thought of near failure and overtaken by a sudden desire to put distance between them—at least for a while.

She went deeper into the woods, remembering the topography of the land, especially a clearing beyond a massive fallen oak tree.

Somehow, she had to turn things completely in her favor, by changing the rules of the game. If not, all her carefully laid plans could pale into insignificance with one incalculable blunder, and she definitely could not afford to let that happen.

It was at this point that she shuddered as she remembered the fierce struggle on the muddy earth. There, she had felt the innate violence beneath his skin like the deadly tropical piranha gathering momentum to snare yet another hapless victim.

In her heart, she really wanted to continue running, but she couldn't. She saw herself back in the woods where she was raped, and right then, she understood that the defining moment could not be postponed. She had to act decisively or continue running for the rest of her life.

She ran on for a few more yards and then stopped.

A shout of "Got ya' ended her cogitations and endorsed her recent decision to stay and face the enemy.

His shout was followed by a familiar boastful prediction: "It's going to end right here and now. No more pussy-footing."

She was prepared and ready with her countermove.

"Ha! Ha! So why are you trembling?"

He couldn't help but protest in arrogance, "Me, trembling?"

At the same time, he stretched out both hands, and indeed, in the subdued light of the clearing, he was puzzled to see a slight movement like a nervous quiver.

The golden opportunity proffered was more appreciated than the most sought-after gift at Christmas, and Lizzie said a hearty thank-you for the unguarded moment with a bone-crushing right hand, followed by a precise chop to the bridge of his nose. Blood smeared his upper lip and he snorted in pain.

He swung wildly, but the intended target proved elusive, and before he could regain his balance, she stepped behind him and delivered a flat-palmed double blow to his ears. The action could be likened to that of an East Indian woman in a village in Guyana hurriedly clapping the traditional roti for her family's late dinner—but using excessive force.

The ensuing sound reverberated harshly among the trees like a clap of thunder, and it must have been the same in the interior of Dominic's ears. He collapsed, as his eardrums seemed to rupture. The thousands of nerve fibers that collected vibrations from the tympanic membrane imploded, disrupting all other senses and immediately triggering incoherence, disorientation and total confusion in his brain.

As he flopped around like a broken doll, Lizzie completed the humiliation.

She ripped the boxer shorts from his body, leaving him completely naked; then, taking two plastic cords from her back pocket, she tied him to a sturdy young tree.

Froth, expletives and unintelligible Spanish flowed from his mouth as Lizzie pulled him to a kneeling position and secured his feet and hands behind the tree.

Next came a thriving ant nest that she had nurtured for three days. It was placed between his quivering knees.

Tears and viscid mucus fought for prominence on his face as a metamorphosis unraveled under an invisible banner that could easily have read "Anatomy of Violence."

"Anything you need to tell me before I go?" Lizzie asked.

Apparently he had a lot to say because the sentences poured out. Garbled words were superimposed on others like a voluble old man attempting to speak without his dentures.

"Guess not," said Lizzie as she pulled something like a silk handkerchief from her side pocket and tenderly wiped his eyes and mouth. When she was finished, she dropped the cloth at his feet and walked off without a backward glance. He didn't have to look to know it was the same panties that he and his friends had ripped from her on the way to violating her body.

At that moment, he unceremoniously said goodbye to his lunch of spaghetti and meatballs, the culinary evidence joining the other excretions collecting in a puddle between his legs.

A long line of ants had already started the uphill climb. And he could smell the fecund odor of his own fear.

Many people knew it, but only one person—a psychiatrist—dared to say it. For this, he was no longer a confidante.

Dominic was psychotic and had graduated from Valium to a strong depressant called Cooladol; he needed one now.

A five-hundred-milligram tablet, like the one he had put in Lizzie's margarita would calm him and take his mind off the advancing army of ants moving purposely up his legs. He had heard of the queen bee, always at the head of her column, now he wondered if the lead ant was also of royal persuasion.

He tried to shake his body, legs and hands-all without success. There was no give in the cords, and he accorded grudging respect to his conqueror, figuring her for a Green Beret or Special Forces specialist. Look how easily she had suckered him with that taunt about his hands shaking.

He didn't know how he was going to get out of the tight situation he was in, but when he did, he was going to move heaven and earth to confront her again.

Losing was a bitter pill, worse than the physical ordeal he now faced. But even as he brooded, the picture of a sleek, powerful feline moving purposely away remained with him.

Lizzie walked off, thanking the Lord for allowing her to capitalize on Dominic's lapses. In a straight fight she would not have lasted two three-minute rounds. But vanity had proven to be his downfall.

She could not hold back the smile as she flashbacked and saw him with arms outstretched, as if in supplication, trying to prove his invincibility.

Father O'Hara's often-repeated exhortation to take advantage of macho hesitations had roared into her head, like Brooklyn's no. 5 subway express. She had gratefully hastened the end.

She was walking away victorious. She had avenged her rape and should be exultant. But she was not.

Instead, she harbored misgivings as she retraced her path of revenge.

She had felt unfulfilled after dealing with Lucifer.

With Slick, she had stepped away from the filth and confusion with absolutely no regrets.

And now, after this latest confrontation, she was cool and calm.

What am I becoming? she wondered.

A fiend? An avenger? An assassin?

She lingered on that final thought, walking slowly past Dominic's BMW and into his cheerless love nest.

Chapter 12

The Curtain Comes Down

The phone rang twice before it was answered.

"Hello, DC. May 1 help you?

"Shanchez, please."

"May I ask who is calling?"

"You may not."

Wow! That must be Sanchez's bitchy wife calling, the young clerk thought, shivering from the ice in the voice. She shouted for the number two man. He came right away.

"Sanchez here."

"Sanchez, 1 have no time to waste, so listen carefully. If you look at the caller 1D, you will see this call is originating from Surrender Point. 1 left your boss naked in the woods behind the house, and he may be hurt, his pride mostly. 1 suggest you come quickly."

"What ... who are you? This is not April Fools' Day. Let me talk to Dominic."

There was no response from the other end as Sanchez waited to turn the monologue back into a dialogue. Dial tone soon signaled an end to that expectation.

For three days, Lizzie had driven the rented Jetta to the private playground of Surrender Point and unobtrusively reconnoitered the large forested area adjoining the exclusive property that boasted a swimming pool and a tennis court.

Her odometer had docked the distance between the country house and the store on Flatbush Avenue at 84.5 kilometers. Travel time was between forty minutes and one hour.

So there was no need to hurry after she had hung up on faithful Sanchez.

In the bathroom, she rubbed her body vigorously, using an

herbal soap and shampoo she knew she could not afford. She replaced the nun's habit and put the coronet back on her head, then paused at the wet bar displaying an intoxicating blend of liquors.

The alcohol beckoned like a lover, and feeling the need for a little spiritual fortification, she took a swig from a bottle of her favorite, Hpnotiq, washing down the unpleasant memories and remorse without the benefit of a chaser.

She picked up the computer monitor and took it to the rented car, then quickly returned for the CPU, the four-in-one machine and finally, a-large bundle of cash held together by thick rubber bands.

It wasn't haste that propelled her, although she preferred to be well away when Sanchez and his army came looking for their boss. It was the will to finish what she had started. The miasma that had polluted her thoughts since the sexual assault weeks ago had dissipated; the fog that had clouded her head had evaporated.

Suddenly, a new and clear perspective was evolving.

It was time to head home. She just had to clear the last hurdle and complete the circle, which had begun with Roger selecting her for the course. She had made a promise to herself, and as Father O'Hara would always chide, "Don't make promises if you can't keep them."

She had just one more significant deed to perform in New York—just a small matter of pulling the curtain down on a brazen charade.

Lizzie watched from a promontory half a mile from the house as three SUVs streamed through the gate of Surrender Point. Sanchez led the charge, sending one man into the house and deploying five others among the trees.

In less than five minutes, a sharp whistle pierced the air and another answered. Soon, the entire group reassembled, Sanchez and Zapata supporting Dominic between them, his head drooping as if he were in pain or discomfort. One man had donated his T-shirt to the boss, and it provided adequate coverage. It belonged to Big Joe, who was over six feet tall and had a beer-belly girth.

Lizzie had seen him outside the store sitting in a van with a large styrofoam container in his hand. When she left DC half an hour later, he was still eating.

She ungraciously felt that all his T-shirts should proclaim to the world, "I eat, therefore I am."

She brought up the rear some distance back as the entourage blazed towards Brooklyn and then into the side entrance of

Queensbrook Hospital. A doctor, two interns and four nurses were already at the entrance, for Mr. Dominic Chavez was a member of the hospital's board of directors, elected more because of his considerable annual contribution, than civic qualifications.

Two policemen were chatting up a full-bosomed receptionist. She bent down for something, and gravity went to work on her breasts, giving lie to the frailty of thread.

The few strands holding the top button of her frilly cotton top were indeed defying the logics of containment.

The spectacle was transfixing, but when the policemen learned who the new patient was, they regretfully tore themselves away and ran after the fast disappearing gurney.

They caught up with the twelve-man team in a huddle waiting for the elevator.

"What happened to you, Mr. Chavez?" asked Jose Perez, the younger of the two cops.

"Nothing," mumbled Dominic.

"All those marks on your body, bloodstained clothing, you're obviously in pain, and you tell me nothing is the matter?"

"Leave it alone, junior. I have nothing to say."

They were both from Puerto Rico, but they had never liked each other, and it had taken a long time before any discernible level of congeniality had been negotiated.

"I have to report this one, buster," the rookie persisted, grabbing for his radio.

His robust sidekick, Alexander Kingsley, a veteran of twenty-four years, held his hand and signaled for him to cool it. He took over, aware of Chavez's influence and spending power in the community.

"Mr. Chavez, it is our duty to investigate crime, assaults and altercations, among other things. Are you sure you don't want to make a report?"

"Okay, Kingsley, you want a report. Here's what happened: A woman dressed like a nun robbed me of all my money and clothes. She beat the shit out of me after drugging, tying me up and leaving me in a monstrous ant nest. You got everything down in your damn book, or do you want me to repeat the details?"

Dominic knew from experience that the more convoluted the lie, the rnore people were wont to believe it. No matter, he had added a liberal dose 0f the truth to further confuse the two policemen, who always appeared happy making their living off the pain of society's suffering.

Both cops laughed uproariously at Chavez's effort to get rid of them, and it was the effervescent Perez who touched Dominic and asked jokingly, pointing at an approaching figure. "Did the nun look like her?"

The immaculately dressed sister was about six feet away, solicitously enquiring of Dominic's health when the gurney-ridden patient sprang upright, yelling incoherently and gesticulating wildly. "She ... she ... that's her! She tied me up and stole my money and clothes! Arrest her, officers!"   .

The lawmen again convulsed with laughter. They figured that Chavez was really going overboard with his chameleon performance. It seemed as if he had a nun fixation.

But mirth turned to concern as Chavez, though restrained by Sanchez, aimed a kick at the holy lady, missing her by just a few inches.

The nightstick cleared Perez's sheath and landed squarely on Chavez's chest as he fought six pairs of restraining hands.

"Check her green eyes and hands! She ain't no sister. She is some sort of karate nut, beating up men for revenge," Dominic ranted.

Kingsley glanced at the nun's eyes. They were light brown and innocent. Whatever happened to Mr. Chavez today had also made him color-blind.

In the meantime, the Sister seemed nonplussed, muttering softly, more to herself than anyone else, "I can't believe Mr. Chavez is anything other than a decent businessman. Why is he accusing me of hitting him and stealing his money? Dear God, please forgive him for he knows not what he says."

She wanted to add the Guyanese Creole rationale "Thief from thief mek God laugh," but she declined.

The young policeman looked at the pious, delicate lady of the church and wondered how a deranged cretin like Chavez could tell such a lie on a nun. It was outrageous.

According to the law, he should ask the good sister just to remove one glove and display her dainty fingers, which would debunk the foolish notion that she was some fearsome karate juggernaut.

But he would look like a fool to his fellow officers, and with promotion just around the corner, he would not want the brass to hear that he had suspected a nun of committing mayhem on an army veteran with a background of thuggery and other unwholesome activities.

"Sister, thank you very much for your help. It would be more than helpful if you can drop by the precinct during the week and sign a denial statement. Thanks again."

Her eyes cloudy with concern, she peered at his badge and said meekly, "You've been a great help, Officer Perez. I will drop by."

That was the last any of those persons gathered at the hospital ever saw of the nun.

✳   ✳   ✳

After the war comes the mop-up operation, followed by the strategic withdrawal.

To the victor the spoils.

She was back in her YMCA room, which had become her shrine, her safe house, where she kept her modest collection of personal belongings.

She had opted for self-service rather than thrice-a-week maid service, not for economical reasons, but because she had amassed a considerable sum of money from the three rapists. She felt no guilt about the acquisition. She looked at it as an inheritance, a requitable, though enforced, contribution to assuage and absolve them of their sins.

She was always a neat person, and even amidst her tribulations, she never allowed disorder to intrude. The moneybox bought from Staples had only three items—three bundles, each bound with rubber bands, each carrying its own sticker. The first read, "Lucifer—$362," the second, "Slick—$2, 105" and the biggest wad, "Dominic—a half day's taking from DC—$8,310."

She sat yoga style on the bed, pen hovering over a pad that already had three notations:

l. Renew passport
2. Can't leave country with more than $10,000
3. Use circuitous travel route

Within the next half hour, a complete list of dos and don'ts appeared, penned in her neat calligraphic hand.

The miniature Bible on the nightstand was conveniently opened at Proverbs 16: 9—"We should make plans, counting on God to direct us."

Chapter 13

Farewell to New York

It was her last night in New York, and sleep was a foreign concept. For a long time, she sat staring at the wall. The television was on, but the insipid sitcom humor had not been able to hold her attention.

She got up and stood at the window of her room. The sky was bright by moonlight and the air abuzz with ambient noises. Lampposts stood like robotic sentinels along a winding passageway meandering all the way to the Brooklyn Bridge.

Those same posts sported smiling faces and empty slogans, the better-funded campaigns in clear evidence. Some messages had no subtlety-"Don't stay back. Think black." Others openly slandered opponents. At election time, it was open season in New York.

Contradictory thoughts tumbled in her head like a washing machine in the spin cycle—a modicum of satisfaction commingled with doubt, compassion integrated with hurt, and futuristic payback mixed with misgivings. They continued to whirl around in the same way a blender would feverishly work to produce a satisfying puree.

But ever so slowly, the confusion and disquietude subsided to become just a slight throb and she found it propitious that as soon as that happened, the soothing voice of Johnny Nash drifted up from a nearby music box, crooning the latter day hit "I Can See Clearly Now."

Lizzie had had a hectic day, accomplishing the four major tasks she had set for herself.

First, she had gone to the Guyana Consulate on Seventh Avenue in Manhattan, a stone's throw from the famous Madison Square Garden. The officials there were very cordial and efficient and in a short time she left with her passport renewed.

She had gone through an elaborate scheme, advising the consulate personnel, via the telephone, that she was authorizing her sister to transact business on her behalf, but she later discovered that the subterfuge was unnecessary and that her name was not on a blacklist.

The trip was uneventful but for a lesson in the interpretation of good old-fashioned manners while she rode the elevator on her way up.

As soon as Lizzie boarded the electronic behemoth, she said, "Good morning" to the only other occupant—a wiry, aged man with Asian features. He responded with a startled Look on his face, simultaneously cowering in the farthest corner. He found enough courage to jab one of the numerous buttons at the side of the door, but if his intention was to escape, his middle finger betrayed him, and the well-used contraption groaned perceptibly on its way up.

Another quick finger jab stopped progress at the third floor and when the door opened, Lizzie uttered a pleasant "Bye."

The reed-thin man squeezed through the aperture like a startled rabbit, his destination as far away as possible from the woman with green eyes.

As he darted away, he was certain that she was new to New York and he figured that in a few more days, she would understand that one never spoke to strangers, especially in an elevator. In his book, that was the first law of the concrete jungle they lived in. As for the subways and buses, whether you sat or were a straphanger, one kept one's mouth shut and minded one's business.

Back in Brooklyn, she had gone to the outdoor market at the corner of Flatbush and Caton avenues, a tropical bazaar at any time of the year. She had walked around bemused, bonding with the West Indian ambience and aromas. It was a potpourri of cultural divergence, an amalgam of Diasporic productivity.

One man displayed a ten-tier layer of caps, the peaks peeping out from all 360 degrees of his head—Jamaican, Haitian and African colors dominating.

Next to him was a pyramid of cups and mugs with the maps of Caribbean countries. And opposite, a conglomeration of leather key-rings, bracelets and handbags in creative designs, spread out.

Music blared from two boom boxes the size of large refrigerators while bootleg CDs and DVDs were neatly stacked on custom-made racks.

Books on Malcolm X, Martin Luther King, and a host of brothers, whose messages had never been heard, lay on a blanket, nestling with the salt of the earth.

Sandwiched between stacked tinned food, cling-wrapped pigtails and salt beef in buckets, was an exquisite display of edible panties and sex-oriented paraphernalia, attracting quite a lot of attention.

The same seller, Guyanese from his idiom, had on display small bundles of kapadula, granny-backbone, man-piaba and other herbs ascribed with aphrodisiac propensities. He stridently sang their praises, knowing that virility was always a money spinner.

Barbadians, Jamaicans and other islanders remonstrated with their own, while Guyanese and Trinidadians flashed golden smiles. They were all haggling for best prices, seeking bargains and "trying on" items for the perfect fit.

A few blocks away, the giant conglomerates, Sears and Macy's, would have to wait until after the Caton experience.

Travel always played havoc with Lizzie's gastronomic juices, and now her stomach was telling her what her head already knew. But she still had an hour before the rendezvous with her uncle, who was coming all the way from New Jersey.

She took the Flatbush no. 41 bus to the junction with Nostrand Avenue and walked across to the Brooklyn College campus, looking like an eager first-year student.

She sat on the lawns amid crammers, studious-looking scholars and outright nerds. Jews, Blacks, Chinese, Puerto Ricans and Caucasians—the campus was alive with them, burdened with massive backpacks and dressed in every conceivable type of outfit.

In the midst of hectic academic activity, T-shirts, denims, short skirts and dirty sneakers were fashionable, and she blended easily in the crowd as she took in the orderly tertiary ambience that she would certainly seek if ever she returned to New York.

The alarm on her watch buzzed insistently, and she reluctantly retraced her steps to catch the no. 44 going the other way, up Nostrand Avenue.

Even before 9/11, New York had always been a city in the constant throes of simultaneous destruction and construction, and the area of Crown Heights showed that as clearly as anywhere.

The bus made a detour but slowed to a crawl as a group of men dressed in black surveyed boarded-up properties. Traffic waited without fuss. It was common practice. The ubiquitous Jews were returning to reclaim and gentrify the structurally sound townhouses they had ill-advisedly sold when ambitious immigrants moved into "their" neighborhood.

Approximately eighteen minutes later, she walked into Tripee's West Indian Restaurant on Nostrand Avenue and Crown Street in mid-Brooklyn.

The immediate warmth was exhilarating and the atmosphere friendly. Laughter and tantalize pervaded as she approached the serving counter and asked to speak with Mr. Tripee, the owner.

"Who wants to see me? Let me see your face. Tripee ain't got 'Mister.' It's either Tripee or Mr. Gordon. What can I do for you?"

Her uncle had warned her about his egregious friend, whose colorful language was not for the ears of the bashful.

But today must have been a special day, she thought, for the voice addressing her was genteel and almost boyish.

She was mesmerized by his cheerful demeanor, which, along with a portly figure, gave him an avuncular look. However, her uncle had said his friends could attest to the age-old saying that "looks can deceive."

Tripee was a chef par excellence, but it was not only his culinary expertise that had made him famous. It was also his remarkable, uninhibited lifestyle, which had produced a score of offspring. Many were coevally aged.

"Did my uncle John leave a message for me? I'm supposed to meet him here," Lizzie asked.

"Uncle John, Uncle John? 'I don't know any Uncle John," replied the restaurant owner.

In a flash, she remembered. None of his friends ever called him by his given name. It was always Pompey this and Pompey that.

"I mean Pompey," she stammered.

"Oh, Pompey. You had me baffled there. Yes, he says the train is running late. I've been instructed to offer you whatever you want. So don't be shamefaced."

She smiled, not at the last comment, but the manner in which he spoke. All those short sentences without pause, without inflection. It was music to the ears, transporting her back to Albouystown, where she had been nurtured.

Lizzie considered herself a gourmet. In Guyana, her choice of a super meal would have been cow-foot soup, followed by curried hassar atop cook-up rice, and accompanied with fruit salad and a mouth-watering crab back. Carambola or awara drink would be the choice to slake her thirst.

She liked bangamary, tilapia, lukanani and snapper, but the river fish with the dark curved scales—hassar or cascadoo, as the Trinidadians called it—was a delicacy for special occasions.

However, the current choice did not include her preferences, and ever the connoisseur, she took her time selecting pepper pot and white rice, fried plantains, a huge bowl of salad and a tall glass of ice-cold mauby.

Her uncle arrived, and soon afterwards, he dragged her over to where the old boys' network was in full cry, reminiscing about long-forgotten girlfriends, daring episodes that had attracted police attention and personal achievements barely remembered. Nicknames :flew nonstop—Prezzie, Legge, Short Man, Puree, Kincaid, Sarjo, Sack, Cutty, Fake Head, Boogey, Doc, Kid, Cotton George, K-Shoe, Cardo, Mallet. It was unending.

Then miraculously, an hour later, Uncle John proclaimed loudly, "See you later, guys. Time to rap with my niece. And if you see her again, pass her straight."

Amidst shouts of "no way" and "impossible," they moved to the other end of the restaurant where Lizzie recounted her time in New York, minus details of the assault.

Her uncle disclosed that during the past weeks, he had been extremely worried because some official-sounding person had kept calling his home, asking to speak to her. Rude instructions to desist had put an end to the irritation.

A tearful farewell followed their discussion, and Lizzie, bolstered with a hefty two-hundred-dollar "raise" from her favorite uncle, headed back to her haven. There, she packed the computer equipment that she had taken from Surrender Point into two boxes and with the help of the YMCA's security guard, took them up the block to post by air to Guyana.

At the same shipping office, she paid for special delivery of a thick, padded envelope, which had her name and address. It contained almost $5,000, the bills flattened between sheets of carbon paper and old newspapers.

Way past midnight, Lizzie climbed into bed and badly needed sleep came—dreams intruding with blurred lines of demarcation between fact and fiction.

A wake-up call at five o'clock, followed by an invigorating cold shower and hot breakfast, spurred Lizzie's enthusiasm and anxiety. She was the first to check in at the airport.

Chapter 14

Long Way Home

"Ladies and gentlemen, please return to your seats and fasten your seatbelts. We are going to land at Boa Vista, Brazil, in a few minutes."

The voice of the clearly bored stewardess droned on, but Lizzie heard nothing. She was tired from the cross-continent jaunt, going first to Mexico before heading south to the Brazilian border town via the Dominican Republic. From there, she would cross over to Lethem, a Guyana town bordering Brazil. She would then journey overland to arrive incognito at her village. She wanted her arrival to be kept secret for a while.

The Brazilian Airlines Airbus touched down smoothly and she was past immigration and customs in a jiffy, with just one piece of carry-on luggage. She took a taxi to Bon Fin, the border crossing point, and then hired a private speedboat to cross the Takuru River and put her among the people she loved.

Home was still many hundreds of miles away, obliquely across the heartland of the country, but she felt good, better than at any time over the past weeks.

A beat-up Ford that had seen better days took her to Lethem's only guesthouse to secure a room for the night and then it whisked her to the Interior Airlines office, where she booked the last seat on a nine-passenger charter, leaving at six o' clock the following morning.

Mosquitoes and disquieting thoughts plagued her sleep, and she was thankful when her new watch alarmed at 4:00 a.m. and an antenna like probe tickled her wrist. It was the only luxury she had allowed herself from the money she had taken from the three cruel musketeers.

The Islander aircraft sprinted down the pebble-strewn runway, headed for the skies. One Canadian schoolgirl, so happy to be in the tropics, began reading aloud from a glossy magazine named *Explore*

Guyana, Land of Many Waters: "Guyana is socially and politically a Caribbean destination, though geographically and anthropologically part of the South American continent."

"Is that true?" the young tourist asked, turning to Lizzie.

Lizzie nodded her head in the affirmative, and this gesture suddenly opened a floodgate of questions.

Lizzie, who before enlisting in the army had been a teacher like her mother Margaret, slipped easily into that familiar role, and for an hour she held the visitors spellbound with facts about her beloved country.

As the small plane skirted the Pakaraima Mountain Range, she pointed out the majestic Kaieteur Falls, careful to underline that its 7 41-foot perpendicular freefall with thirty-five thousand gallons of water per second, made it the world's largest waterfall. She then quietly reminded the passengers that it was five times the height of Niagara Falls.

She spoke with pride when she told of the vast mineral wealth found inland—gold, diamonds, bauxite, and manganese. And as if on cue, the pilot banked a sharp right over the Canadian-owned Omai Gold Mines where, in 2002, a total of 319,600 ounces of gold had been mined. At $214 per ounce, the schoolgirl paused to do the math while visualizing Indiana Jones or Crocodile Dundee in such a setting, searching for the legendary El Dorado, Sir Walter Raleigh's fabled city of gold.

They soared over miles upon miles of vast tropical rainforest, replete with a variety of wildlife, and mouths fell open when Lizzie casually mentioned that Guyana's area of 215,000 square kilometers was roughly the size of the United Kingdom, and that its landmass could swallow almost all of the Caribbean.

But Lizzie was not one to hide the negatives. She related how ethnic strife, even before independence in 1966, had continued to severely splinter the country's infrastructure and prevent the nation from fully developing. She told how, in 2002, the per capita gross domestic product was a mere $760, making Guyana one of the poorest countries worldwide. And she mentioned the nation's massive foreign debt, which had been $1.4 billion in 1998, but had been reduced to $850 million four years later.

"Wow! Are you an official guide with the airline?" asked the young lady, in awe of the narrator's matter-of-fact erudition.

"No, I'm just an ordinary local returning from abroad. I really miss the culture mix and laissez-faire acceptance of life. The grass is definitely greener here."

The schoolgirl was not done yet. She turned to her mother and spoke with the openness of unbridled youth. "Mommy, this lady is brighter than any teacher I know. Can't you get her to come to Toronto and teach? You're with the department of education."

The mother, conscious that everyone in the aircraft, including the pilot, was looking at her and waiting for a reply, said, "It isn't as easy as you think. But I'm going to take her name and address, and hopefully, we can keep in touch. I do agree that she is marvelous with her facts and delivery. She's an asset to her country."

Lizzie accepted the compliments, fully aware that she was never going to drift into the vast Caribbean lumpen proletariat, hustling a living, doing what the indifferent North Americans no longer wanted to do.

She had returned to settle a score and then to fulfill her potential in an underdeveloped and unappreciated paradise.

There was no respite for her as the plane bucked and bounced on air currents.

The young lady was at it again.

"Why do the people look so different from one another?"

Lizzie knew exactly what she meant. She looked into her briefcase and extracted a sheaf of paper. "Only yesterday, I downloaded this report by the Council of Hemispheric Affairs (COHA). Two relevant chapters will enlighten you.

"Originally, the Dutch, English and French established colonies in what is now known as Guyana. Subsequently, Britain gained control of the majority of the area during the Napoleonic Wars and established British Guiana in 1831. During that period, African slaves were introduced to the land to work the sugarcane plantations, propelling the colony's economy forward. After slavery was abolished in 1834, a wave of indentured workers arrived from India, Portugal, and China.

"A century later, the nation has one of the most diverse populations in the region—approximately 50 percent Indian, almost 40 percent of African descent and substantial populations of Amerindian, Portuguese, Chinese, and mixed ethnicities."

Chapter 15

Back Home

The plane landed in misty conditions at Bartica, the gateway to the gold and diamond districts of Guyana. The inquisitive schoolgirl and her mother deplaned after a spirited exchange of addresses and phone numbers.

The next stop was Charity, a major settlement on the Pomeroon River, and finally, her destination—Mabaruma.

Lizzie could have flown directly from John F. Kennedy Airport to Guyana's Cheddi Jagan Airport at Timehri, but she wanted to avoid attention. She wanted to go back to her little Catholic village of Mora Mission, one of thirty-eight in the sub-region.

She wanted to be one with her past and to let memories swirl and eddy. She needed to draw strength from a gentle, fructiferous land before venturing into the big city to confront intrigue and deceit.

Mabaruma, nestling alongside the Venezuelan border, was one of the first communities in which Amerindians settled. During the Spanish War of the eighteenth century, many settlements were uprooted, as the Dutch who occupied the country at that time did nothing to prevent the Spanish raids. Then in 1890, the British proclaimed the North West District, to which Mabaruma belongs, a British possession. This was followed by powerful religious crusades through which many natives were converted to Christianity.

Over the years, Mabaruma had evolved into a developed community with approximately eight thousand Amerindians occupying a geographic area of three thousand square miles. Most of the villages were accessed by road from the Mabaruma Compound, which was the center of all administrative 'activities. Travel by steamer was provided biweekly, but a reliable service of speedboats operated from Charity on a daily basis.

Lizzie let the oxen-drawn cart drop her off some fifty yards from the house her mother had inherited from her parents. No interior walls, no glass windows, no doors. Just like the typical Amerindian village where there were no discernible boundaries, only tacit landmarks serving that purpose.

She walked quietly, hoping to surprise Maggie, but just before ascending the stairs, she heard voices, and then her mother's easy laughter.

She felt guilty about eavesdropping but stood transfixed, listening.

The other voice belonged to a man, and for a brief moment, Lizzie wondered if it could be her father.

She rapped on the door. When Maggie asked who it was, the answer was a curt "It's your daughter, remember me?"

A chair toppled. The door was flung open. Mother and daughter embraced for an eternity, oblivious of the visitor.

"Ahem." A polite cough brought them back to earth and Maggie pulled Lizzie by the arm to effect introductions. Lizzie tugged back, her eyes flashing the question. Is he my father?

The tears of welcome gave way to a wholesome, unfettered burst of laughter. Maggie had to control herself to reply; "No, he's not."

"Jeffrey, this is my daughter, Elizabeth."

The stranger took the extended hand and said, "Don't think me presumptuous, but I think I already know all about you, Ruth Elizabeth. Your mother never stops talking about you, and I now see why."

"A sweet talker, Mom, you'd better watch out."

"Jeffrey Blackwell is the new government administrative officer for the region. He's here to entice me to become a civil servant and education officer for the region. I was just telling him that I would only consider the offer after I had heard from you ... and poof, you are here. By the way, girl, why were you incommunicado so long?"

Mr. Blackwell got up quickly; saying, "You girls have a lot of catching up to do. I'll be staying at the regional guesthouse until tomorrow. I hope to have your answer by then."

"Sure will ... and thanks."

"I'll work on her, Mr. Blackwell. She needs to get away from home for a while."

"Thanks, Elizabeth. I may have a job for you too."

"No thanks, I'm still a commissioned officer in the Guyana Defence Force. But I'll keep the offer in mind.

After the government officer had departed, via a taxi summoned by cell phone, Lizzie kicked off her shoes and lay contentedly in the hammock inside the house. Her mother sat comfortably on the floor nearby.

They talked and talked about everything that had happened during Lizzie's absence, but the daughter could not bring herself to speak of the assault in the park. She willed herself to elaborate on the aborted SMET course and her weeks in New York.

Maggie knew her daughter well and suspected that a vital part of the American drama was not being told. She said nonchalantly, ""Whenever you feel like talking about the missing part of your story, I'll be here to listen. It hurts to know you are hiding something from me, but take your time."

"Guess you know how I feel about you withholding information about my father's identity."

Maggie was startled, not by the statement, which was true, but by its frankness. She said no more on the subject.

Later, Lizzie felt a thirst for the cool juice of the water coconut, so she slipped a sheath with a short, sharp cutlass over her shoulders and climbed a tall tree overlooking the river. She drank the contents of three nuts and devoured their thick, pulpy jelly.

From her perch among the branches, she gazed on the murky Essequibo waters rushing to meet the Atlantic-turbulent and infinite. Her thoughts roamed far and wide but invariably returned to her own disturbing situation.

For a while, she was alert and wide awake; then she dozed off as the eloquent silence of rural life palpably engulfed her.

She dreamt of her pet dog, Ginger. She saw herself talking to him and observing how his prominent ears moved, responding to a range of emotions. She could see him in Lamaha Gardens, where she had left him with Roger, scolding the two compact and dangerous Dobermans with a dour, paternalistic expression that demanded obedience.

She was always happy in this kind of environment, where the forces of nature seemed to pay special attention, and although she knew she would soon have to head back to army headquarters, she still wanted to slip back in time to relive precious moments.

She returned to her bedroom and retrieved a strong box from under the bed.

It was her reliquary, where she kept everything sacred—the

rosary made of beads, lovingly put together by Father O'Hara; the gold broach she had gotten at her baptism; the silver dollar heirloom from her grandmother's brother, a fierce Amerindian tribal chief; her first ever doll, still attired in its original clothes; her first attempt at drawing.

And most prized of all was the intricately designed pair of eighteen-carat gold bracelets given by her mother when she, Lizzie, earned top marks at the Caribbean Examination Council's secondary schools' exams.

Her feet next took her a mile away to the small Catholic Church where Father O'Hara used to tutor her.

The new priest was an amiable red-faced Englishman named Henry, and he had no objection to her browsing through the refurbished library.

The room had always been her solace, her chamber of peace, lined with hundreds of tomes, most of which she had read.

She smiled as she saw the derelict lazy boy chair, which squeaked with the slightest movement, and the converted love seat, worn bare by generations of sinners.

Father O'Hara liked to make people feel at ease. He mused that the more comfortable one was, the more likely one would unburden. "Free-up" was the word he used frequently.

Still tacked to the wall was the faded caricature of a male figure, vital parts and points of the body highlighted. She could almost hear Father O'Hara's voice: "Never concentrate on hard and bony parts. Always aim for connective tissues, nerve centers, vertebrae and blood vessels."

He never pressed her to remember medical names like "ischemia" and "cerebellum." He only wanted her to appreciate the essence of the lesson. She had done so with gusto, and later, assurance.

It was now time for an afternoon river swim and she sought company. By then, the entire village knew of her return and it was easy to get volunteers.

She only swam when the sun was up, mindful of Father O'Hara's warning that the repeated abuse of cold water on the ear caused it to constrict, thus narrowing the ear canal and developing an exostosis. She knew this for sure because there were many half-deaf villagers, all of whom loved to swim in the river, especially early in the morning. They found the cold water invigorating and refused to "bow to newfangled ideas."

The first four hundred yards were torturous on the muscles

in her arms and legs, but gradually, the tightness disappeared and she found her rhythm to easily outdistance five others to the halfway buoy in the river.

She approached river swimming like long-distance running. The first mile was the hardest-before the mind and body had a chance to synchronize. Then controlled breathing took over, and later, the monotonous silence, into which the participant could inject pleasant thoughts and memories. It was Father O'Hara who swam alongside her for years, calculating distances and signaling the changes in phases. Now, she needed neither guidance nor instructions.

Back ashore, she accepted the praise and congratulations of a large group of villagers gathered at the river's edge. For although her mother had been a super athlete, a scholar and teacher, it was Lizzie's exploits and achievements that had gained hero-worship status throughout every Amerindian community in. the country.

Every district library carried facsimiles of everything in the press about her, the latest being a photograph of the SMET course participants waving exaggerated goodbyes at the airport. Even that fuzzy reproduction could not hide the enthusiasm on her face.

Maggie arranged a twilight "bush cook" in her honor and invited the entire village.

Everyone turned up with a contribution. Some came with live chickens and wild geese, others with meat—labba, deer, peccary, wild cow. Giant-sized cuffum fish, morocut, patwa, and the freshwater delicacies, lukanani and rilapia, were also in abundance.

A big pot boiled dasheens, tanias, eddoes and plantains, while fresh fruit lay in heaps—sapodilla, watermelon, monkey apple, soursop, golden apple, awara, and psidium.

Jars of chilled liquid were hauled from various creek beds and passed mostly among the men. The earthen containers held bush rum, the unlicensed potent alcohol distilled clandestinely in a homemade still, from a mixture of molasses, ammonia, lemons and a lot more items.

Drums, shanto singing and tribal dancing enlivened the impromptu festival, and at midnight, the end came with an arm-wrestling contest between Lizzie and a cocky teenager with bulging biceps.

Lizzie's fully developed right arm was more than a match for the opposing bulk, and given her competitive skills, she had the edge. But she had seen the adoring look in the eyes of the combatant's girlfriend and relented in the third and final stanza.

The animation of the two lovers and the haste with which they departed could only mean that his reward was assured.

Margaret enjoyed the night as much as anyone else, but Lizzie noted her displeasure when the bush rum and another lethal concoction called piwari started to take their toll. Even the elders, noted for their rectitude, seemed to abandon caution as they challenged. one another "to drink like a man."

After everyone had departed, Lizzie asked Maggie what had been bothering her during the festivities. "Why were you hiding the bush rum and piwari?"

"Nothing!"

But even as she spoke, the tremor in her voice betrayed. the lie.

Lizzie grew angry.

"Is it always going to be this way? You never give me a straightforward answer whenever I ask certain questions. From childhood, you have been evasive with your answers, shunting me off and advising me to ask Father O'Hara. Go to Father. Father will explain. What about you explaining?"

"Lizzie, please."

"Please what, Mom? Don't ask questions about my father? Don't ask why you won't have a man in your life? Don't ask why you were hiding those jars?"

Maggie stopped picking up the discarded plastic cups and plates. She lowered the partly filled twenty-gallon garbage bag to the sand and walked over to her daughter to hold both hands and address her.

"Guess you're right. I keep forgetting you are a big girl now. Every day, I solve problems for others, yet with you, I skirt the truth, attempting to protect you."

"I need truth, not evasion."

A slight hesitation, a moment of indecision, a flash of inspiration.

"Good, let's start with tonight."

They walked to the river's edge in the moonlight that lit up an azure sky with puffs of clouds and countless stars.

Maggie began simply.

"Piwari is a drink made largely by fermenting burnt cassava with grated sweet potatoes and sugarcane juice. The longer it stays in a dosed container, the more potent it becomes. I know you already know of its alcoholic power and also that of bush rum, but I want to make a point."

She paused as if it were painful to continue.

"Twenty-eight years ago, I saw a good man challenged to "drink like a man." It was that man's farewell party-his last night in this region for a while. He was the last person standing when all the homemade alcohol was finished and he just barely made it to the island in his speedboat. He had never been drunk before—and I am sure never since—so it was distressing to see him stumble and fall flat on his face. It was a moonlit night like this, and I witnessed a proud, decent man—the man I loved with all my heart—lose his way in an unfamiliar world of alcoholic stupor."

Lizzie glanced at her mother. Her face looked pale and there was a faraway look in her eyes. She was obviously back in time, remembering every moment as she dealt with the man's alcohol-clouded sub-consciousness.

"I don't know how I got him up the steps and into the house, but I had no choice since there's hardly any kind of communication technology in the village. I held him in my arms for most of the night, listening to his ramblings, his hurts and his pains. He clung to me like a lifeboat in a rough sea and I mopped his brow with my dress. And sometime before the sun rose the next day, you were conceived. There was neither a courtship, nor a love affair as we know it. Just that one time. And the irony of it all, your father knew little or nothing of what occurred."

There was a long, uneasy pause as Lizzie wondered how an intelligent woman like her mother could behave so impulsively.

She answered the question herself. Of course, intelligence was not a factor when other parts of the body were doing the thinking.

Still wrestling with confused thoughts, Lizzie found her voice. "Please answer two questions."

Maggie felt a tendril of panic, but stoically said, "Shoot."

"Is my father a non-Guyanese? Does he know I am his daughter?"

"Yes to the first, and no to the second."

Minutes later, they returned to the house.

Lizzie couldn't help but wonder if her father was married to someone else or if he had left the country before she was born. But she brushed aside those thoughts as soon as they entered her head. She lay on her bed thinking until the night embraced her and she drifted off to sleep.

In the adjacent room, Maggie had sought refuge in the safety of silence, dreading the day when her daughter would confront her and demand the truth.

Both slept peacefully as a gibbous moon hung placidly in a cloudless sky.

Chapter 16

Off to Georgetown

It was time for Georgetown.

She was well prepared to face Father O'Hara and then to confront the manipulative enemy soldier. She had confidence in her ability to handle the first task and silently prayed to be able to deal with the second challenge.

She felt sad at saying goodbye to her mother, but it was an unpleasant task that had to be handled.

"Mom, where are you? It's time for me to go," called out Lizzie.

Margaret came through the door fully dressed. "Are you sure you don't want me to come to town with you?"

"Mom, we went over this many times before. It wouldn't be convenient and I'm uncertain of the time frame. I've got to do what I've got to do. I'm going to see Father first and then report to headquarters."

"Lizzie, please don't go blaming Father for anything. He suffers every day, not knowing where you are and if you're safe. Then you have me keeping your return a secret, not even telling him. I don't agree with that at all. But you have assured me you know what you're doing."

Lizzie frowned, then laughed. "I was just about to ask you to pray for me, but who is there to listen to useless prayers?" She provided her own answer: "No one."

Maggie looked to the heavens before saying, "I am going to pray for you with every fiber of my being. One day soon, you'll realize how wrong you are. Don't blame God and Father O'Hara for Roger's twisted personality."

She moved to the bedroom and snatched up an overnight bag, already packed. "Not another word, I am going with you, even if it's only for a day."

Lizzie knew there was no point in arguing. She shrugged mutely, hoisted her backpack without one word of dissent, and together, they walked down a narrow lane, which took them to a broader path and finally to the river's edge. There, they took a speedboat to Charity and then the inter-island steamer to Georgetown

Father O'Hara was sure the figure in front of him was an apparition, a specter. He refused to believe his eyes. This was not his Lizzie, who had boarded the aircraft at Timehri, ebullient and effervescent, eager to serve her country.

For a priest, it was easy to gauge the wear and tear on the soul, What he saw shocked him, and his eyes probed searchingly for deeper trauma. Her discomfiture was apparent, her expression wavering from confusion to pleading.

For his part, he had seen her troubled many times before, but rarely had he felt as concerned.

The air was filled with uncertainty, she opting for restraint, and he wary of openly displaying raw emotion. She could not allow herself the luxury of tears, he dared not rekindle the fire of godfatherly love.

The awkward moment passed, and Father O'Hara found his voice. "Lizzie, my God, where have you been? Your mother is sick with worry and I have been praying for you to be safe. Where have you been?"

"Praying! Safe! There is no God" Lizzie said without a waver.

"Why, Lizzie, why do you blaspheme? What happened to you in the weeks you have been away?"

"My whole life has changed."

Father O'Hara had known her to be mysterious in the past, but never quite as enigmatic as this. He uttered a quick prayer, staring into his wrinkled palms, looking for answers like Aunt Cleo, the widely advertised palm psychic in Florida with the fake Jamaican accent.

He had so many questions, but he knew he would not get enough answers. Lizzie was single-minded when she wanted to be. He would be told only when she thought the time was right.

"Father, you taught me well. I owe my education, my career, and my life to you. But along the way, you told me things that are not true. The God you taught me to love does not, in turn, love me. He abandoned me when I needed Him most. I am no longer good for Him or any man now."

The priest heard the trembling voice, but all he could do was gaze into her troubled eyes and silently appeal to her to let it all out.

The silence stretched on. He could not control his anxiety.

"Exactly what do you mean?" the priest asked, his eyes widening in entreaty.

Lizzie was in no mood for commiseration. She carried on in a detached state of indifference, her voice cold and bitter.

"I just wanted to say hello to the man I love more than my biological father and to tell him face-to-face that he might be a good priest but a bad mentor. Father, I heard a voice like yours in a Brooklyn church, telling me to do what I had to do. That's the last piece of advice I'll ever take from a priest again."

With that, she walked away, looking as vulnerable as a puppy stranded in the middle of a busy intersection.

It took considerable time for him to regain his composure. He wasn't sure if it was Mark Twain, but familiar words rushed into his head—*How swift are the feet of the days of the years of youth.*

Only yesterday, he thought, Lizzie was a precocious elf, with a torrent of questions and a myriad of suggestions. Not yet three years old and swimming in the Essequibo River. At six, she was a barefooted Easter bunny staying atop a bucking bronco longer than any of the vacqueros at the Rupununi Rodeo. At eight, she had paddled a canoe more than a mile to get help for a critically ill villager. At ten, scoring the winning goal in the final of an annual schools' soccer competition.

At that time he had a hard time convincing the organizers that the winners had breached no regulation. However, the next year's tournament made it clear that the competition was only for boys.

But the memory that brought a tight smile to his lips was when she had hoisted his fast ball high into a coconut tree and ran between wickets for one hundred runs as he struggled to climb the tall tree in his cassock. It was one of her many fruitful innings in their favorite game of cricket.

In answer to her uncharacteristic outburst, the priest responded with downcast eyes and becalming honesty. "Lizzie, I made a vow so many years ago to make the church my whole life without a single distraction. I broke that vow the day you were born. Your eyes locked onto mine, and your lungs told me and the rest of the world to take notice of your arrival."

"Father, don't put me on a guilt trip. I know I owe you my life."

"Stop it right there!" The words were harshly expelled, an uncommon and unfamiliar reaction. "You owe me nothing."

Margaret had stayed in the taxi outside the Catholic presbytery on the Brickdam boulevard and had heard the raised voices of Father

O'Hara and Lizzie in heated conversation. That kind of confrontation was unthinkable and unacceptable.

Her heart beat wildly as she watched the two people she loved most, moving in ragged circles, remonstrating, censuring and telling it like it is. Two multi-layered persons, different but the same—patient teacher and avid student, perfectionist and protégéé, crusader and loyalist.

The sun sank below the only dark cloud in an otherwise blue sky, as if in somber acknowledgment of the situation's gravity. She peered through the car's tinted window, hearing snatches of the dialogue, the wind distorting or completely obliterating full sentences.

However, the tempo was gradually subsiding and a semblance of normalcy was returning to the robust exchange.

At last, they walked towards the car, speaking in hushed tones. The priest signaled for Maggie to wind down the back window.

"What you saw and might have heard did not present a pretty picture, but it was necessary. Now, I have to appeal to my God. Stay close to her and keep me informed. We're all in this together." His strong, rugged hands had found each other and were now clasped under his chin.

He kissed Lizzie's fingers even though he wanted to buss her cheek. For a moment, she thought of her biological father and what it would be like to embrace him and feel his presence, if only ephemerally. Her mother not telling her about him troubled her, although she didn't show it. She felt that no one should have to live in the limbo of not knowing something as important as that.

A nascent thought pegged at her. Something her mother had inadvertently said a few days ago. She tried to pry it loose, but it steadfastly refused to budge.

Lizzie faced her mother who was looking much more relaxed than when they left home.

Maggie said without preamble, 'I'm going right back home tomorrow. I'm happy that you and Father reached some common ground."

"Mom, I was selfish. I only thought about myself and craved for the personal attention he usually showered on me. He has a congregation, a whole lot of sinners, plus his own private pain."

"What exactly did he tell you?"

"He berated me for letting myself drown in self-pity. He said I should always remain a prisoner of hope and take back what the enemy stole. He reminded me that nothing was over until God said so. He made it dear that I had a mission to accomplish, and if I walked along the right path, I would come back twice as strong. He took the venom right out of me and replaced it with hope and faith. Mom, he was born to be a healer."

"Do you still love him?"

"I love him more than the father I don't know. I love him more than any person other than you. By the way, Mom, when are we going to talk about my father?"

"You just had a long conversation with the best father you could ever have."

"One of these days, you will have to tell me the truth. I don't want it to be a wedge between us, but you owe me the right of knowing. Let me decide how to handle it after that."

"Okay. But let's get a room at the hotel by the Sea Wall in Kitty. I'm tired."

Lizzie sighed. Her mother was probably trying to keep some deep dark secret from her. She, however, had a right to know. But now was not the time to dwell on paternity.

Other important matters beckoned.

Next morning, she rented a pedal cycle from the hotel's management and she sat next to it on a bench outside a neighborhood shop on the fringe of Lamaha Gardens. From her vantage point, she could see the front door and the entire eastern side of Colonel Benson's house.

At 7:40 a.m., the officer emerged from his home, accompanied by a pretty young woman in army fatigues. Whatever had transpired earlier, she did not look fatigued.

Somehow, she appeared chirpy and eager to get back onto the battlefield. Three dogs barked and performed calisthenics to gain last-minute attention, and the senior soldier obliged, ruffling the dewlap of the short terrier and then tickling the backs of the two Doberman pinschers.

Colonel Benson's polished black Mercedes was already on the bridge and Lizzie could visualize him pressing the remote button on his key and waiting for the chirp as the door locks disengaged.

The car pulled off and she adjusted her shades. She watched as he drove past, chatting animatedly with his newest conquest.

Despite his deceit and betrayal, Lizzie could not help noticing that his skin remained smooth and his face cleanly shaved. It was always that way no matter how early a meeting or exercise was scheduled. It was one of the tenets of military discipline to which he adhered with fanatical obsession.

She watched as the vehicle turned north onto Sheriff Street, then she pedaled to his entrance, aware that he believed that turning back brooked bad luck. Only an emergency would cause him to return immediately.

The dogs rushed to the gate, barking excited greetings. They had not seen her in weeks and they all wanted to show how much they missed her. She opened the gate and slipped through, leaving the bicycle lying on the perfectly manicured outer lawns.

Ginger, her own dog, was all over her while the two others kept their distance, looking on enviously. She hugged all of them in turn and shared the hamburgers she had brought—two Dobermans capable of speedy evisceration and one dachshund with almost human traits. They were happy together, unaware of the treachery in the air.

While they wolfed down the treat, Lizzie opened the sturdy greenheart door with the key Roger had forgotten to reclaim when she was leaving for the trip. She was up the stairs and into the master bedroom, where the bed was unmade and the air reeked of licentiousness.

But that was of no concern to her—the massive safe and its contents were—and she had just about fifteen minutes before the maid arrived.

Seven, six, zero, five, two, then spin. Nothing happened.

She was sure of the combination. She was lying on the bed in the dark one night when Roger had opened the safe to get ammunition for his firearm. He had shielded the combination with his body, but one of the overhead mirrors had displayed the numbers in reverse.

She tried again.

Seven, nine, zero, two, five, then spin. Bingo.

On the top shelf lay ten bundles of U.S. currency. Each had a marker that said $10,000. A total of $100,000 that, at the local bank rate of 150 to 1, amounted to a nest egg of $15 million.

Lizzie froze. So the rumors she had heard were true. It was now a fact that the colonel had found a cache of money when he had gone into Jonestown after Jim Jones's mass suicide pact that had claimed the lives of more than nine hundred people, mostly Americans, in the Guyana jungle.

The tragedy on November 18, 1978, had gone down in history as one of the most catastrophic events, with commune members either murdered or forced to drink a cyanide-laced cocktail.

Somehow, the colonel, with the first batch of soldiers to reach the area, had gotten his hands on a portion of the large sum of money reported to be in the camp. After all the years, he still had a considerable amount.

She whistled under her breath. The colonel was something else.

On the second shelf was an old album with only two pages of faded photographs. Lizzie plucked one showing a woman and a boy in loving embrace and, together with eight bundles of cash, stuffed them into a backpack She closed the safe and spun the dial.

Quickly down the stairs, she relocked the door and exited the yard after bonding again with her three canine friends.

Ginger nuzzled her aggressively and when they made eye contact, it was just like looking into a mirror. There was neither intrigue nor deceit. No wicked intentions.

Always reflecting, she wondered why dogs could not be allowed to manage national affairs. There would be a lot of good to go around.

She remembered someone writing, "The more I think of people, the more I love my dog."

As usual, Ginger seemed to read her mind, and he did a tail-thumping acknowledgment.

Lizzie spotted the maid walking briskly in the distance. She turned the first corner and rode back to the hotel.

Margaret looked at her enquiringly, but Lizzie offered no explanation for the bulky bag or its contents.

After breakfast, she hired a car and deposited the U.S. currency in her safety deposit box at a bank on Regent Street. Then she took her mother to the Ogle Airstrip for a flight back to Mabaruma.

Margaret sensed her restlessness. She put both hands on her shoulders, declaring, "Nothing I say to you will make you stop whatever you are embarking on. Just be careful. Don't bite off more than you can chew. And remember, stay in close contact with Father O'Hara. He has more resources than you can possibly dream of. I'll be praying for you day and night."

Chapter 17

Finding Answers

The aircraft was in the air but Maggie could still see her daughter following its upward trajectory. She pulled down the shutter against the window, but while the action blotted out the sun, it seemed to simultaneously open another window, this time in her head. She made herself comfortable as she remembered ever so clearly.

Tragedy and bad luck were sometimes like brother and sister, and in her early years, they stuck together in filial bondage.

Her mother had suffered four miscarriages before she was born, and when she was twelve, her parents drowned in a senseless river tragedy on their way from church.

She would never forget that Sunday morning. In fact, she blamed herself for their deaths.

She had feigned a cold, and her parents departed for church on a nearby island, approximately two nautical miles from their home. After listening to two hours of God's word intoned by the cherubic Father Mike Sullivan, they departed for home, worried that Maggie might have come down with a severe infection. Out of nowhere came a speedboat full of laughing teenagers, and though they narrowly avoided a collision, the backwash created a massive swell that immediately capsized the canoe. Her parents were capable swimmers, but the tide at the confluence of two rivers proved too strong for them.

Maggie blamed herself and openly carried the guilt, slipping from prim and proper to disheveled and disorganized. Precipitated by an untruth, her world had come crashing down. She told herself that if she had been there, like every other Sunday, she would have saved them. After all, she was the undisputed champion female swimmer of the school district, and she had twice forded the dangerous channel.

From an A-plus student, she slipped precipitously and struggled to maintain a C. Nothing motivated her. Little things repelled her and learning seemed more an impediment than a foot on the climb to womanhood. She ate little, soon becoming a victim of anorexia nervosa,

But one day, a month short of three years since the tragedy, a young Irish priest arrived in Mabaruma as a temporary replacement for Father Sullivan, who had returned to Scotland.

She was standing by herself at the stelling, watching the ferry moor while the entire village observed this twice-monthly spectacle a little distance away. The Catholic priest could not take his eyes off the carelessly dressed, yet striking young woman, hair flying wildly on that windswept day.

The sun provided a natural backdrop and he could see the outline of her body through the translucent cotton shift. It would be the memory he would always have of her—a model's figure silhouetted against the skyline.

On her guard, she stared at the new arrival, harboring doubts that such a young person could be a priest. She thought that priests had to be old to be wise in the ways of the world. She was confused and continued to stare until he said, "Hello there."

Shocked out of her reverie and unaccustomed lately to easy banter, she wheeled and walked hurriedly away without the courtesy of a reply.

"Maggie, Maggie, are you stupid or what? What's the matter with you? Walking around like a zombie and insulting people who just want to be friendly. Who the hell do you think you are?"

This was coming from her best friend, Gabrielle.

No one had ever spoken to her like that. There was no need to because she had always been a pleasant child. Now, as a young woman, approaching her sixteenth birthday; the ring of sincerity and worry in her friend's voice tore through the veneer of inscrutability and pricked her heart.

She stopped suddenly and paused, as if summoning courage to make a big decision.

In twenty seconds, the debate in her head was over.

"Thank you, Gabby, thank you and thank you. Why didn't you do this before?"

"Before! The entire village has tried to get through to you. Your family came from town and could not get past your wall. Father Sullivan has given up and the teachers refer to you as catatonic and schizophrenic."

"Wow, that's serious. Do you know what those words mean?"

"Yeah, I looked them up in the school library's dictionary. Tell me you're not going mad.".

"No, Gabby, girl, never."

And soon, a miraculous transformation took place, galvanizing an entire community. The improbable had happened and all praise went to the young priest. Letters were written to the bishop in Georgetown, seeking a permanent parish at Mora Mission for the newcomer. And their wish was granted.

As the single-engine aircraft with her mother aboard took off, Lizzie suddenly felt an overwhelming urge, a compulsion to know everything about Colonel Benson—her lover, yet a stranger, a seemingly loving man, yet becoming a monster overnight. She thought about the contradictions that characterized their lives-wisdom and naiveté opposite cleverness and deceit.

For no reason at all, she reflected on Father O'Hara's method of questioning, his tone devoid of opinion or judgment. He would ask how she felt about this or that. Or, did she think it was the right thing to do?

Now, she was asking herself similar questions, the main one being, *Is getting even with your deceitful lover the way to go?*

She pared away the layers of reasons, and over and over came to the same conclusion, which was that somebody had to prick the bastard's giant insidious bubble.

With eyes devoid of infatuation, she was clearly seeing what she had avoided observing.

She would not be able to live with herself if she did not spend some time investigating his background and his game plan.

It was odd that he never spoke of his parents or his boyhood days. As she remembered it, a vague look would take over his face whenever those subjects came up, and he would adroitly switch to another topic.

She felt compelled to painstakingly traverse his path of life, trace his roots. He was obviously living a prodigious lie, and it was possible that the debris he would have left in his wake might turn up some interesting facts.

Every man had a weakness, some two or more. Through his actions, the colonel had shown two major ones: his lust for power and his insensitivity to others' feelings.

How had he become so ruthless? she wondered.

Had his parents shown him any love? Did they flog him often?

She vowed to find answers to those burning questions.

She knew where to start. The back of the picture carried the address of the photographer, and even though the lot was indecipherable, the names of street and town were dearly visible—Main Street, New Amsterdam ... in the "Ancient County" of Berbice.

Chapter 18

The Berbice Trip

Lizzie had made the trip to Rosignol on the west coast of Berbice more than a dozen times. But each occasion had been on army business. She was determined this time to enjoy all of its sixty miles, and the minibus driver, who insisted that she sit up front with him, proved a tolerable guide.

The early-morning traffic was light going in their direction as the coastlands opened up alongside the Atlantic Ocean.

Parallel to the roadway snaked a massive chest-high concrete wall, the only obstacle between the mighty waters and the hardy rural folk living happily below sea level. It was called the Sea Wall and was built by the Dutch.

Village commerce encroached on the East Coast Highway, primary conduit to the rural expanse of Berbice, open-air mini-markets and boutiques existing happily alongside regulated businesses.

For the most part, human and animal traffic coexisted on the roadway, each species grudgingly giving way to the other in silent acceptance of each other's rights.

Lizzie listened to the driver while watching the villages flash past her window—Plaisance, Ogle, Beterverwagting, Annandale, Buxton. They stopped at Mahaica to buy gas, and she purchased luscious mangoes from a vendor who conducted business without pausing in her cell phone conversation.

The villages were now spread out over larger areas, and signs were far apart—Mahaicony, Abary, Enmore, Clonbrook-and soon, the cool ocean breeze had all the passengers dozing.

"Wake up, everybody. We're almost at Rosignol Stelling," said the cheerful driver. Turning to Lizzie, he asked, "Did you enjoy the trip?"

"Yes," she replied. "It was wonderful."

He looked pleased, and beamed even more when she handed

him a one-thousand-dollar bill and told him to keep the change. Even though his quick calculations told him the gratuity from the overseas lady was the equivalent of just over $6 in U.S. currency, he was pleased. He would be able to fill his tank for the trip back to Georgetown.

Lizzie could see the ferryboat on the other side of the Berbice River moored at the New Amsterdam Wharf. She bought a one-way ticket, then walked to a cake shop and purchased a newspaper.

Slowly, the two short lines of vehicles waiting to make the crossing began to stretch, trucks on one side, cars and vans commanding the other.

It took half an hour for the boat to arrive, disgorge passengers and vehicles, and then load on its eastbound cargo.

Lizzie was happy to go. If she had thought displays of good manners were few and far between in the city, they were an endangered species at Rosignol. Instead of "Good morning" greetings, she received only crude solicitations and snide comments.

She was the second person off the boat as it berthed, having to dodge scores of touts hustling passengers for their minibuses. She walked slowly to the main road, then retraced her steps and stopped at a fruit vendor's stall.

"Can- I have a water coconut?" Lizzie asked.

"Sure, how much you want one for?" was the query.

"It doesn't matter. I want a young one with jelly."

"Good, I got the right one here for you. A little bit of steel drops and you're good until you pass by here again and buy another."

Lizzie couldn't help smiling.

The pleasant middle-aged East Indian woman expertly took off the top of the coconut with a sharp cutlass and then inserted a straw into the jelly-fringed opening.

"You're too young. You don't need the drops. That's for old people like me. And I don't believe in vitamins from a bottle. Eat plenty fruits, drink plenty water, and the drugstores will soon close down."

Lizzie marveled at how easily this woman, who had never set eyes on her before that day, could have established such rapport in a few minutes despite the historical and political divisions in the country between East Indians and blacks.

Lizzie pulled out a faded photograph from her handbag and showed it to the vendor. 'I'm looking for this lady. She may have lived in the town a few years back."

The vendor took a good look, then passed the picture back. "I don't recognize the person, but I only got this stall three years now. I don't know everybody.

Though this was Lizzie's first try, she was disappointed.

The stallholder must have realized this, for she immediately said, "If you have time to wait for the boat to come back over, you can talk to Rainbow. He knows everybody in the town, maybe in the whole of Berbice."

"Is that his real name?"

"Everybody calls him that, though the little children got to call him Mr. Rainbow. As soon as you see him, you'll understand why he has that name."

Sure enough, the ferry returned. Soon, a dazzling figure of iridescence burst through. He was astride a big-framed bicycle, silver bell ringing incessantly while yelling to no one in particular, "Out de way, out de way." He narrowly missed an old man walking with a limp, then took enraged umbrage at a young man's suggestion that he was "cockeyed."

Lizzie was prepared for a colorful character, but the harsh onslaught on her retina made her hastily slip the sunglasses from its perch atop her head onto the bridge of her nose.

The vendor uproariously hailed the apparition. "Rainbow, you must be working with some optician. You will hurt people's eyes. Look, this young lady wants to talk with you."

"Good morning, Mr. Rainbow at your service," the character said, bowing and whipping off a double-peaked red cap. He may have sported the popular afro hairstyle some years back, now however, the few tufts of silver gray hair spouted at forty-five-degree angles, as if wary or scared of one another.

Rainbow looked liked he was fast approaching seventy—a beanpole of a man, with boyish enthusiasm. And he spoke as loudly as he dressed.

Behind the safety of her sunshades, Lizzie observed that yellow and green were not colors restricted to his clothes. His yachting boots had a tinged yellow hue with pea green laces. The socks were aquamarine, the tie polka-dotted with turquoise prominent. And as if to relieve the variegation, he sported a black vicuna double-breasted jacket, shining from a thousand brush strokes. It went without saying that the lily white handkerchief in the jacket's pocket was for mere decoration.

As she prepared to return his greeting, she thought that if Sol was the sun god in mythology, then Rainbow had to be the color god in real life.

"Good morning to you, Mr. Rainbow. Do you have a moment to spare?"

"Certainly ... anything for a charming young lady like you."

"I hear you have a phenomenal memory. Nobody told me to look out for flattery."

"I've been known to remember a thing or two that others might have forgotten. And I'm also known for telling the truth. You are beautiful."

"Thank you for the compliment."

Lizzie extracted the photograph from her purse once again. She asked him, "Do you know this woman?"

Rainbow, the Memory Man, cocked his head to one side as if searching his archives, a pose with which she would become familiar.

"Before I answer your question, you have to answer one of mine. What is she to you?"

"I have never met her but I need to get in touch with her desperately to find some links to connect a chain."

Rainbow was quiet for a long time. Then, as if arriving at a major decision, he said, "I suspect this has more to do with the boy than with his mother."

A cloud seemed to pass over his face as he continued, his gravel voice reduced to a whisper.

"I know people like to get away from the limelight to live below the radar for a while. I feel sure that's what Robert has done. Most people looked upon him as intelligent and kind, but he was always a crude manipulator. He has never visited his mother in the mental hospital since she was sent there more than twenty years ago."

Rainbow paused again, once more cocking his head to one side, getting ready to spew out more details.

Lizzie knew she should be patient and wait for him to lead the way, but she wanted to hear those details from the horse's mouth, as they say.

"Can you arrange for me to see her and speak to her? I'll make it worth your while."

It was as if he didn't hear.

"They first called her Sweet Yvonne. Now she is Mad Yvonne to the few who know that she still exists. She took the blame for that evil son of hers, yet all he ever gave back was ingratitude."

Lizzie took off her dark glasses and Rainbow was able to look into her eyes.

"Is he dead, in jail, or a big shot some place?" he asked.

"I can't go into details right now, but he's very much alive and climbing the ladder of success rapidly. Self-preservation is his watchword. He doesn't care whom he hurts along the way."

Rainbow's dark brown eyes had never left hers.

For him, the message was clear. What he had feared had come to pass. The smiling little Dr. Jekyll had turned into a big bad Mr. Hyde. The dual personality was always there, but no one bothered to look beyond his bewitching demeanor.

He rose, telling Lizzie to follow him. But not before locking the cycle with a heavy iron chain and instructing the vendor to keep an eye on it.

Rainbow hailed a passing hire car. After a ten-minute ride, he announced that they had arrived at their destination.

He led her past a broken gate, along a well-trodden pathway, up a creaking flight of stairs into a huge colonial-style, unpainted building with a crooked sign proclaiming, "Mental Hospital."

Lizzie held back a little, aware that she was headed smack into the core of insanity, where the detritus of mental chaos was visible from the main road, but few felt constrained to offer a helping hand.

Two women in heavily starched white uniforms stood behind the wire mesh of the reception station, one a serious-faced Portuguese with black waist-length hair, and the other, a smiling brown-skinned woman sporting a low-cut afro hairstyle.

"Hello, ladies. All is well?" asked Rainbow solicitously.

"Well, well, if it isn't Mr. Rainbow come to brighten our day," quipped the black nurse.

Rainbow ignored the barb and said to Lizzie, while pointing to the smiling woman, "This here is Henrietta, and the other lady is Delores."

Without pause, he continued, "Girls, this is Miz Elizabeth from the States, come to visit Sweet Yvonne."

However, before the conversation could continue, up sauntered a satisfied looking man in a tattered multicolored outfit, possessively clutching a battered suitcase, more commonly called a grip by country folk.

"Bye," he said to no one in particular.

"Bye, bye, Sugar Foot, see you later," rejoined Rainbow.

Lizzie was a little puzzled by the exchange and asked, "Isn't he leaving the institution?"

Rainbow let out a raucous laugh that had heads turning, his flashing gold teeth contrasting against bright pink gums. He held his sides as he continued laughing, then between guffaws, he contrived to explain.

"Mr. Sugar Foot leaves this place every day at noon and walks up the road heading for the ferry stelling. Everyone in New Amsterdam knows the charade. One person just has to say "Got ya, Sugar Foot" and the old dog hightails it back here. This month makes it a dozen years he has been officially discharged, but he's still here."

Nurse Delores broke up the discussion. Addressing Lizzie, she asked, "Are you a relative of Yvonne Boatswain?"

Lizzie had concocted a story to present to the authorities, but an inner feeling told her to stay as close to the truth as possible, hoping that Delores's stern mien was just a temporary barrier erected to ward off the inquisitive and uncaring.

"Actually, no. A family friend asked me to check on her and to leave some money for her upkeep. She gave me a picture. Is this the same person?"

Delores took the aged photograph, and Henrietta moved to her side to have a look. For a while, they said nothing, just shaking heads in unison, labored breathing drowning the melange of strange sounds from somewhere beyond their cubicle.

It was Henrietta who broke the uncomfortable silence. "That's her before she was sentenced to this institution for almost killing one of her lovers. She was the most beautiful girl in this town and knew it. It was easy for her to sell her favors."

Henrietta continued to shake her head from side to side and her irises, which a moment ago had been brown and dear, were now clouded.

Lizzie moved quickly to bring things back to an even keel, asking politely, "Who is this next to her?"

Rainbow had told her, but she wanted to hear it again.

It must have been a lifelong habit with Henrietta. Her head again rocked, but this time, she could not hold back the tears. "That's her son, her only child. God, that kid was bright, but he had a mean streak. Come to think of it, he was more clever than brilliant. He could outmaneuver kids twice his age. No one has seen him since the night his mother was held by the police. Guess he must be some part of the world breaking hearts."

Lizzie could have told her which part of the world she could lay eyes on him, but she held her tongue, keeping her expression blank.

It was Delores's turn now. "It's already lunchtime. I'll take you up to her room, and then maybe you could have lunch with her or go for a walk around the grounds. She hardly goes out."

The distance from the nurses' station to Yvonne's cell-like room was perhaps less than fifty yards, but it turned out to be the longest walk she had ever undertaken in her entire life, one that she was not likely to forget as long as she lived.

By the time she had taken her first few steps, she was in the total grip of confusion. All around she could hear strange sounds, voices raised in terror, voices bellowing in rage, voices appealing for divine direction.

The air was suffused with tension and lost hope. Sounds that made no sense continued to cascade all around her in a symphony of dementia.

But the most disturbing feature was the eyes. They told a thousand tangled stories and mirrored a myriad of scattered emotions-uncertainty, confusion, guilt and curiosity.

Lizzie was frightened.

At Father O'Hara's insistence, she had read extensively about psychiatry, but the textbook had not prepared her for what she was seeing. Outside looking in was vastly different from inside looking out.

Lizzie had read that there was a thin line separating real from fantasy. She could now bear witness to this phenomenon.

Only a few minutes in the building and she had moved from reflective conversations with the nurses to the vortex of insanity. The forces of madness had quickly assaulted her senses, effectively buffeting her ability to think straight.

She saw a slender woman, radiant in childlike beauty, walking with mincing steps and making the sign of the cross at regular intervals. Nurse Delores whispered that she had been abused by her stepfather at the age of nine. Since then, she had descended into a confused world where prayers were her only decipherable words.

She had been robbed of her youth, her hopes and her dreams because a beast took something he wanted without considering the consequences of his actions.

Lizzie felt a bond with the abused young woman as she followed her progress along the crowded corridor, her own face an obsidian mask of incomprehension.

The nurse must have seen the look of concern on her face because she held her elbow and said, "Don't let it get to you. It's confusion in here every day of the year."

If the statement was meant to reassure, the next sound certainly didn't.

Somewhere deep within those cavernous halls, someone let out a long plaintive howl like a coyote. The sound soon trailed off like the whimper of a chastised puppy.

Men and women moved about wild-eyed and unsmiling-a motley collection of lost folks of all ages and sizes.

Robes, housecoats, petticoats and pajamas blended with pants and skirts too short or too tight and shirts and blouses too Loose. Color combinations screamed for attention.

Hairstyles that would make a stylist cry, displayed hair exploding from scalps while others were so matted that no ordinary comb dared to venture.

Stringy beards sprouted like stalactites in abandoned caves.

Lizzie moved in a daze.

One man, who obviously didn't embrace the concept of sartorial elegance, advanced on her, lifting a skeletal arm and pointing a bony finger. He shouted, "You are sent by the devil to create havoc. Stop it now!"

Without missing a beat, he marched off, his mismatched socks and shoes flashing among a mass of ankles. The left side shoe appeared too tight while the other side flapped loosely.

Sizes and styles, like so many other things, were obviously unimportant in the institution.

They had almost reached Yvonne's quarters when a rotund bundle of corpulence, quivering like jelly in the hands of a nervous person, waddled past, arms festooned with ornamentation. It was difficult to determine the sex of the being. The man or woman was accompanied by a tall, cadaverous male wearing a black suit and gray felt hat. He waved his black umbrella in an absurd parody of Agatha Christie's fictional detective M. Hercule Poirot.

The nurse hustled Lizzie along. Suddenly, they arrived at

Yvonne's room.

The grill door was open. A single overhead bulb threw permanent shadows, offering just enough illumination to reveal a bed, and its occupant who seemed as comfortable as a rich lady in her expansive boudoir.

She was alone on that elevated part of the building and the place reeked of eeriness.

Lizzie froze for a moment. Her throat constricted as she looked at the woman who might well have been her mother-in-law.

She couldn't trust herself to speak, so she just held out the photograph.

The woman uncurled in an exaggerated movement and languidly walked forward to look into a small hanging mirror and adjust her wild hair. Then she took the proffered picture extracted from Roger's album.

The stuffy silence became chilling as Yvonne seemed to suddenly stop breathing. A shadow of fear flashed across her garishly painted face.

Seconds expanded into an eternity.

Her legs faltered as she sought refuge on the bed. She didn't quite make it, falling heavily to the floor, where she curled up in a fetal position, her body racking with sobs. She gradually squeezed herself into a corner, shrunken and etiolated, like a crumpled piece of paper in a garbage can. There was nothing to set her apart from the withered flowers and misshapen objects scattered haphazardly about the room.

Lizzie moved to help her, but Nurse Delores clamped a restraining hand on her shoulder while whispering, "No, no, no. This unraveling has to take its course. It's been long in coming. The doctors say it's her only hope."

The nurse patted Lizzie's shoulder. 'I'm going to leave you two together. I suspect there is more in the mortar than the pestle. Don't worry, she is not violent. And when you are finished, go with her to the dining hall. I'll join you there.

By now, Yvonne had dissolved into mournful wailing, beating the bed with her fists. Lizzie did not interrupt, mindful of the nurse's caution.

After the prolonged outpouring of bottled-up grief, Yvonne slowly regained her composure. Her swollen eyes obtusely reflected the years of emptiness. They were blood red from hundreds of sleepless nights and years of tear-shedding, the burst capillaries zigzagging like the varicose veins evident on her thin legs.

"Tell me the truth. Who are you?" She whispered, but her voice had a force of authority. It was obvious that Colonel Benson had gotten his confident manner from his mother.

"My name is Ruth Elizabeth Ferreira. I foolishly thought that Roger was as much in love with me as I was with him. He betrayed me and caused me to suffer badly."

"Is that what you call him ... Roger?"

"That is his official name in the army. He is now Colonel Roger Benson."

A surprisingly controlled burst of laughter, more like a tantalizing snigger, lit up the stale air, beating back the gloom. Lizzie marveled at the magic that could make madness and sanity coalesce to produce clear moments of lucidity.

In just over an hour, Yvonne's entire being had metamorphosed into that of a well-mannered, middle-aged schoolteacher. Her bearing took on regal poise and her diction had almost reached perfection.

"Your eyes have already told me that you are speaking the truth, so it's my duty to tell you some things. But remember, he's my only child, and there are details I might never disclose. By the way, his real name is Robert Orville Boatswain."

Chapter 19

A Mother's Tale

The two women walked towards the dining room and heads began turning, slowly at first, then brazenly. The hushed whispers evolved into loud catcalls and shrill whistling.

At first, Lizzie thought it was her unheralded presence that had caused the stir until she glanced sideways and saw fingers pointing at Yvonne.

The inmates had always alternated between calling her Mad Yvonne and Sweet Yvonne, but today the chorus was for the more appealing version.

Yvonne had left Lizzie for a few minutes to go to the bathroom. When she returned, she was magically transformed. Gone were the streaks of watercolors and crayons from her lips and face, and so too were the multicolored strips of ribbons from her hair.

Her hairdresser, if she had one, might not have been impressed, but to the less fashion conscious, the bun at the back of her head, held in place by two rubber bands, was a rave in those surroundings.

Yvonne walked as if she were floating, gliding noiselessly in her bedroom slippers, a too-often washed housecoat held in place by a broad, frayed leather belt.

That day, the meal was supposed to be stewed beef with potatoes topped with fried plantains. However, the congealed mess looked like a burnt offering, especially the plantains, which resembled charred cardboard. Any hope of a vitamin-rich fare would have long since evaporated in the sizzling oil of the huge stew pan that hissed in the smoky kitchen.

Lizzie picked at her meal, skeptical of its provenance, while Yvonne wolfed down her portion and gratefully accepted her guest's untouched plate.

All the time, patients and staff were finding excuses to stop by their table, all eyes on the new Yvonne.

The image of institutional discord was evident as patients trooped in with pain plainly written on their faces—hallucinations, manic depression, unresolved anger, delusions, and many other undiagnosed ills. It seemed that forces outside the recognized plane of existence—whether divine—or demon-driven-were constantly manipulating them.

Lizzie wanted to put her hands to her ears to shut out the noise of inhumanity and, in her mind, to escape the flying debris of misery. But she steeled herself to closely observe Tommy punctuating his imaginary conversation with wild gestures and to listen to Robot Man, who spoke without moving his lips.

Thankfully, Rainbow joined them just before Yvonne finished her second plate of food. In his right hand, he had half a pineapple, which he energetically bit into, rivulets of juice trailing down his fingers onto his shirt. He made a few ineffectual dabs at the affront with the white kerchief, but it was certain now that that bit of cloth was just for decoration.

Yvonne rubbed her stomach and belched behind cupped palms.

"Let's go for a walk and talk."

She was all business, the self-erected closed door torn down, a tunnel of sanity beckoning.

Yvonne turned to Rainbow, saying without rancor, "You can come with us. There are general things I want to talk about, things that have been locked away in my mind for a number of years. Later, I must talk only with this young lady."

"That is as it should be," replied Rainbow.

"Okay, Elizabeth, let me just say hello to Nat over by the window then we will be on our way."

Nat was severely cross-eyed and sat at a small table with a child's twelve-piece puzzle in front of him.

To the sane, this exercise would seem uncomplicated, but as the nurses attested, many times it proved too intricate. And the acute strabismus did nothing to help him find the solution.

Rainbow playfully slapped Nat on the back, then when the latter looked around, quickly slotted a piece of the puzzle into place.

As if jolted by a sudden charge of electricity, an emaciated arm shot out, scattering the puzzle off the table onto the ground. Eyes flashed crossly, and had it not been for the presence of a nearby orderly, Rainbow might have lost some of his luster.

He apologized profusely and attempted to retrieve the pieces, but whether Nat was staring at him or someone else, the intensity was enough to dissuade him.

As the trio walked, a procession followed. Inmates and staff were witnessing a miracle unfolding and no one, sane or insane, wanted to miss its conclusion.

The two nurses abandoned their cage of protection to simultaneously hug both women, tears flowing freely.

"Hey, what's up? Who's dead? What's all the crying about? Aren't you glad to see me clean and going for a walk?"

A chorus of platitudes, encouragement and praise answered her four questions as the crowd grew.

Yvonne held up her hand and addressed the throng as if it was something she did every day of her life. "God sent an angel to me today. She said not a word, just showed me a photograph, and my sanity has returned."

Hands still aloft, she continued, "Give me some space. I need to talk to Elizabeth. Don't think you all getting rid of me just yet."

The crowd seemed relieved and began dispersing. The triumvirate descended the stairs and took a path that traversed the grounds.

"Where do you want to start?" she asked Lizzie.

"First, I think I should let you know a little about myself and then my involvement with your son."

"Please don't refer to him as my son just yet. I'm still trying to reconcile his absence all these years."

They walked, talked and paused under large trees providing shade. Lizzie narrated as if reading from a script. Her details were so graphic that her captive listener rarely interrupted.

When it was her turn to listen, Lizzie had to work hard to quell her impatience and not interrupt the monologue. Yvonne had method to her oration. She started from her early years and worked her way to the present. She refused to take any shortcuts. For her, expiation or exorcism, or both, had to be complete—no leftovers.

For his part, Rainbow took a backseat, listening to a fascinating tale of good that had taken a sudden evil turn. He let the two sharp minds interact, conscious that a bond was slowly and inextricably entwining them.

He might dress like a fool, he thought. But he was nobody's fool.

∗   ∗   ∗

Yvonne Audrey Boatswain had been a young orphaned girl living with an English family on the Blairmont Sugar Estate across the river from New Amsterdam. One summer, when she was almost seventeen, her adopted parents' only son, Gerald, came to spend the holidays. He was eighteen and as handsome as she was beautiful.

Within a week, they had become an item, unknown to the parents, but common knowledge to the servants and anyone else with eyes to see. A month later, she missed her period for the first time in her life.

Gerald, like a true English gentleman, accepted responsibility and even contemplated marriage. His parents were furious and dispatched him posthaste to the Motherland. Yvonne was given marching orders and a hefty check, with advice to quickly get an abortion.

She, however, moved to New Amsterdam, bought a small house in the heart of the town, and to the mortification of the British overseer and his wife, settled down to set the stage for her baby's arrival.

Robert Orville Boatswain was born a few days before Yvonne's eighteenth birthday, a large bundle of squealing joy. She lived only for her son, turning her back on academia and opportunities to learn a skill.

She quickly blossomed into a ravishingly beautiful young woman and soon began to attract the attention of men, young and old. Most of those suitors were married, and she made them pay dearly for the precious stolen moments.

Her looks and body remained rewarding assets until one man stepped into her life, demanding all her attention. He was the captain of an American fishing trawler, snaring fish and shrimp in the Atlantic Ocean. He came ashore twice a month. His name was Albert Sampson, but his friends called him Big Sam.

Robert had disliked him from the start although the seaman showered him with large sums of money. He resented the fortnightly visits when Big Sam would turn up, tap him crudely on the shoulder, and order him to stop whatever he was doing and disappear for the next few hours.

It was during those hours that he was transformed into a cruel being, acting out his revenge on children he hardly knew, exploiting them with Sam's bribes.

He was just fifteen years old, but fast approaching six feet. That August, he was heavily into a new version of Nintendo and hated being away from his expensive toy.

Big Sam came, handed Robert the usual bundle of notes, and, with a sour expression, headed for the kitchen where Yvonne was preparing dinner. Five minutes later, Robert was still preoccupied. with his game when Big Sam came back into the sitting room and snatched it from him, shouting drunkenly, "You haven't gone yet. Why do you think I gave you that money? Go and buy something nice for you and your friends. Me and your mom want some privacy. Take three hours tonight."

Robert could see the concern on his mother's face fleetingly turn to fear. And though he was a little alarmed, he walked away, down the steps and out of the yard.

But he soon retraced. his footsteps to crouch under his mother's bedroom window, something he had never done before.

Just like he had suspected, a raging row was on. He heard Sam accuse his mother of "giving it away to every man in town" and making him the laughingstock of everyone. He predicted. that she would soon have another bastard like the one he had just paid off, and he called her all manner of names, "whore" being one of the more moderate.

Then, amid the strident "busing," Robert heard a dreaded. sound—an open palm connecting to flesh. Then followed the sounds of clothes being ripped and mumbled protests from his mother.

Yvonne and Lizzie were still walking side by side. Without eye contact, frankness had seemed to come more easily. Now, Yvonne stopped to face Lizzie. Her tone was resigned.

"Somehow, Robert had heard me protesting loudly about having my period, and he must have looked through the window and seen the blood on the bed. My vision was blocked, but I heard the dull thud of something against flesh. Six times--each blow accompanied. by a blood-curdling scream.

"I managed to extricate myself from under Big Sam's crushing weight, and when I realized what had taken place, I cleaned off my son, packed a few pieces of clothing in a bag, gave him some money and ordered him to stay out of sight for a while. Obviously, he took that to mean forever."

Yvonne continued, "I walked to the police station and told them that I had left a man bleeding to death on my bed. I was covered in blood and I had a bloodied hatchet, but I told them I could not remember anything about the incident. I stuck with that story throughout the trial. Big Sam was flown out to Trinidad for emergency surgery and returned months later to give evidence at the trial. He swore under oath that I had inflicted the wounds when he fell asleep."

She sat down on the grass and went on with her tale. "The authorities knew nothing about lie detector tests or hypnosis. If they had administered any one of those, they would have discovered the truth. But the official diagnosis was that had intentionally blocked out the memory of the incident and that it might be years before it returned.

"Since there was no separate institution for the criminally insane, I wound up at the mental hospital. It was an open sentence with talk of an annual examination to determine competence, whatever that meant. The authorities forgot about me, and I crawled further and further into my shell. There was no Robert to live for."

Lizzie glanced surreptitiously at Yvonne picking strands of weed out of the ground and tried to reconcile the bloody encounter with this seemingly sane woman, who obviously had more than a passing acquaintance with class and culture.

The afternoon sun was slowly slipping behind the horizon when they got back to the main building. Among them, they had eight plastic bags containing new clothes, frilly underwear, hair and body lotions, cologne, powder, scented soap, shampoo, and a pair of sandals. Those items and a host of other minor ones were bought from an all-in-one store just beyond the boundary of the hospital.

The welcoming party comprised almost the entire patient population and all the staff. Some were anxious to see Yvonne return, and many others had hoped that she would take the first opportunity to walk away from her self-imposed exile. After all, her period of incarceration for wounding with intent and attempted murder had long since been served. She was still there because she refused to face the outside world.

Their arrival with the bulging bags had spurred inquisitive looks, and the scores of faces before them mirrored a conflation of emotions that was difficult to decipher.

"I see you're back, Yvonne. Thought you were on the ferry boat headed for the bright lights of Georgetown," Nurse Henrietta teased.

"That will take some doing and all in good time," quipped Yvonne in response.

"Is that you speaking, Yvonne?" enquired a querulous blind woman. "How come you talking such good English and all the time you here you talking madhouse gibberish?"

"Dorothy, let's not delve into that right now. Suffice it to say a veil has been lifted from my inner being and I can now see the light."

A melodious suck-teeth rent the air as Dorothy sauntered off mumbling, "All of a sudden, you is an English duck. 'Inner being' me ass." She was dabbing furiously at her eyes with a wadded face towel already heavy with long-dried phlegm.

Smiles and unbridled laughter lit up the drab surroundings as news continued to spread throughout the institution that a soul had been saved and its owner might soon demit their palatial quarters.

Lizzie had bought a wide range of sweetmeats, aerated drinks, biscuits, several loaves of bread and a dozen tins of corned beef. To top it off, she had purchased three bottles of wine that boasted of some kind of connection to California grapes but, doubtlessly, had originated in one of the many back dams at the rear of local sugar estates.

At dinnertime, while all shared in the consumption of the unexpected treat, one man unnoticeably drank all the wine and soon passed out. Lizzie engaged one "Speedo" to "run to the shop" to replace the bottles.

Taking her literally, he was back in minutes, perspiration cascading down his face, the back of his singlet wet with the effort. He later clutched a five-dollar tip as if it were the only life jacket on a boat in the heart of a storm.

The ecology buff who spent all day serenading trees and plants, was a rich tenor and he broke into song—"Soon She'll Be Gone."

Yvonne sniffed.

Then it was "For She's a Jolly Good Fellow."

The floodgate flew open.

Yvonne cried like a baby. The ambivalence of wanting to remain in the safety of anonymity, as opposed to finding her son and facing him, tortured her.

She walked to a window and bent over the sill. The deep silence of the wooded area beyond was almost oppressive, in complete contrast to the bedlam within.

With no trace of the psychotic depression that had controlled her mind for so many years, Yvonne turned to face her friends, saying calmly, "I'm leaving tomorrow, but I'll be back to see you guys."

The noise and unaccustomed merriment continued unabated, and it was easy for Lizzie, Yvonne and Rainbow to slip through the door and head towards the town. Rainbow pleaded a headache. The taxi dropped him off at the ferry stelling to collect his cycle, cross the river and head to his home at Rosignol.

The two women were driven to a guesthouse, and there they booked a double room. Yvonne reacted to her new surroundings with elan, looking comfortable and positive. She sat with her legs folded, like an Amerindian chief conducting a tribal council meeting, and Lizzie wondered if, somewhere along the way, one of her breed had left a mark.

Lizzie, comfortable in her yoga posture, faced her on the other twin bed.

The dialogue went past midnight, stopped short only because of the incessant pounding on the paper-thin wall by someone who claimed he had not slept in two days.

Yvonne was the first to awake. The clock hanging on the wall said five o'clock. She filled the bathtub with hot water and added liquid soap before stepping in to endure the oppressive heat. The clear water turned light gray and then became darker as she scrubbed every inch of her body, cognizant of the many missed baths over the years.

Twenty minutes later, her undernourished body tingled with a new sensation, and she finally stepped from the bathtub after accepting the realization that she could not cleanse what was inside her. Her hair glistened. And when she pushed the door and emerged from the oasis of mist, Lizzie gasped in astonishment.

Yvonne instantly drew back. "Do I look horrible?"

"Horrible? Girl, you look like a slightly anorexic forty-year-old model. A little bit of filling out here and there and you will be a smash hit on the catwalk."

"Lizzie, please don't tease me. Tell me how I really look."

She removed the turbaned towel from her head and her long black hair fell to her shoulders.

"Here's what we'll do. I won't answer your question. You will not look in the mirror, and later you'll judge for yourself after we go to the hairdresser. Now let me see if you left any hot water for me to have a bath."

Lizzie had a notepad. As they devoured ham, bacon, eggs and waffles, she wrote in bold letters: HAIRDRESSER, NAIL SALOON, BOUTIQUE, BANK, HOUSE.

Fortunately, the first three objectives could be achieved in one building across the street from the hotel. And this they did in less than three hours.

Nobody recognized Yvonne, and the duo was very happy with that situation.

The bank proved to be a bother since Yvonne had lost all identifying documents. A thumbprint sufficed, and the new Yvonne emerged from the financial institution with a passbook that felt as heavy as the $1 million written in it.

The lucky recipient looked at her benefactor, stammering, "Lizzie, forgive me for asking, but why are you giving me so much money? What have I done to deserve this?"

"Don't think of it as a lot of money. It's only six thousand U.S. dollars, and there is much more where that came from. By right, some of it belongs to you by default. Trust me, you have every right to it. But later for that. I'll tell you everything as we go along. We must set a timetable and stick to it."

Yvonne was still confused and uncertain, looking askance at Lizzie. The latter, however, was all business. She added, "This money came from your son's safe. Ir cannot buy love, but we're going to make sure it acts as a good substitute."

Only the visit to the house she owned remained on the original agenda. But Yvonne was apprehensive. Since her confinement, the building in the central part of the town had been taken over by an extended Rastafarian family; whose members had stoned her the four times she had attempted to enter the yard. She hadn't been back in five years.

"Just show me the house," Lizzie said evenly.

"Be careful, they look like mean people."

"Don't worry; if I can't move them with my charm, I'll do so with my arm."

Yvonne was not in a facetious mood. She remembered the headache from one of the bricks finding its mark. "I hope you know what you're doing."

She pointed out the building, a solid one-storied structure perched on eight sturdy concrete columns. It badly needed painting, and the front picket fence clamored for urgent attention. Under the house, a dreadlocked woman was washing clothes in an aluminum tub while three naked children plaited a maypole with the hem of her long skirt.

Lizzie pulled a reluctant Yvonne over a treacherous-looking bridge, minus a few planks, and walked through the gap where the gate should have been.

"Greetings, sister, is your husband at home?"

"Rasta man selling by the market."

"Good. When he comes home, tell him the owner of the house and her attorney will be back at nine o' clock tomorrow morning. Tell him it would be in his best interest to be here."

"Owner! The owner is ah old woman in the mad house. We have prescriptive rights. You know how long we living here?"

"We are not here to argue. Just give him the message."

A long "suck-teeth" heralded their departure.

The rest of the day went by in a blur, but a lot was achieved.

They chose the traditional siesta time between two and three o'clock to slip into the mental hospital to say hurried goodbyes. Yvonne paid a final trip to the room that had been her home for so many years and returned with her favorite doll, all dressed up in wedding apparel. Under her left arm, she carried a foolscap-size manila envelope, yellow with age and perusal. It contained every report published about her arrest and trial.

The farewell was uneventful, not because of the time of the day, but because few inmates recognized the former resident, dressed in fashion: hair glistening in a coiffure.

The facial treatment had done wonders, an oil-free foundation smoothing out the skin tone and texture to give a healthy, natural-looking complexion.

But Sam, the painter, was not fooled. He was mimicking a real-life tradesman and testing Newman's Law on a rickety ladder when he saw Yvonne departing. He stopped his imaginary brush stroke to wave and say quietly, "Ta-ta, Yvonne."

Yvonne was shocked to the core. She had met Sam in the institution when she was incarcerated and, like every other inmate, had never heard him utter a single word. Some said he was born dumb, others opined that some mishap had befallen him. But after all these years, the mystery deepened—the man's muteness was elective.

142

Yvonne said a parting prayer for him.

Numerous falls, broken bones and skin contusions had not dissuaded him from his endeavors. His fellow inmates regularly pointed out that black and blue were obviously his favorite colors, taking their cue from his skin hue.

The next day, at nine o'clock, the women returned to the house where a thin Rastafarian man with a ragged beard and a hostile manner greeted them. It didn't take long to dislike him.

"You the daughters who been here yesterday? Let me tell you up front. I man is the owner of this house. Who say different?

Lizzie was angry and not afraid to show it. She moved forward and said in a powerful tone, "I woman say different. This here woman standing next to me is the lawful owner with a transport to prove this claim. You have until the end of the month to vacate the premises."

"Or else what?" asked the Rasta man mockingly, adopting a pugilistic stance.

Over the last few weeks, Lizzie's patience had worn thin with men who were no more than bullies, taking advantage of situations without regard to consequences.

She didn't respond immediately to the question.

She simply covered the distance between them in three lightning strides, slipped her right foot behind his legs and pushed. It was the first offensive maneuver taught in judo, and over the years, she had perfected it to a fine art. He fell flat on his back.

The toppled man struggled to get up, but the sole of her right boot under his chin did not accommodate his efforts.

"Listen carefully. We have no time for drama. There are thirteen days left in the month. When we return, we expect to find this lady's house vacant. Take all the furniture, equipment, and utensils. Leave all the fittings. Do we have a deal?"

A mumbled reply, like a dog's growl, suggested that an agreement had indeed been reached, and Lizzie turned her back to walk away.

Infuriated, the floored man jumped up, determined to "rain fires on the daughter" who had desecrated his sanctuary and humbled him in the clear view of his nosey and unfriendly neighbor, Gertrude. He sprang to grab her from behind, but there was no body to hold on to, since she had anticipated his move and had adroitly dropped to the ground with one leg outstretched. He tripped and went flying headfirst.

Strange, he couldn't remember buying an airline ticket, yet he was flying, moving through the air, propelled not by the thrust of Rolls Royce engines, but his own momentum and aided by gravity, which soon brought him quickly back to earth.

This was becoming a familiar scenario. Lizzie was again standing over him. This time, she was dead serious, and so was her tone. "One more stunt like that and I'll whip your ass for the whole of New Amsterdam to see. You now have twelve days to move."

Yvonne looked a little stunned by the morning's whirlwind events, but she stared at the Rasta man malevolently, repeating firmly, "Twelve days."

The man knew that they meant what they said. "Jah" could not help him now.

*　　*　　*

A sand truck blasted past them, the eddy physically redirecting their paths, dust flying everywhere. Two cyclists, bells shrieking, zipped between gossiping housewives while harried pedestrians elbowed those whose feet moved slower than theirs.

Cows stood in the center of the roadway, unfazed by engine sounds and blasts of horns, and innocent-eyed sheep nuzzled one another on the tarred surface before casually mincing off to grassy pasturing.

New Amsterdam was fully awake and thriving.

As they trekked to the ferry stelling toting their overnight bags, a battered Wolseley pulled up with Rainbow in the passenger seat, grinning expansively and gazing at Yvonne in gap-toothed amazement.

The car looked like the last surviving one of its kind in the hemisphere. It had a cracked celluloid windscreen, battered doors and fenders, and an engine that emitted an angry, flatulent response whenever the ignition was engaged, which was often. The paint job was a self-help effort, the color a far cry from what the manufacturers had intended.

Miraculously, the dashboard was intact, and if one were brave enough to enter the museum piece, one would have heard an eight-track tape mangling Millie Jackson's "If You Can See Me Now."

Chapter 20

Back in the Army

The army was preparing for its big anniversary celebrations—route march, divisional competitions and promotions.

That particular day was the first full rehearsal and all the senior officers had taken their positions on the platform. Having gained entrance to the camp through the rear gate, Lizzie had hurriedly gone to her quarters to replace civvies with army fatigues.

She approached the platform from the back and when the band had completed a selection, she walked forward briskly, stopping in front of Chief of Staff Geoffrey Sinclair. The salute was crisp and professional, the command authoritative, "Reporting for duty, sir."

"Good to see you, Captain Ferreira. When did you get in?"

"A couple of hours ago, sir. I heard of the rehearsal and I hurried in."

Lizzie was addressing the army's commander, but her eyes were fixed on Colonel Benson sitting next to him, wearing a stony expression, which made his face impossible to read. She supposed that that was his objective.

She saw him as a serial plotter and a consummate actor and she watched as he carefully masked the surprise of her unexpected arrival with a cold, ingratiating, practiced smile while his eyes spoke volumes. She could decipher every line. What she read evoked feelings of fury, indignation and deep hurt, but she wasn't going to let emotions override direction. She had to combine all the hurts into a pool of energy and use the resultant electricity to fully charge her batteries.

The brigadier turned to the colonel, saying jokingly; "Your top athlete is back. Perfect timing."

Roger sprang to his feet to greet her. She got the full politician's handshake--strong forearm grip, shoulder brace and back slap. It seemed he had been practicing for the future.

His eyes bored into hers, searching for signs, ready to deflect and deny. She was prepared and her emotions were under control, cauterized in anticipation of all the lies she knew would soon flow.

"How are you, Officer Ferreira?" he asked, his voice echoing concern.

In company, Roger had always referred to her as his smart young colleague, his protege, and quite often, as just Elizabeth. Back then, she had wondered when the formality would graduate to more endearing affectations.

Now it was back to Officer Ferreira. And she welcomed the adherence to convention, aware that the forces of betrayal had ruthlessly ripped out the roots of loving memories.

"I'm fine now, but I'm sure you were being kept up to date with my progress."

"Why would I know all the details of your course?" he asked, his hands appealing for a reason.

The question got an A for "ambiguity" and seemed to take the edge off her rising hostility. But she already knew his cunning game of answering a question with one of his own, using the courteous emphasis in the midst of an abrasive confrontation. The ruse had a devastatingly soothing impact if the timing was right, and for years, that had been the colonel's ploy, his trump.

As far as she knew, it had never failed.

However, she was determined that nothing along those lines would transpire.

The script had now been rewritten.

Scores of inquisitive eyes were on them, so she smiled pleasantly and said softly but firmly, "This time, you will lose."

She walked down the line, saluting and shaking hands, none more vigorously than that of Major Belgrave, who let out a whoop of joy. It was unmilitary and unconventional, almost like laughing at a funeral. She was aware that she could be censured later, but the two women knew any type of discipline would be accepted without a murmur. She, Lizzie, was alive and well, and Yolande felt energized with the knowledge.

The colonel was offering her a seat next to him, and although every fiber in her body screamed in the negative, military discipline propelled her to the empty chair.

Her senior officer spoke as if he had not heard her last profound statement addressed to him.

"I couldn't understand it. I heard you had gone AWOL the night before you were supposed to proceed to the advanced part of the course. I kept it quiet. No one knows you didn't actually go the distance. But you know you can trust me to be discreet."

She closed her eyes, not only to picture him telling his CIA friend to find her at all costs, but more to blank out his baleful, lying eyes. Again, she willed herself not to become upset by his vapid equivocations and cloying web of deceit. But what was even more disturbing was the fact that he seemed to believe his own spiel.

"We have to celebrate your return with a special dinner tonight," he continued casually.

"Really!" exploded Lizzie, turning to stare into his eyes. The single word ricocheted around the army base and needed no expansion. Heads turned in their direction. She fought for control while the visibly embarrassed colonel scrambled to regain his seat and his composure.

Lizzie was irritated. She was a woman given to controlling herself in any situation, but now she was riled and ready to shoot down explanations and protestations, which she saw only as self-serving lies.

Her mind was a kaleidoscope of images. She saw Roger making love to her, smiling in her face, putting a birthday ring on her finger. She saw him with countless women and the politician's daughter he was grooming to be his wife.

She saw him for what he was, and now, so close to him, she noticed that his face, the visage she had so adored, was devoid of emotion and held a pair of vacant, cruel bluish eyes.

In her mind's eye, she could see him in his stiff prison warden's uniform, yelling and baton-whipping a hapless prisoner. What she couldn't understand was how she had not noticed the signs before.

Was love always so blind? she wondered.

In truth, she thought he really was a jailer through and through, always locking people and things away, erecting barriers at will to suit his own purpose. She had read somewhere during her university days that the absence of parental love could make a person look for a substitute in different directions, such as a surrogate parent or many sexual partners.

She was painfully aware of his choice.

Now, any vestige of respect that might have lurked in her mind was completely eradicated. There could never be that level of trust and confidence that existed before. For her, losing respect for your partner was as reprehensible as infidelity itself.

She closed her eyes again—this time, in final renunciation, acknowledging the end of their relationship.

Utter indifference shrouded her like a mummy as she glanced at him disdainfully and walked away without a parting word.

It was the first round of a salvo that would drill holes in the image he bad craftily constructed.

And for the first time in his life, Colonel Benson understood what real fear was—a terror, which was mirrored in his inability to sidetrack and. woo a wronged woman with irresistible charm and words of silk.

*　　*　　*

It was considered a breach of protocol to leave the presence of the chief of staff without his permission. Having done so, she moved to a rear seat and followed the rehearsal. An idea suddenly struck her, and she waited animatedly to discuss it with the senior members of the Women's Army Corps.

While waiting for the activities to end, Lizzie cast her eyes around the parade square where she had left pints of sweat, drilled mercilessly by Sergeant Major Telford.

She reeled back to her most precious moment—the passing-out parade after a grueling six-month course.

Lizzie smiled as she recalled that day as clearly as if it were yesterday.

She had heard her name being called, but couldn't move. A strong voice was saying, "For the first time in the army's history, a female officer has finished in the top three in the best all-round category. Come forward, Second Lieutenant Ruth Elizabeth Ferreira."

The same legs that had carried her twenty-five miles with full military gear, the same legs that had propelled her across a turgid, shark-infested river, were now leaden impediments.

She had looked confusedly at the head table, and the colonel, at that time a major, had inclined his head, as he always did when giving his legendary curt order: Move, soldier.

Automatically, she had moved, feet gliding over the tarred surface in the pristine compound, ablaze with color and pageantry. Astride the podium, the president of Guyana pinned a gold medal on her tunic, an impish smile on his face. The band played "For She's a

Jolly Good Fellow," and then followed tremendous applause from the hundreds of dignitaries, army brass and regular soldiers.

Afterwards, in the officers' mess, the president had walked over to her and said, "I hear you are from the Essequibo region, where exactly?"

She had replied, "It's a very small village in Mabaruma called Mora Mission, not accessible by air. I doubt you know it, sir."

The president had shot back, "Hey, little girl, do you think I only travel by aircraft. I once visited that village and was very impressed. I seem to remember two persons vividly ... a Catholic priest and a stunningly beautiful young woman who garlanded me with a bouquet. Meggie or Maggie was her name. See how much I remember of your village?"

"It is Maggie, short for Margaret. She is my mother."

"I knew it from the time you named the village. You're as beautiful as your mom. Tell her I said that."

She could not believe her ears, the leader of the country chatting easily with her and paying compliments. She had come a long way from a sleepy, rustic paradise in the belly of the interior to a high point in the urban social setting.

Lizzie blushed as she remembered a period of her youthful years when she had held fast to the adolescent creed "I can do that, it's easy. I can handle that, it's no problem." At that time, she was propelled by teenage hormones, which had no place for fear.

She had seen Sylvester Stallone's Rambo: First Blood more than a dozen times, and if the opportunity presented itself, she would see it again. In some strange way she had—bonded with the badly treated Vietnamese veteran, and on Career Day her winning essay was read to the entire school population. It was titled: "Preparing to Be a Combat Soldier." No one took Lizzie seriously at that point, except Father O'Hara. On reading the brilliant essay, he immediately knew it was not done in a fit of hubris. Conversely, he felt sure that the vaguely supercilious tone was just an embodiment of the arrogance of youth, hoping to be taken seriously.

The priest did not try to dissuade her. Instead, he quietly made her abandon the "I can do everything" doctrine and consciously began to fashion her military aspirations. It was done systematically, although, at that time, she was blissfully unaware of the scope.

Now, she was at the core of military operations, and soldiers respected her.

After the rehearsals, Lizzie invited four female officers to her quarters for a private discussion. She got straight to the point.

"For years, we have been asking for WACs to compete in events as a unit. For years, they have treated us like an appendage to be conveniently stuck here and pushed there. We can never command the kind of respect we deserve if we don't show our collective strength. We have to underline our importance, and now is as good a time as any."

One tough-looking thirty-year-old veteran interrupted, "All of this is lovely rhetoric, but don't you remember how many times they turned the request own.

Lizzie rejoined, "I have an outside chance of swinging it this time. Do we have the backing of all the women?"

"Is tomorrow coming?" sneered a sultry, athletic-looking subaltern.

"Good. Spread the word. We have just over two weeks before competition begins, so training and fine-tuning are important. We are going to let them notice we are not only good for the kitchen and the bedroom."

"Girl, I hope you know what you're doing. Don't let us start spreading the word and you can't come through with your end of the bargain. All the women will hate you for raising their hopes and the men will laugh you down for thinking you could pull off such a coup." This admonition came from Captain Jesse Weston, the longest-serving female soldier in the force.

Yolande Belgrave was the last to speak. She stood while doing so, more to make her point than to relieve the cramp in her legs. "Don't ever doubt Elizabeth. If she says she can do something, give her the opportunity. Believe me, I would stake my rank and reputation on her word."

"Thank you for that vote of confidence, Yolande. On second thought, wait until I leave the chief's office tomorrow morning. When I give the thumbs-up, I want the word to spread like wildfire so there will be no reneging."

A querulous voice interjected, "I see you said 'when' and not 'if.' Are you that confident? You really think you can get past your friend, the colonel, who thinks women should know their places and stay there—in bed, that is."

Lizzie sighed. "In normal circumstances, I would say 'Leave it to me.' But on this occasion, a little bit of prayer might help."

"Not a bad idea," said Belgrave. "Let's pray together now, and don't leave anything to chance. I'll be on the lookout for you at lunch tomorrow. Good luck."

A circle was formed and simple prayers said.

Precisely at 9:00 a.m., Lizzie approached the commander's secretary and requested an audience with the chief, citing matters of national importance. Three minutes later, she was seated in one of the four chairs arranged in front of his colossal desk. Her hands gripped each other as her elbows rested. on the arms of the chair. She clenched her teeth and then began slowly and purposefully.

"Brigadier, there are a few things I have to say to you personally and then I am going to ask for Colonel Benson to be present. I have every respect for you and your office, and you in turn, have praised my intelligence and sense of purpose. I will not waste your time with inanities.

"The colonel used and abused his authority as a senior officer to handle personal matters. He wanted to be rid of me, so he sent me on a course where his friends in the CIA could tamper with my brain. I barely escaped, but I later had to endure a horrifying experience that will scar me for life. I hold him and the army responsible.

"I have here a copy of the release I intend to make available to the press if my requests—you note I didn't say demands—are not met. I can assure you that they are not unreasonable. But the colonel should be here before I go any further. I don't want to have to repeat myself and take up time unnecessarily."

The brigadier commanded his secretary to summon the intelligence officer immediately. Then he smiled with tolerant humor and asked, "Officer Ferreira, are you sure this isn't about another woman—a love triangle?"

Lizzie's icy smile and lack of response wiped the smirk from his face, and he wordlessly continued to pay attention to the scattered bits of paper on his cluttered desk.

Soon, Colonel Benson pushed the door. Right away he asked, "You sent for me, Chief?"

It was only then that he noticed Lizzie.

"Colonel, what the hell is going on? I just heard something that worries me immensely." The brigadier's voice was low, but its intensity was like sound waves in an empty room.

"I wish I knew," answered the colonel, shifting positions and making eye contact with his highly polished shoes.

"Elizabeth, the floor is yours," said the chief of staff, tossing aside his Parker pen.

"As I was saying, the release to the press will expose the army's involvement with the CIA, all the way to Jonestown and, specifically, my escape from the devious setup to scramble my brain and remove memories of my personal association with the colonel. I have also detailed a list of other infractions which should make interesting reading locally and on the Internet."

"Don't do anything stupid, Elizabeth," hissed Roger, his tone devoid of any sweet talk."

Lizzie dressed him down with her blazing eyes, dismissing the arrogance, and then said chillingly, "I was not addressing you, Colonel Benson. My remarks are intended for the commander, but if you are speaking on behalf of him and the army, so be it."

Brigadier Sinclair did not want to believe what Officer Ferreira had said, but he had no evidence to refute her. "You have not told us what you want" was all he could muster.

She could feel strong currents and contrary winds at work in the room.

But before she could make her request, the colonel jumped back in the fray. "Chief, you cannot bow to this junior officer. We have to remember that the individual must always be subordinate to the greater good. Let me deal with her. She went AWOL in America and I sat on the information. Now that she is back, she must have heard that I'm seeing someone else and she is displaying typical female paranoid emotions. All her imputations are preposterous."

All the months he had been courting her, each word spoken had said one thing but meant another. His mind must be like concrete, thoroughly mixed up and permanently set. She shook her head in wonderment, fully realizing that the most pernicious aspect of his awesome authority was the fact that he could distort and manipulate information under a personal blanket of intelligence and security.

Through shaded spectacles, the brigadier was shooting penetrating looks her way. Ordinarily, those visual barbs would send soldiers into some sort of paroxysm, but she was beyond caring. She was about to blend hard-nosed negotiations with long-scoffed-at ideas.

"Brigadier, I am suggesting that the Women's Army Corps compete in the upcoming competitions as a separate division. I also want to be paired with Colonel Benson, overtly or covertly. I don't care. I want the opportunity to whip him in most, if not all, of the five disciplines. At the conclusion of the last event, I will submit my resignation."

The very audacity of the two suggestions produced a coarse laugh from the colonel and a burst of anger from the head honcho.

The room was now gyrating to the rhythm of angry voices.

"Officer Ferreira, you could be court-martialed for attempting to blackmail the army," said the brigadier. "But because I suspect you underwent some sort of suffering in the United States, and in the interest of strengthening our divisions internally, I'm prepared to listen, but nothing out of the way or preposterous, mind you."

Lizzie spent the next half hour persuading, pleading, and, as a last resort threatening. In the end, the talks bore fruit. The women would get their independence on a trial basis and she would get her desire.

She had made it appear as if the women's issue was the key component in her demands, so she was fully satisfied when the brigadier said, in closing the discussions, "As to the other matter, there will be no one-on-one. Whatever points system you want to rig up is up to you. Good luck to both of you. I hope at the end of the exercise there will be some kind of closure. The army is not a vendetta camp."

The parameters were quickly drawn up, then the brigadier's aide-de-camp and the force's press officer joined them. It was explained to them that Lizzie had just returned from overseas with a few interesting ideas to spice up the upcoming celebrations, and the experimental shift of women competing as a unit would have to be made known immediately. There was no mention of the personal duel between Colonel Benson and Captain Ferreira. That would remain a secret among three persons.

The charade she was witnessing was a military opera designed to make it look like the brass was not capitulating to a junior rank. And the two newly arrived officers were astute enough to understand that what they were hearing amounted to some form of "bowing to pressure" ironically and brazenly being perpetrated by a woman in their man's army.

Both wondered, but dared not ask, what she held over the two senior officers.

By lunch time, the camp was buzzing with the new development. For years, this separation had been sought but never given any serious consideration. The argument had always been that the women were scattered in various divisions and should, therefore, represent those sections. As the years went by, the Women's Corps continued to expand rapidly but was denied the opportunity to compete as a group.

The new development represented a major step of recognition, and they were going to work doubly hard to make it permanent.

At lunch, the four women officers, who had met with Lizzie the night before, cornered her in the mess hall, and each offered heartfelt congratulations.

They would never doubt her word again.

Chapter 21

A Safe Is Not Always Safe

The colonel was furious that the brigadier had hauled him slowly over the coals and wrung the truth from him. He headed back to his office in the closely guarded intelligence unit and was barely civil to his secretary who handed him an envelope.

He threw it on his desk and reached into his bottom drawer for a flask, which usually contained warm milk, It did have milk, but its alcoholic content outweighed the dairy product two-to-one.

The first swig merely tugged at his hoarse throat, but by the third, he was feeling relaxed enough to reach for the unopened envelope. He slit it open with a gold letter opener, a birthday gift from a long-forgotten conquest, and a U.S. hundred-dollar bill fell out. Under the famous words "In God We Trust" and on the picture of Independence Hall was stamped one explosive word in bold black ink. It screamed, "JONESTOWN."

The colonel's heart stopped beating. He struggled to breathe.

A portrait was slowly forming in his mind, but he had neither brush nor crayon to capture the image. In his desperation, he visualized Lizzie kneeling in front of his safe, confidently selecting the combination, opening the door, and extracting bundles of bills, one of which now lay before him.

He saw there and then that he had seriously underestimated her, and now, she was toying with him. He had committed the cardinal sin of not taking the key from her when she was leaving for the United States.

As for his two dogs and her terrier—his first line of defence— they loved her even more than him.

He had watched her through the brigadier's window as she walked to the officers' mess for lunch. He steeled himself and rushed out to confront her, determined to keep his cool. But when he saw a group of women toasting one another, he blew a fuse.

"Elizabeth, come here a minute," he commanded.

"It's Officer Ferreira, don't you remember?" she countered, rooted in the same spot.

"You're determined to make this difficult, eh!"

"Are you in any way threatening me, Colonel?"

He gave her a piercing stare. She returned one as unwavering as a laser beam.

The room became dead silent. Madame Tussaud's wax museum, with its world-famous, lifelike caricatures, would have brought a distant second; so frozen were the officers.

They had never heard anyone speak to the colonel like that. And Lizzie was not giving ground, seeming to embrace hari-kari with her defiant stance.

"Did you send this to me?" he asked, displaying the defaced note.

"Why would I? I only send gifts to my friends." Her smile was radiant with sarcasm.

Roger looked hard at her, his countenance an opaque dark mass revealing nothing. Lizzie stared back at her deceptive ex-lover, her face revealing everything.

Not a single word was uttered. No nuances. No overt threats. Yet the silence provided its own form of communication—a man's arrogance against a woman's indignation.

He knew he was being outmaneuvered in a human chess game, but he had to continue the moves.

"You haven't heard the last of this."

His wavering voice belied the truculence of his statement. He spun on his heels and hurried out the door.

There was a collective sigh of relief as the entire mess population rushed over to congratulate the fearless officer who had made Colonel Benson back down.

Lizzie was however quick to downplay any talk of heroism, quietly warning them not to do as she had done.

Meanwhile, the colonel drove his Mercedes Benz at breakneck speed to his home. Filled with misgivings and paying no attention to the dogs, he unlocked the front door and rushed to the safe in his bedroom. He knew that she had been there; he just needed to see what she had taken.

He saw two bundles of American currency sitting forlornly on the top shelf. At least she was kind enough to leave something, he thought mockingly. Then he looked at the album, slightly askew, and a sinking feeling took control of his stomach. An empty space on the front page confirmed his guess.

It was obvious that Lizzie had been back in the country longer than she bad reported and had carefully plotted her course of action. There was nothing haphazard about the chain of events. He was a chump, thinking that he had always held a winning hand.

He slowly withdrew his revolver from its holster and gazed down the barrel. He wanted to kill somebody. He wanted somebody to feel pain and beg for mercy like that bastard who had hurt his mother so many year; ago.

The dogs slobbered all over him, and the wet tongues seemed to be easing the commotion in his head. He grabbed a full bottle of carbonated water from the miniature refrigerator near the bed and downed its contents.

He was calm now, though a low, persistent ringing somewhere continued. It was a while before he realized that it was his cell phone, and as he reached for it, it suddenly stopped. Digital technology told him it was the chief of staff trying to get a hold of him.

One thought penetrated the symphony of discord in his head-that if Elizabeth had single-handedly achieved so much, he had to seriously regard her as a rival. He could handle disappointment, but not defeat by a woman. Even to think of such a thing was degrading and emasculating. He had better get quickly into perfect shape.

✶   ✶   ✶

The giant gymnasium had more than a dozen running machines, but Lizzie had an aversion to working up a sweat while going nowhere. Running on the roadway had always been her therapy, and every morning, she led a bunch of women around a five-mile circuit, getting them in shape for the ten-mile full-kit run. She herself ran fifteen miles on bitumen surface thrice a week with Yvonne pacing her on a brand-new black scooter.

For both, the bright sunshine provided a naturopathic elixir. Lizzie soaked it up as part of her training regimen while Yvonne needed it to color her pallid complexion and replace nonexistent vitamin C.

Yvonne was relaxing and regaining her strength at the hotel in Kitty, and twice, Lizzie took her into the compound to observe her son, walking with brisk strides and issuing orders.

Once, she had purposely passed him closely, going in the opposite direction, and he didn't even spare her a glance. In turn, she could hardly recognize him from the chubby boy she had borne and loved so much.

She felt no urge to greet or meet him.

Any offspring who could orchestrate an estrangement of more than a quarter of a century from his mother after seeing her institutionalized-when he was the one being protected-was not worth being thought of as a son.

Somehow, that seemingly harsh judgment did not disturb her.

Her own fear was not what she had already seen of him, but what she might find out about a dark past.

Chapter 22

Revisiting Albouystown

L izzie decided to take a one-day break to look after personal matters that had been left unattended. And later that same afternoon, she belatedly remembered that she had promised her cousins and teenaged friends in Albouystown a treat of pizza and ice cream.

Shortly after five o'clock, she walked through a narrow passageway, and a chorus greeted her before she could reach the steps of the Rodrigues' house.

"Cousin Lizzie, we thought you weren't coming."

"Auntie Lizzie, where is the pizza you promised to bring?"

"Miss Lizzie, I was waiting here since school closed at three o'clock."

Lizzie gleefully hugged her second and third cousins, along with other children living in the same yard and close by. She counted twelve heads—an ethnic potpourri—as she marveled at the collective memory of the promise she had made more than a week ago.

"All right, kids, just a few more minutes. Where's Joaquin?"

"He's by the YM. He told me to call him as soon as you arrive."

"You haven't reached yet?" Lizzie teasingly asked the serious-faced, light-complexioned girl approaching puberty. Like a gazelle, she was off in a flash.

Lizzie extricated herself from the cluster to enter the house, enquiring loudly, "Good afternoon, good afternoon, anybody home?"

The living room was small, but somehow, a three-piece suite, an oblong dining table, an oval coffee table and a stereo combination fit snugly, leaving minimal space for a walk to the tiny elevated kitchen and a makeshift bedroom.

On a worn, square piece of carpet, an antique round-shouldered refrigerator rested. And on its door, dozens of message jostled for

159

attention stuck haphazardly in place by obedient magnets. There was no space within the house for toilet and bathroom. Those facilities were accessible at the rear of the yard.

Two paintings and one framed portrait of the ubiquitous Last Supper hung forlornly and crookedly on a papered wall, waiting for attention, which no doubt, would come at Christmastime.

"Who's making all that noise? Not Elizabeth, she's more considerate than that."

"Aunt Marie, it's me Lizzie. I'm sorry if I disturbed you."

"C'mon, girl, one voice cannot disturb me when 1 have to deal with more than a dozen children and a 'botheration' husband. 1 was only joking. Come and give your aunt a hug."

Just as Lizzie responded, Joaquin arrived to plant a kiss on her cheek as he complimented her. "Liz, girl, you look as fit as a fiddle. Got any fights coming up? Who's the victim?"

His mother answered for Lizzie. "You're always talking about fighting, and it's Lizzie who has to represent you. Remember Bully Jack? Why don't you stick to your hip-hop and rap foolishness?"

Lizzie immediately jumped in. "Auntie, 1 have to disagree with you. True and clean rap and hip-hop are the expressive sounds of today's young people. Think of them as the spoken word with a beat added. This art form might be young in definition, but it is as old as time."

Joaquin could not contain himself. "Beautiful, Lizzie, beautiful. 1 could never express it the way you've just done. Hold the thought right there, let me get a pencil and a piece of paper."

Her aunt also expressed surprise. "1 didn't know you were a hip-hop fan. I know you play Beethoven, Bach and the other long-name man on the piano. Rap seems a big difference to me."

Lizzie replied, "The long-name man you're talking about is Tchaikovsky, and if you put a compelling word beat to classical music, you will get hip-hop. Music soothes the savage beast and we should encourage it no matter what form it takes."

Her aunt was not done with the subject.

"Lizzie, 1 still think hip-hop and rap are bad for young children. Listen to them on the way to and from school, comfortably repeating lyrics referring to females as 'bitches' and 'whores.' Their little minds are like sponge, oaking up everything they hear, unable to differentiate between good and bad messages."

Joaquin returned with pencil and paper, but Lizzie said to him, "I'll write it down while you're gone. Here's a receipt with your name on it, Grab a taxi, pick up the boxes of pizza and the ice cream, and get back here quickly, Hip-hop Man. The kids are getting restless."

Her cousin had grown into a handsome man. He was not noted for his physical prowess, even though he could now take care of himself. It was his mental acuity that had secured him a senior civil service job within the ministry of finance. But when it came to his dress, his peers in the neighborhood influenced that.

He was wearing a University of Penn singlet over an NBA jersey, a do-rag over plaits, and a cap cocked rakishly over the rag. Just barely hanging on below his waist was a pair of oversized blue jeans, the crotch inches past his knees.

As he moved briskly to collect the goodies, Lizzie joined her aunt on the couch. Marie was a little over sixty, but looked older, having to cope with the daily chaos of an extended family. She bore twenty-one children of her own, was surrogate mother for countless others, plus grandchildren, washed clothes at a standpipe, cooked dual pots daily, kept a scrupulously clean home, and still found time to go to church regularly.

Looking sideways at her aunt's weather-beaten face, Lizzie wondered how men could labor under the misapprehension that women were the weaker sex. She had long since known that that was just a delusion.

She knew that when God created women, He gave them an inexhaustible supply of innate power to tackle life head-on and to bear insufferable pain, especially in childbirth. Their power was as old as creation, and they knew it. It was a credit to them that they never sought to exploit it.

Her aunt was now looking curiously at her. "So what gives with you? Still seeing that big boy? What's his name?"

Lizzie never had the luxury of living with a grandparent since they both drowned before she was born. Aunt Marie was her most senior elder and after living so many years with her, she knew that untruths were always stillborn.

"Robert is his name, and no, we are no longer seeing each other. He is out of my life for good."

"It was always in his eyes, but you never took the time to look. He is a user and a manipulator. Good riddance."

"Thanks, Aunt Marie, I was blind, but now I see."

"So how many events are you competing in during the anniversary celebrations?"

Lizzie was puzzled. She asked, "How did you know?"

"I read the newspapers and saw that women were going to compete as a unit for the first time. I knew you somehow had a hand in wringing that concession. Did you.?"

"You're extraordinary. Yes, I did "

"One final question and then let's talk about your mother and the trip to America. Are you competing against him one-on-one?"

Lizzie was completely floored. She had tried so hard to camouflage her intentions and felt she was doing a good job. Yet her wise old aunt had seen beyond the screen.

"No, we've agreed on a points system and the commander is the only other person who is aware of the personal contest."

"Be very careful. He would stop at nothing to maintain his lofty position. Sleep with one eye open. And oh, by the way, how is your precious Father O'Hara?"

"Still very precious to me. He suspects what I am about to do, and although he hasn't endorsed it, he hasn't tried to dissuade me. I think he looks at my decision as the final expiation, an expurgation of sorts."

Uncharacteristically, her aunt sucked her teeth and mumbled, "He should have been man enough to leave the church and marry her."

"Marry whom? What are you talking about? Auntie, are you off on that tangent again?"

"No tangent. Father O'Hara fell in love with your mother the first time he saw her and carries that weight with him all the time. Since he couldn't have her, he poured all that love into his relationship with you, so much so you resemble him. God would have forgiven him for making that worldly choice, and God knows your mother had strong feelings for him."

This was not the first time that Lizzie had heard her aunt's preposterous suggestion, and it was unlikely to be the last. She laughed heartily and leaned over to tousle Marie's dose-cropped hair, saying with a gentle reproof, "Imagination, imagination, imagination."

Joaquin was back, and the mini-feast began in earnest. Uninvited kids gazed longingly until they were eventually invited to partake while cats and dogs fought for scraps, angry sibilance and growls filling the air.

Soon, it was time for homework and then bed, or what passed

for that luxury. Bed meant used clothing, old window blinds and discarded sheets—any scrap that would serve as a cushion between the body and the hard, unyielding floor. Each person knew his or her treasures by sight and texture and guarded those intimate possessions with a passion that often escalated into serious arguments and, many times, fisticuffs.

After all, "Flora McDonald" as the sleeping turf was facetiously called, was not a matter to be taken lightly.

Lizzie left amidst a profusion of thanks and enquiries as to when the kids would see her again. She had decided to enjoy the moonlit night by walking along Sussex Street and into Cemetery Road, where no two streetlights in a row functioned. If they did, they would have been celebrated far and wide.

Halfway down Sussex Street, just past the Dharm Shala, a sanctuary for the dispossessed and transient, two youths rode up on a bicycle and brazenly attempted to snatch a chain from around her neck.

She skillfully avoided them and sprinted away, slipping through two broken panels in the gate of nearby Le Repentir Cemetery. The young bandits stopped and watched from a distance as Lizzie casually strolled among imposing tombs and twisted headboards, waving to them every few steps.

She casually ran her fingers along the larger gravestones, the handiwork of local masons long obliterated by the harsh tropical elements.

The two culprits departed, confused as to whether their intended victim was spirit or human. They did not understand that she chose that route because Amerindians were not afraid of the dead.

She continued to walk purposefully along the main road in the burial ground, alert for signs of more intrepid villains. As always, she was impressed with the sight of hundreds of lofty palm trees with their huge overhanging branches as they blotted out the noise of constant traffic. Yet, she thought, it was such a shame that the designated place for souls to rest was no longer honored with tranquility and reverence. A national treasure, steeped in tradition, was now overrun by criminal elements, using the vast acreage to their unlawful advantage.

If she had a choice, she would choose night over day. The air at that time always seemed cooler than its predecessor, less erratic. She walked unhurriedly, kicking at the unruly grass that converged on the narrow, pot-holed pathways.

Soon, she came to the gate at the Princes Street entrance of the massive burial place. It was in worse condition than its companion at the other end, and she passed through without any special effort.

After a potentially dangerous shortcut, her long walk to army headquarters at Thomas Lands proved uneventful.

Chapter 23

Ready for Action

There is inherent knowledge of right and wrong in every human being.

And so, the determination to seek revenge or wreak havoc requires an overwhelming desire to forge ahead regardless of consequences.

Lizzie had once listened to Father O'Hara painfully chastising himself for losing control and doing harm to his childhood sweetheart's wicked stepfather. She was not yet a teenager when he told her of his wrongdoing, but the priest knew the level of her intelligence.

She understood clearly, and she let him know that the lesson was well documented in her head. What she didn't tell him then, and never would, was that she agreed with the exacting of punishment.

She couldn't understand why the justice system did not make it mandatory for a criminal to feel the same kind of pain he or she had inflicted on a victim. Tit for tat. Rape a rapist. Execute a murderer. Brand a thief on his forehead..

She felt that she could not rest in peace until she had her revenge. She wanted to go even beyond that, but could not imagine what that feeling would be like. And after she had gotten revenge, would she be satisfied?

No answers were forthcoming.

She absently played with the ring that Roger had given her. Its metal was cold. Over the past few days, she had caught herself doing it occasionally, and she wistfully remembered how she had been willing to put her career on hold if he had wanted them to start a life together.

Then he had coldly concocted his dastardly plot.

A bugle destroyed the silence of the early morning. It was reveille—the normal summons for a soldier to get up and prepare for a new military day.

But that day, it had ominous significance for a few.

Lizzie was up and alert, immediately kneeling at the side of her bunk, saying regular morning prayers, plus Psalms 23 and 27. She prayed in a soft tone, quiet and authoritative. Her roommates had grown accustomed to her morning devotions and were still catching the last few desperate minutes of shut-eye.

But it wasn't her voice that Lizzie was worried about.

She was sure every person in the room could hear the pounding of her heart and the roaring of blood in her veins.

Dizziness swirled through her brain, and hollowness, not caused by the absence of breakfast, entered her stomach. Nausea also played seesaw along her esophagus.

Elbows on the bed, she began to rise, but a sudden sensation in her temple pushed her back on her knees.

"Hey, girl, you all right?"

Lizzie didn't look up but managed an affable "Yes, thank you."

"C'mon, girl, you sound terrible. What are you doing with a hangover on the first day of competition? Bad example. You know all the girls are counting on you."

Lizzie turned to Lieutenant Sandra Turpin, whom everyone, including the commander, called "Mother Turpin."

Forcing a smile, she said, "Good morning, Mother. It's not a hangover, nor is it morning sickness. Rest your fears."

"Well hallelujah! Our star is all right. So let's rise and shine and kick some ass." Those words of encouragement boomed from the muscular Ensign Ann Trim.

But before they could move on, a raspy voice intruded. "I don't know why you all seem so confident when our star looks so much like a scared rabbit."

Major Belgrave, always the pacifier, jumped off a top bunk and rushed to add her voice, but Lizzie stopped her with a finger to her lips.

"Second Lieutenant Greaves. Fear is easier to control than overconfidence or, more to the point, bed-hopping. You see, every one of us, some time or the other, has been in a position where fear was a major factor, and we were forced to deal with it. On the other hand, you seem to have absolutely no fear of the danger of warming every officer's bed in this compound and outside."

There was complete silence for almost a minute, and Lizzie immediately regretted the didactic tone. She hastened to add, "Let's say a collective prayer that we put a serious dent in the arrogance of our male counterparts. Remember, there is no one star. Everyone must perform above and beyond."

Even the chastened Greaves joined in the prayers calling for the strengthening of moral weaknesses and physical foibles.

✶   ✶   ✶

The first event of the day and of the week-long competition was pistol shooting, beginning 9:00 a.m. at the Timehri ranges. In the afternoon, the big rifles would boom.

Since men outnumbered women, the latter had first use of the range; then the men took over both.

Dozens of triggers snapped back and their firing pins slammed home. Guns roared around the range. The results would be based on a per target ratio.

The WACs had carefully selected their ten representatives, and not surprisingly; they recorded a 79.1 percent average. The male soldiers competed in their respective divisions and their selected team averaged 90. It was a no contest, but it represented a significant statement for the ecstatic women.

There was further honor for them, as Lizzie, using a Smith & Wesson 9 mm semi-automatic pistol, recorded 98, 97 and 99 out of a possible 100 at three different ranges. She was second only to Colonel Benson, who stood supreme with scores of 99, 98 and 99. His weapon of choice was a .357 magnum Colt Python.

In the Timehri mess hall, at lunchtime, there was definitely a mood of intense rivalry; and the women seemed to be walking with a spring in their steps. However, by afternoon, the spring had turned into a hop, for although the rifle shooting results read "WACs 69 percent; Male representatives 90.2 percent," the individual competition was going down to the wire, and Lizzie was right in there with the best.

Once again, "Dead Eye" Benson shot an amazing 118 points out of a possible 120 with 15 V Bulls, dropping just one point each, at three hundred and five hundred yards.

Lizzie hit the bull's-eye with unerring accuracy and needed just one more to top the colonel when she dropped two points at her favorite five hundred yards.

She would not blame anyone or offer any excuse, but she was sure a sudden movement had willfully distracted her. When she looked in its direction, she saw the colonel smugly cheering, the expert sharpshooter's badge—with bars for rifle and pistol—glistening on his shoulders.

She thought fleetingly of making an appeal to the shooting judges but abandoned the idea. She knew that adjudication of official complaints was heavy with procedure and gravid with technicality. She knew everything about the committees, the panels and closed-door meetings. It would do no good to go that route.

The announcement blared through a loudspeaker system. The grand aggregate for both competitors was 118 points. Lizzie and the colonel had tied for first place.

The IQ test was held the following day. And even though she was aware, she did not object to the fact that the questions were set by officers within the colonel's intelligence unit. At the end of the day, all scores were posted next to names in alphabetical order. Benson, Roger-98 marks. Not far below, Ferreira, Elizabeth-94 marks.

Those results did not displease her because they did not count in the match-up.

Less than twenty-four hours later, she was sitting at the open door of one of the army's planes, waiting for the tap on her shoulder that would signal her turn to parachute onto the force's football field, the perimeter of which was dotted with thousand of citizens gathered to witness the daring aerial feats.

She consulted her compass, making mental adjustments for any drift that might be caused by the slight Atlantic breeze, focusing on the red painted roof of the officers' club, which she would use as a landmark.

The pilot circled and climbed to the point high in the sky regarded as the ideal altitude for a parachute jump.

When the shoulder tap came, she was perfectly psyched. She eased off the edge and fell gracefully into space. She counted off a certain amount of seconds then pulled the chord on the chute. It ballooned over her head with a slight tug to her shoulders.

She landed textbook fashion in the large painted circle—her knees bent and arms tucked into her sides as she hit the ground. She lay without moving while offering a silent prayer, then made the sign of the cross.

Jumps always unnerved her. Opening the chute too soon could

cause the parachutist to be blown away from the drop point and into dangerous situations. Too late, the chute might not open properly-- disaster.

Lizzie folded her parachute expertly then marched off to where a large throng of excited women soldiers were jumping up and down, yelling and pumping their arms in the air.

"We're proud of you, girl."

"You were perfect, Liz. You looked like a descending angel."

"Girl, only you and Colonel Benson landed in the circle. The others missed the mark, and one unfortunate ensign broke a leg when he landed in somebody's mango tree over there."

She was pointing in the direction of nearby Kitty village, where an orange chute was still billowing.

Someone took her bundle, and suddenly she was hoisted aloft and carried into the club. She remained airborne until a round of drinks was served, courtesy of Major Belgrave.

A roar went up and they lifted glasses, offering a toast to "Equality."

$$\ast \qquad \ast \qquad \ast$$

Friday! It was the grueling ten-mile run with full kit. Each division had selected its fittest representatives to tackle the course along the Timehri roadways and sand slopes.

The sun was scorching hot. Birds were reluctant to fly, quietly hugging the shelter of the smallest leaf. No one lingered to see if the tar on the road would melt, accepting it as a matter of faith.

After three miles, soldiers were strung out in single file, many walking. By the halfway mark, "the fittest of the fittest" had easily outdistanced their tiring brethren and were settling down to outpace one another.

The lead group of eight included two young officers. The second bunch had six soldiers, and Lizzie was the only officer there. One senior officer, Colonel Benson, not far behind, led the third body of twelve.

With a little more than a mile to the finish, Lizzie glanced over her shoulder. It told her what she instinctively knew. The colonel was closing the gap rapidly on the most steep hill, his sturdy legs an asset in that climb.

She unhooked the shirt from around her waist, where she had

secured it from the start of the race. With practiced fingers, she formed a kata—a round pad placed on the head to ease the carrying of load—and donned it. She slipped her arms out of the knapsack's straps and placed the pack atop the kata, her rifle now across her shoulders.

The colonel's group had caught up with Lizzie's, and he was observing her unorthodox transfer of Load at such a crucial point in the race.

The officer flashed a confident, sardonic smile, which Lizzie noticed. She had been on the receiving end of that grin often enough to know that conceit and smugness lay at its core.

Still grinning, he cocked his thumb, took aim with his forefinger and fired, mouthing, "Pow, pow, pow." He blew smoke from his fingertips, pushed his knapsack high on his back and strode briskly ahead of his group, as well as hers.

A storm was fast approaching.

In a few minutes the sky had changed from azure to dark gray. It seemed contusive and angry, and the wind had picked up noticeably, carrying a whistling sound.

Then, as if summoned, a bolt of lightning split the sky with frightening flashes. Thunder shook the surrounding trees and torrential rainfall pelted down from the heavens.

Faces streaked with sweat and rain, the competing soldiers moved inexorably on, some jogging, others trudging wearily. However, all eyes strained to see familiar landmarks that would signal an end to the grueling ordeal.

While the rain proved an impediment to most, ironically it served to invigorate Lizzie. She greeted the downpour with relish, fondly remembering her youthful days when games and contests were regularly conducted under similar conditions. She began singing a popular old classic as her walk turned into a purposeful jog.

Colonel Benson's bunions were giving him hell. His back felt as if he had been whipped and his arms and legs were leaden. He was one of the fittest and toughest officers, but this was going to be his last year of competition. It was only because of the challenge from Elizabeth that he was now pushing his body in this monster of a run, or walk, as was his current pace.

He couldn't believe that she would try that knapsack-on-the-head stunt. By now her neck should be into her shoulders, hurting and slowing her perceptibly, he thought satisfyingly.

He glanced back to verify his prediction, and the breath choked in his throat. Ten yards behind, Lizzie was jogging merrily along, singing some infernal song with the tantalizing chorus of "raindrops keep on falling." By some form of magic, the backpack was still atop her head, her boots now held together by their laces around her neck and the rifle in both hands across her chest.

He looked ahead and saw the army's ensign fluttering above a five-ton truck. That was the finish line. A quick calculation told him that his destination was a little over six hundred yards and he mentally adjusted his strategy for the final surge.

His feet were protesting, but he dismissed the thought of removing his boots. A true soldier must be properly dressed at all times, his manual said.

Lizzie was now abreast of him, singing and smiling teasingly. She removed her right hand from the rifle, cocked her thumb, took aim with the forefinger, and shouted derisively, "Boom."

Roger Benson's temple throbbed with umbrage. He was being tested and pushed to the limit by a woman. Not any woman, just the woman he had wronged—a woman scorned.

But she was not going to best him. He was going to effectively blunt her challenge. He was going to trip her up and claim an accident. No other person was in the immediate vicinity to witness his action.

His face told a tale of pain and suffering, his breath coming in rasping, uneven gasps.

He veered right to shorten the distance between them, but Lizzie must have seen the mischief in his eyes.

Barefooted, she sprinted hard for twenty meters, then settled into an easy lope.

When she crossed the finish line, there were a few soldiers ahead of her.

But that did not concern her.

She was happily looking back and savoring the sight of her arch-enemy lirgping painfully to the finish.

For a long time they sat on the sand, a few yards apart, eyes locked in a struggle of wills. There was a kind of lethargic silence, but she heard his thoughts louder than if he were speaking.

The sun reappeared, but its blistering heat did nothing to assuage Benson's pain.

And for all the quiet civility between them, the soldier athletes could sense the undercurrent of hostility; and they kept a safe distance.

In all the years, they had never seen the stalwart senior officer in such ragged condition. He was a legend in the field and, in the arcane world of military intelligence, held widespread respect, not ostensibly for his tactics, but for their results.

On that day, however, he looked a thoroughly beaten man.

The disappointment that invaded the colonel's stomach tasted like gall. He dropped his head on his chest and closed his eyes. He had known loss before, but had never tasted that kind of absolute defeat. It took a superhuman effort but he walked over to Lizzie and, in front of hundreds of eyes, said loudly, "Good run, soldier."

The absence of a reply was reply enough.

Her face remained a mask of neutrality as her small fingers interlaced in a prayerful tent.

Chapter 24

Looking Back

Colonel Benson walked away, beaten and insulted. Compassion for the beautiful young woman flooded his veins, yet he could not yield to the indignity of apologizing to her and seeking forgiveness.

Wrestling with the implications of whatever new choices lay before him, he knew that he had lost ground and face over the previous days, and he would have to top his best performance in the river swim on Sunday.

It was the clincher. Whoever finished ahead of the other would have won the contest. For him, it could only be one person—Roger Benson.

A moment ago that look in Lizzie's eyes—always a barometer of her moods—had told him everything he needed to know. Gone was the vulnerability of the past. The love, the emotions and the trust were replaced by a penetrative glow of willfulness—a personality trait he had never seen in her.

He could feel her eyes on him and he willed himself to keep on putting as much distance as possible between them. But without understanding why, some unknown force seemed to whip his head around for a quick look.

His face flushed with embarrassment as she met his furtive glance with an unblinking stare. He felt as if he had been caught with his hand in the cookie jar.

In the brief glimpse, he saw a woman that he was a fool not to have loved unconditionally. She appeared like a beautiful wild flower, so fragile looking, yet imbued with surprising strength.

He also saw a woman with a strong sense of purpose, clinging to the will to survive and to be as good as anyone else.

His right hand slammed into his left palm six times in staccato fashion, a ritual he performed only when he was thoroughly angry with himself And that was not often.

It was therapy, subconsciously reenacting the scene when he had chopped his mother's lover six times with a hatchet.

The act was a penance, reminding him how he had once lost control and, by a sickening twist of fate, barely escaped crushing legal consequences.

He continued to berate himself Like a fool, he had fallen victim to overconfidence and been hit by complacency. Plain and simple, he had underestimated Lizzie. He had taken her for granted, lumped her with all the other vapid women, even though he was aware of her special qualities.

For years he had lived with the dreadful thought of someone disclosing that he was not the person he claimed to be. And he had always been curious how he would deal with it when it happened.

Because he was driven by a consuming ambition to head the army he loved so dearly, he had always been able to rationalize a variety of scenarios in which he could avoid detection.

Up to that point, he had done a good job of hiding his adolescent past. 1t was so well hidden that he didn't even consider it deceit anymore. He had done a lot of work on himself, moving from a chubby youngster to a superbly fit athlete. He had enjoyed the odyssey and the constant female attention his appealing personality had garnered. But none of the encounters held any meaning for him ... until Lizzie.

He continued to walk towards his Land Rover and found himself praying to a god in whom he had never fully believed, praying for his world not to come tumbling down.

As he prayed, contradictory messages echoed in his head. You love her, don't you?

No, you don't. You love the idea of having a brilliant and perceptive woman under your control.

Don't trust her. She wants to bring you to your knees.

You really miss her. Remember the ache of emptiness when she left for America.

But one particular echo persisted. You can't let her beat you, Robert.

No one had called him by his correct Christian name since he had hastily departed New Amsterdam so many years ago. This must be the voice of authority, and surely, he ought to heed its counsel.

Don't let her do it, Robert, the echo, now a voice, commanded again.

At that stage, he knew he had to stop her forever.

*   *   *

Sunday began casually. A nine o' clock church service at St. George's Cathedral was followed by a sumptuous brunch in the army's gymnasium, during which the chaplain prayed for an uneventful swim contest across the Demerara River later in the day.

The women soldiers were in high spirits, knowing that they had exceeded all expectations, and that they had earned grudging respect from their male counterparts. But they could not contain themselves, aware that their trump card was one of the favorites in the race.

A placing among the top order would be the crowning glory since that would put Lizzie in line for Best Performing Soldier, an honor never given serious thought before that day.

And despite the lack of evidence of any leak, it was obvious among the soldiers that there was a personal contest between Colonel Benson and his junior officer, once his lover.

Table manners were forgotten. Conversation was everywhere.

The clink of glasses and the sound of knives and forks against plates provided the background for the symphony of satisfying mastication. But for the conviviality, the scene could have been mistaken for the Last Supper.

Twenty-four swimmers awaited the starter on the Vreed-en-Hoop Ferry Stelling. Only two were women.

Lizzie wore the conventional one-piece bathing suit and seemed anxious for the race to start, pacing up and down. To the casual onlooker, her irregular movements could be labeled as nervous energy. But she was actually remonstrating with herself for the indiscretion of downing two glasses of rum the previous night when she knew it was foolhardy to follow a tough physical exercise with hard liquor.

A contingent of senior women officers had invaded her quarters near midnight and insisted on a "drink" to celebrate her sensational victory over the enemy colonel. She had acquiesced, and now her stomach had a funny feeling.

She was anxious to get into the murky waters before the tide turned. She had mapped her strategy based on information gleaned from the Web site maintained by the Caribbean Institute of Meteorology and Hydrology, and timing was important.

An official arrived breathlessly on a noisy motorbike and immediately pulled out his starter's pistol.

A snotty young officer, known to curry favor at will, slapped the colonel on his back and said encouragingly, "C'mon, Colonel, we can't let a little country girl embarrass us men."

The colonel bristled and glanced sideways, immediately realizing that the wind had carried the comment. Although he had heard others refer to the subservient junior officer as a "fairy," he was never one to make hasty judgments. But right then, he conceded the likelihood.

Lizzie's eyes smoldered with indignation and the clear message was there is now one more reason to whip your ass.
She moved quickly to his side and said, "Just to let you know, Robert, your mother will be on the barge to greet you."

He gasped audibly.

Did she say Robert?

Nah! It must have been a slip of the tongue. She couldn't know his real name. He never used it. And mother? What could she know of his buried past?

He dismissed the matter as soon as he heard the starter's voice. "On your mark! Get set! Go!"

The gun cracked and two dozen swimmers plunged into the river.

Twenty-three of them struck out at a forty-five-degree angle in a direct line to the finish at the army's naval base at Ruimveldt. One contestant swam almost in a straight line as if heading for the Stabroek Market.

For one hour, doubts were cast about that swimmer's strategy. But suddenly the wind picked up noticeably and the tide, once ebbing, was now flowing. At that stage, Lizzie's strategy made sense.

She was upriver doing an unhurried backstroke and the tide was accelerating her speed. Head back, eyes to the heavens, she listened to the sound of her own breathing as she was propelled, with little effort, towards the finish line.

The other fifteen—eight had abandoned their efforts—were now struggling as the tidal movement worked to push them beyond their target.

Colonel Benson led the pack. With his smooth freestyle action, he scythed through the softly rippling waves, and ever so often, he would flip over on his back to check the progress of those behind him.

He smiled to himself. This win would decisively settle the one-on-one battle with Lizzie, and it would also help him to retain his place as one of the best all-round soldiers. He lowered his head and glided the last forty yards to the large decorated barge where officials and a few dignitaries sat.

The last rays of sunlight blinded him as he stretched his hand to accept a "leg up." He was about to say "Thank you" when the person offering the hand blocked the sun for a fleeting moment.

As he stared into the icy eyes of Lizzie, two words were wrenched from between clenched teeth. Though each was of one syllable, together they stretched into an extended wail that blanked out all other sounds- "Not you."

His brain registered the fact that only contestants who had successfully completed the event were allowed on the barge. Lizzie's presence had to mean only one thing: she had beaten him in the race and in the contest.

Still in the water, his eyes traveled up those shapely legs that he had caressed on numerous occasions, up past the mound, flat belly, pert breasts, perfect nose, and thick black lashes shading emerald green eyes that were now surveying him with ill-concealed apathy.

Now that she had won their private contest, he had no way of knowing whether she would keep her promise not to expose him.

He thought of the irony of a distinguished career ending on such an ignoble note, and he suddenly realized that the shockwaves of her devastating disclosures could be averted if somehow, he could take her down with him.

The commanding voice in his head bellowed, Don't let her abort you career.

And without thinking, he grabbed her ankles and heaved her off the barge, into the water. He was upon her in a flash, locking his right hand around her neck, pulling her into the depths of the recently dredged river.

Onlookers were confused by what they were witnessing, unsure whether it was real or staged.

Meanwhile, the surface of the river was alive with bubbles and other eruptions of thrashing legs and flailing arms. Then, after what seemed like an eternity, two heads appeared, six feet apart, mouths gasping desperately for vital oxygen.

Treading water, they circled each other warily until Lizzie disappeared under and then reappeared at the steps of the barge, climbing groggily aboard.

The colonel followed and, as he scrambled aboard, shouted, "No one interferes. This is personal."

Chapter 25

Final Curtain

A sudden gust of Atlantic breeze rocked the barge. It produced a whistling sound, eerie and funereal.

The colonel grimaced with fatigue. In his eyes, she could read the question, How did I allow myself to be outmaneuvered?

It was now clear to Lizzie that she would have to engage in pure street fight tactics, and although she was well schooled in that exercise, her guess was that it would be no cakewalk.

There was no time for textbook style and fluidity of movement, so she acted first, lunging and drawing back her elbow to drive it into his cheekbone, careful to avoid the lethal zone directly in front of the ear.

It was a paralyzing blow, but the colonel was agile enough to grab the elbow on contact and cruelly twist it. The movement toppled both soldiers to the floor of the vessel, and there they wrestled furiously—he, fuelled by the disdainful prospect of again being overshadowed by a woman, and she, suffused with the knowledge that he was mortal.

Each felt and quietly respected the undeniable strength of the other.

She hooked a slender but powerful arm around his neck, attempting to compress the trachea. But the senior officer was naturally strong from exercising every day and his hammerlock grip slowly began to impair her breathing, causing little colored stars to dance before her eyes.

All muscles in her body seemed to be failing her and she felt a little like someone caught in a strong current, being tugged inexorably along, powerless to offer resistance.

Suddenly, she felt the hasty release of the vice-like grip, and as she fought to catch her breath, she saw Yvonne stabbing the colonel in his ribs with the shiny tip of the large black umbrella, which until then had been providing shade from the relentless glare of the sun.

Life was slowly returning to Lizzie's eyes, even though she remained rooted to the rough texture of the floating vessel. Rational thoughts surfaced sluggishly. Coherence followed. Then the door of dear thinking burst open and she jumped up, swiveling to locate the cagey enemy soldier. She was on her feet, but her balance was still compromised.

The colonel was also slowly surfacing from the depths of his own exhaustion, struggling to breathe. He let out one single harsh obscenity, feeling the blood pounding in his chest and echoing in his ears.

Lizzie watched in consternation as his face contorted through various frames of emotions--disbelief, cunning, madness.

She was unfazed by the first, wary of the second, and frightened by the last.

Now, he seemed to be assessing the situation anew, circling and plotting, an enlarged vein throbbing noticeably on his temple.

It was now or never.

"Move in the moment of hesitation"-Father O'Hara's famous words.

Her immediate kick to his groin was like fireworks exploding. He looked down to see if there was any kind of dismemberment, but he found it to be only an illusion.

The feeling of something wet running down his legs was not. It was indeed "pee pee" as his mother used to call his urinary discharge as a little boy.

His eyes immediately swung left to look at the woman who was supposed to be his mother. A hauntingly familiar visage confronted him. She gazed at him without flinching then winked twice in quick succession.

He had his answer immediately. So well he remembered that intimate gesture. With it, he had always felt reassured that the bond between the two could never be broken and that he would always have her to look after his welfare.

Then the realization of his abandonment over the years hit him and his knees sagged perceptibly.

Lizzie, unaware of the eye-play between mother and son, and its devastating effect on the officer, went on the offensive again.

In the split second before her move, she became aware that the dynamic could become completely skewed with Roger's mounting anger. Her best bet was to bring about a quick conclusion before he began to think dearly. He would surely prevail in a drawn-out encounter.

A faked kick to the groin earned an opening for a hard chop to the nose and a stiff-fingered jab under the heart. Her hands flew, blocking, deflecting, and countering. The colonel was grudgingly giving ground to the human tornado, but he too was registering telling blows to her body and once to her temple. His left hand was working like a well-oiled piston.

Shouts of derision were mixed with those of encouragement as the swelling crowd of soldiers, media and special invitees realized they were not witnessing any type of rehearsed scenario. It was obvious to all that this was deadly combat, spurred by some sort of simmering animosity.

And from the reaction of the women soldiers, the female combatant was carrying their collective hopes of equality in a male bastion that had grudgingly allowed members of the opposite sex into their prized profession. .

Lizzie's head throbbed with pain, but her thinking was not impaired. She crouched low before springing vertically in the air. As her opponent closely followed her trajectory, she shot out her right foot to slam its heel smack into his face.

He was unprepared for the move, toppling backwards into the river with a loud splash. When the resulting ripples subsided, he did not surface.

Lizzie darted from one side to the other, looking for a sign of the colonel.

She didn't want him to die by drowning. She didn't want him to die at all. She wanted him to live and face up to all the wrong he had done over the years. She wanted him to stand in front of a jury of his conscience and be condemned.

While she was now paralyzed with the fear that she might have killed him, his mother leaned on the closed umbrella and seemed to be holding her breath. Like Lizzie, she wanted him punished, but not in that manner.

They searched the murky waters with their eyes, but there was no sign of the embattled soldier.

Lizzie could not bear the suspense any longer. She looked around once more and, to her horror, saw what could only be the dorsal fin of a shark.

She did not hesitate.

She plunged into the river at the spot where he had fallen and allowed her body to sink below the surface, moving in circles with her hands outstretched. Once, twice, three times, no obstacle. The fourth circle was almost complete when her fingers brushed strands of hair, and she grabbed them as if her life depended on them.

She felt for his face and immediately spun him around, jocking her right hand under his chin and heading for the surface.

She gasped for air as sunlight greeted her eyes, But the same sunlight revealed that she was more than twenty yards from the barge, and on the other side of it, the dreaded shark loomed larger as the distance between them closed.

Lizzie knew she could reach the vessel and safety if she let go of Roger, but she hadn't risked her life to let him drift off into the depths of a watery grave. As it was, she had to get him to safety and quickly administer live-saving cardiopulmonary resuscitation (CPR). Too much time with an excessive amount of water in the lungs was a devastating cause of death. The brain cells starved of oxygen would cease to function.

She was swimming with one hand, moving slowly, and while on the periphery she saw two speedboats thundering from the shore, she doubted that they could reach in time to deny the man-eater a satisfying supper.

She moved purposely along, fear fuelling frenetic fantasy. She looked skyward and prayed and prayed. Suddenly, two figures appeared in the distant sky, only their faces clearly visible. One was Father O'Hara, and the other unfamiliar, but with a halo around a peaceful face.

While her godfather encouraged her to dig deeper for faith, the other head bobbed majestically as if agreeing with the priest's urgings.

Although danger loomed ahead, she couldn't help but rehearse Hebrew 11: 1-"What is faith? It is the confident assurance that something we want is going to happen. It is the certainty that what we hope for is waiting for us, even though we cannot see it up ahead."

Lizzie turned her head to again gauge the distance to the safety of the barge. She stopped in mid-stroke. Yvonne was a spectral shape reflected in the approaching twilight, bareheaded and barefooted, both hands above her head holding her umbrella like a lethal spear.

With remarkable accuracy, she plunged the shiny tip into the open mouth of the killer fish as it was about to glide past the raft. The fish trashed about in confusion, sidetracked from its original prey and fighting with the intrusive object that seemed to have a motive of its own.

The respite was enough for Lizzie to reach the barge and drag the colonel aboard.

Yvonne gently pushed her aside and bent over her son, squeezing his nostrils and locking lips to send badly needed oxygen into his lungs. Two efforts were enough. The colonel coughed once then a series of retching spasms expelled almost two pints of brown water.

By that time, the first speedboat had dislodged the army medic, and he immediately clamped an opaque oxygen mask over Colonel Benson's face.

A stretcher followed but the colonel refused to lie on it. Instead, he walked unaided and looked searchingly at the two women before him.

The hat was off and he immediately recognized his mother. The woman who had brought him into the world when she was little more than a child; the woman whom he had abandoned but to whom he had sent allowances without any concern whether she had benefited from them. That same woman had just given him life a second time.

A series of shudders racked his body as he silently acknowledged that his filial contempt was hard to justify. He had always loved his mother. Yet he wondered if subconsciously he had resented her for bringing so many men into their lives.

His gaze turned to Lizzie and he hung his head in renunciation of his strange behavior. How could he send her off to be a guinea pig in a mind-altering exercise just because she presented a threat to his ambition? Look what she had just done. She had risked her life to save him although he had met her pure, unadulterated love with betrayal.

All his life he had firmly believed that men controlled their own destinies. He did not believe in fate, divine intervention, the church, or God. More significantly, he had always held strong to the conviction that in a toss-up between an evenly matched man and woman, his half would always succeed.

In the explosive silence that followed his examination of them, he could clearly see the hurt and pain in both pairs of eyes. And then, something within seemed to snap with the realization that not only one woman had soared above him, but two.

He longed for a cigarette. The nicotine would coast through

his lungs into the bloodstream, reaching the brain and central nervous system, producing perfect relaxation. He had heard that only addicts and junkies could fully understand the sense of calm after a satisfying smoke. He could now sympathize with their addiction.

The noise and stares of the onlookers pummeled him. A sudden, desperate panic seized him and he shrank from the women, jabbering unintelligibly and warding off invisible intrusions. It took four soldiers to get him into the emergency services boat and keep him subdued.

Meanwhile, two soldiers in the other vessel were busy squirting a yellow substance on the surface of the water. The shark, with the umbrella protruding from its bleeding mouth, was fighting for survival against six of its own species, attracted and excited by the scent of blood.

The liquid was supposed to be a potent repellant to drive away sharks, a goal that had eluded scientists since World War II Recent tests had found the repellant effective on three species; the Caribbean reef, black nose, and lemon sharks. It was called A-2 and was derived from extracts of dead sharks, based on long-noted observations by fishermen and scientists that the voracious fish stayed away when it smelled. a dead shark.

It seemed to have an effect on the six aquatic foragers for a short period, but as Lizzie and Yvonne left the barge, climbed aboard the speedboat and sped the short distance to shore, commotion continued as the tide pushed the carnage away.

The colonel's head throbbed. with doubt and confusion. The boat ferrying him to shore docked and his resolve to crush Lizzie wilted under the intense scrutiny of the press, fellow soldiers and guests. His shoulders drooped in languid resignation as he again stole a hurried glance at the two women glaring at him.

His eyes quickly took in the other female officers, stiff and proper in their uniforms. Then they settled on his wife-to-be, the politician's daughter, finally resting on one of the guests—a young woman with a ring in each eyebrow, one on her bottom lip and, quite repugnantly, a stud on her tongue.

They all paled into insignificance compared to Lizzie, yet he had shut his eyes to all-round class that sparkled with humility, dignity and character.

A wave of regret swept over him. He wanted to change course to go over to Lizzie and his mother to apologize. But two pairs of the strongest arms in the army resolutely restrained him.

Anger and haughtiness churned inside him as he regretfully glanced one more time in their direction. He was shocked to see Lizzie unobtrusively forming a circle with the thumb and index finger of her left hand and suggestively inserting the middle finger of her right. Once, twice, thrice.

The significance of what he saw as a belittling and disparaging gesture hit him like a ton of bricks, and he shut his eyes to the insult.

Then, as if operating to a prearranged signal, the chief of staff's voice boomed over the loud hailer. "Ladies and gentlemen, it's getting late and I know you've had more action that you could have anticipated. It's my pleasure to announce that the Women's Corps has more than justified its right to compete as a single unit. Congratulations.

"Mortar Platoon has again taken top honors. But the piece de resistance this afternoon is this piece of paper that I hold in my hand. It has the name of the soldier who has gained the most points in the all-round competition. That soldier will have the honor of representing the army at every official national function throughout her reign."

The respectful hush subsided into eerie silence. A collective intake of air suspended all movement of persons and things. And the commanding officer, a champion of suspense, let the moment linger.

Then, breathlessly, he continued, "Ladies and gentlemen, my mouth must have slipped when I said 'her' a few minutes ago because nowhere on this piece of paper is the word 'her' written. It must have been a Freudian slip. What it says here is simply this—Winner of the President's Medal for Best All-Round Soldier ... "

He let his words trail off and paused again for dramatic effect, but the pleading looks and a few hostile glares made him continue quickly. He raised his voice a few octaves and said clearly, "The winner is Officer Ruth Elizabeth Ferreira."

Amid the shock of the male soldiers and the bedlam among the women, Lizzie's heart was beating irregularly and performing an inappropriate gig. A few yards away, Colonel Benson felt a loosening in the hinges of his reasoning, like the loosening of the bowels after an overdose of laxatives. Unreasonably, he felt a palpable wave of animosity, as the imponderables rushed to him like a raging tornado with one message: "All is lost."

He heard Brigadier Sinclair offer an apology for him, saying, "Our intelligence officer, Colonel Benson, as last year's winner, should he the one handing the medal to Captain Ferreira, but a slight touch of sun stroke will prevent him from so doing. I'll humbly substitute for him."

Colonel Benson lashed out at the two soldiers, trying to break away and go to the podium to let everyone know nothing was wrong with him. How dare they let two ordinary soldiers put their hands on him? He fought silently and furiously, but almost six hundred pounds of pure muscle proved too much for him, and this time, he was moved to the dark recess of the medical truck and restrained.

His head began to throb violently, and tears clouded his eyes. He was painfully aware that the consequences of his questionable actions would soon manifest themselves in enforced leave, investigations and probably sanctions. His once-glorious future was suddenly uncertain and obviously tainted.

He watched from the shadows in helpless frustration as Lizzie stood proudly at attention, the evening's last rays crowning her in glory. A quick comparison of their respective positions told him what he had learned as a youn gster. Proverbs 29:23 said clearly, "Pride ends in a fall while humility brings honor."
So true, he reflected.

The activities were about to conclude when a cell phone was thrust into the chief of staff's hand. He listened, beckoned to Lizzie, and she damped the instrument to her ear. When the conversation ended, she was invited to the podium to speak

She responded without preamble. "I have been promoted on the spot to acting major by the president, who is the commander of the country's armed forces. I thank him, my fellow officers, soldiers and those who have helped to shape my life and career. But I reserve special thanks for Jesus Christ who has tested me severely over the past few weeks. My perspective and motivation may have been questionable, but nevertheless, I dedicate my success to the Women's Corps.

"I want to close by stating the obvious ... that the army is one of the finest institutions in this country. I urge every one of you to help keep it that way. No single person should be allowed to tarnish our image ... never. Remember what Colonel Benson always says: 'No unit is more valuable that the whole.' I enjoin—Let not one rotten banana spoil the whole bunch. Thank you all."

In the meantime, twilight had imposed its purple visage upon them. A shadow fell across the back end of the medical vehicle, and Robert was not surprised to see his mother. They stared at each other for a long time, then Yvonne asked, without anger, "Why, Robert, why?" He wanted to beg for forgiveness. Tell her how much he missed her love. Show remorse.

But his mind was like a bottomless void, and no such words came. Instead, in a weak voice, lacking conviction, he stammered, 'I'm … sorry … Mom."

Yvonne was torn between anger and pity; love and dismissal.

She shivered, knowing in her heart that she still loved her son.

But she needed time.

Twenty-something years were not twenty-something days.

Robert, meantime, pulled himself into the farthest corner to avoid facing her. His thoughts were jumbled. He visualized lovers embracing, people drinking and dancing, soldiers marching, and sons holding mothers' hands. But all he saw of himself was a ghostlike shadow in weird levitation. He hugged his head between his knees and retreated completely into his fetal hell.

And after a long while, his mother walked away, the silence echoing a challenge to her maternal instincts.

Two days after the swim, Lizzie submitted her resignation as a regular officer, opting to remain on the reserve list. She had things to do, and the regimen of military life would put a crimp in her operations.

Brigadier Sinclair pleaded with her, knowing her greatest ambition was to become the first female full colonel in the force. But it was to no avail. The challenge was now unimportant and irrelevant.

His parting words to her were "If you change your mind anytime, you're welcome back. The army needs you, Elizabeth, not the other way around."

Chapter 26

A Sister's Intuition

Her sixth sense prompted Margaret to travel to Georgetown. When she arrived at the hotel in Kitty where Lizzie and Yvonne usually stayed, she immediately noticed the change in her daughter's personality.

No longer was there the tension and edginess of the last few weeks. Instead, Lizzie radiated warmth and assuredness. She hugged her mother tightly for a long time, then, upon releasing her, regarded her with new eyes.

"Mom, have a seat on the patio. It's nice and breezy out here. What brought you to town?"

"Nothing really, I just wanted to see my daughter. Is anything wrong with that?"

"Not at all. In fact, I expected you at any time. The accuracy of your intuition over the years is still as sharp as ever."

"Everything all right?"

"Everything's fine. I'm now an ex-soldier. I'm thinking of entering the nunnery, and I want you to accompany me to see Father O'Hara. There, you have everything important in a nutshell."

"Well, last things first. I saw Father O'Hara earlier this morning and he wants us to go to the airport with him to meet his sister. She's arriving this afternoon. If you want, you can talk with him on the way up."

"That's wonderful, Mom."

"Now let's move on. I can understand you quitting the army, but what's this I'm hearing about nunnery. Girl, you'd better talk to Father about that."

Lizzie smiled knowingly. "It's always Father when a major decision is to be made, eh!"

"Child, talk to him. He'll give you the right advice."

"Mom, I'm not a child anymore. I've not been a child for a Jong time. I'm a woman. Stop treating me like a child."

"What are you two arguing about?" enquired a voice behind them. Both turned around, and Maggie, grateful for the timely interruption, asked quickly, "How are you, Yvonne?"

'I'm okay, thanks to your daughter. I now have a second chance at life, and I intend to give it a good shot. I have a little surprise for you. This is the last time you'll ever pay for a room at this hotel. I will own it in a month or so. Yesterday, I made the down payment and signed the agreement of sale. The owner is migrating to Canada, and Lizzie squeezed a reasonable bargain out of her."

Maggie shook her head in wonderment; Lizzie was born to help people. She hugged Yvonne then shook the lucky woman's hands, knowing that her transformation was now complete.

From abandoned, emaciated and scorned to accepted, healthy and confident.

All credit to Lizzie.

Yvonne was excitedly looking around. The anticipation of owning something as substantial as a hotel caused her hands to tremble and she quickly stuck them into her pants' pockets to hide the nervousness. But she continued to gaze at the well-groomed flowerbeds that spouted a rainbow of colors. The floral paradise was a far cry from the turmoil and disorder that had dominated her life for so many years.

∗   ∗   ∗

Lizzie, her mother Margaret, and Father O'Hara sat in the VIP Lounge at the Cheddi Jagan Airport, awaiting the arrival of the priest's sister on a British West Indian Airways flight from London. The acronym BWIA was sometimes jocularly used to read "But Will It Arrive?" Today, it had not only arrived, it had landed on time.

The clergyman was restless. He had not seen his sister in more than ten years and he eagerly looked forward to her visit. She was the essence of banter and good-natured teasing. A natural wit with a carefully concealed serious side.

He had made his sixth trip to the entrance before he saw her striding purposefully in the direction of the signs marked Public Health and Immigration. He put two fingers to his lips and the sound of a bird's chuckle rent the air. Immediately, she deposited two plastic bags on the hot tarmac to answer the call. She saw his welcome wave and hastened in his direction, almost running.

Brother and sister clutched each other, memories of all the good times they had in the past rushing to the fore. Reluctantly, they parted after what seemed an eternity, and Father O'Hara steered his sister to meet the two persons who had accompanied him.

The priest began the introductions. "Margaret, here is my only sister, Megan, who most times thinks she is my mother."

Maggie saw a big-boned woman dressed with the conservative flair of someone born or married into money. The fabric of her clothes spoke volumes—a long-sleeved cream silk blouse tucked into a chocolate brown pleated skirt that lingered at the top of her knees. A cardigan that suggested ermine, and soft chestnut-colored pumps, completed the look.

The affable Irish matron smothered a soft yet firm hand that belonged to a handsome middle-aged woman with a creaseless face. She looked much younger than the forty-four years her brother had mentioned, and the slight build and persistent smile added to the youthful appearance.

But it was her voice that gave the hint of maturity. It was firm and persuasive as it said, "I've heard so much about you. I'm extremely pleased to meet you. Please call me Maggie."

Megan wanted to tell her that she had also heard so much about mother and daughter that she felt she already knew them. Instead, she said amiably, 'I'm happy to meet you at last. My brother described you perfectly. And where are you hiding, Miss Lizzie?"

"Here I am, Aunt Megan."

Addressing senior women as aunt had been drilled into her from early childhood and it came naturally. Plus the fact that it was her mentor's sister made it more authentic.

Megan O'Shaunessy was a distinguished-looking woman in her fifties, with tinted gray hair, full and rounded face, dimples and smooth skin—as refined a lady as any. But at the sound of Lizzie's voice, her mouth fell open, and she performed an undignified ballet spin, almost certain that her ears were playing tricks. Lizzie was mouthing pleasantries, but the voice was that of her mother in London, who, up to the day before, had called to warn of the nice, but dangerous tropics.

Megan was facing a beautiful young woman, assured and confident, with the same graceful arch of eyebrow and slight slant of eye like her mother. She was saying, "It's amazing. You and Father Clement look like twins. I bet you are as quietly efficient as he is. I knew I would like you from the start and I hope you don't mind me calling you Aunt Megan."

Megan had recovered somewhat. She laughed easily before saying, "Your voice has an Irish lilt to it. For a moment, you sounded like our mother in her younger days. Don't you think so, Clem?"

Father O'Hara appeared to do a quick comparison then said, "A little, perhaps:"

Lizzie turned to Megan, whipping off a pair of sunglasses. Some people say I have Irish eyes. Do you think so?"

Green eyes mocked her, challenged her, claimed her. They had the same tint as her great grandmother's, and it was firmly believed that such eyes always skipped two generations.

There was no immediate reply to the question. Instead, there was an uneasy silence. Megan had trouble breathing and her head throbbed. She needed air. She needed the silence. A dozen scenarios danced and gyrated. Intuition beat a steady tattoo, and she felt the rhythm at the base of her brain. She was experiencing a strange sensation in her bones and the short hairs at the back of her neck stood up as if electrified.

She could hold her breath no longer. She exhaled and simultaneously collapsed into the soft embrace of the lounge's plush seating.

Lizzie was already at her side, a fan magically in her hand. "Stay still," she commanded. "It must be the heat."

For her part, Lizzie was a little unnerved by the look in Megan's eyes. One minute, there was a brief flicker of shock, the next it was replaced by a look of concern.

The critical examination seemed to continue and then the Irish woman's eyes closed in decision making. Whatever she had seen had startled her, and she looked like a very composed person.

The atmosphere in the usually relaxing lounge at that moment was unsettling and almost inflammable.

Meanwhile, Megan was determined to use discomfiture to mask her confusion until she could think dearly. She gave Lizzie her baggage claim stubs and, in her absence, enquired urgently about the young woman's biological father.

Maggie waved the enquiry away with an impatient movement of her hand, offering a token explanation. Father O'Hara was moved yet again to admonish her for the stubborn withholding of such vital information.

Megan continued to pry diplomatically, and it seemed to her that every uncovered detail only helped to reinforce the incongruity of the situation.

When Lizzie returned with the two oversized suitcases and they moved to depart, the full significance of the family tableau grabbed the visitor, and even in her obtuse confusion, a resigned smile breached the stern demeanor, and words became unnecessary at that point.

In the car, on the way to Georgetown, Megan quickly did some age calculations and threw in the component of human frailty. But one element was patently missing, and for the equation to be complete, she had to find the missing piece of the puzzle. For her, the most important variable was knowledge—whether her brother had a scintilla of suspicion or, as she had suspected, he was as naive as when they were teenagers back in Ireland,

Only one person held the key, and she desperately needed it to open a door to shed necessary light. She was not going to let another day slip by without answers, even if she had to squeeze it out of Maggie. She was a person horrified by disorder and loose ends.

But somehow, Megan felt she needed no confirmation. It was self-evident; right there in the moving vehicle, she thought, casting a furtive glance at Maggie, who seemed to be basking in the intimacy of the two people in the front seats, the priest behind the wheel. Though Maggie's hands moved expertly, knitting some kind of lace doily for a table, and though her eyes were downcast, Megan saw, reflected in the fixed smile, absolute love and satisfaction as the pair up front continued to bond effortlessly. Without the collar, they could easily pass for father and daughter.

It was not too long after they reached the neat, brightly lit hotel in Kitty, with its lovely flower garden and inviting patio, that a golden opportunity presented itself. Lizzie had an itinerary, but she was enquiring whether Megan wanted to soak up the rural hospitality of Mabaruma at an early stage of her visit or at a later date.

"How soon can we leave?" Megan asked, almost breathlessly.

"Tomorrow morning if you wish," Lizzie answered easily.

"Then tomorrow it is. I want to see where my brother had his first assignment, although his numerous letters about the geography and some special people were quite explicit."

Megan looked into the three pairs of eyes focused on her, but only one had a fixed intensity, probing and searching for meaning in what she had just said. She stared back, and with unspoken clarity, a gauntlet had been thrown down. It was easy for Maggie to interpret it. The look said loudly, *no more evasion. Time to talk to me.*

A specially chartered aircraft took them next morning into Mabaruma, and within an hour, they were settled in Maggie's house, drinking coconut water and gorging themselves on a variety of fruits: bananas, cherries, mangoes, pears, oranges and papaws.

As soon as Megan saw the canoe by the riverside, she turned to Maggie and asked, "Can you take me out for a quick ride. I've never been on a river this big."

Maggie was no fool. Postponement of the inevitable would solve nothing. Megan wanted to talk, and now was as good a time as any.

"We can go now and leave Father and Lizzie to jump-start preparations for lunch. They both have the expertise."

Megan had a folksy personality, unpretentious and sociable. She was letting it work at full throttle as they paddled upstream.

Maggie knew this was the calm before the storm, the placatory pat before the bludgeoned swing. As sure as night follows day, the hammer would descend on the anvil.

Although she was expecting some sort of inquisition, she was unprepared when the pertinent question was posed.

Megan was saying, "This part of the world must be God's paradise. Everything is so perfect. So how did it happen, Margaret?"

Like a boxer recoiling from a blow, Maggie's head jerked back and the paddle slipped from her grasp, falling onto the bottom of the small boat.

The sun beat down on her exposed head, but she was unaware of it.

The casual query had swung her back almost twenty-eight years.

She thought for a long time, and Megan patiently waited. She contemplated whether to bluff her way out or tell the truth. Each alternative carried a heavyweight.

She continued to stare ahead, but neither the rippling of the tide nor the murmuring of the wind offered any solution. Instead, their combined sounds came across as conspiratorial whispering.

Suddenly, memory came floating back on a river of atonement, and without fuss or trappings, she told it all during an uninterrupted monologue that lasted almost an hour.

On shore, Lizzie and the priest had finished cutting up greens, slicing meat and fish, and baking cassava bread. A jug of sorrel drink, the contents already chilled, was nestling in the small creek running at the back of the house.

Lizzie asked worriedly, "What could they be talking about so long? Do you think there is any kind of friction?"

"Hold up, Lizzie, hold up. When you reach their age, you will operate the same way. My guess is that Megan is grilling your mother about me since we have known each other from the time I came to Guyana. My sister has always played the mother to everyone because she has no children of her own, despite being married for many years."

Lizzie still had her misgivings as she looked out the window again. At one time, they had been facing each other at opposite ends of the canoe; now they were huddled together.

Whats going on? she wondered.

The next time she looked, they were walking up the path from the river. They were bronze from the sun, but the strain and uneasiness Lizzie had observed earlier were gone. There was now a kind of buoyancy, an animation. Something had passed between the two women—an acceptance, a truce, an understanding, whether territorial or familial.

Their hands brushed each other's as they walked, their eyes made regular contact, and when the big Irish woman flashed the peace and love sign, Maggie gave the thumbs up.

"What were you guys doing out there so long? What could you have been talking about so long?" Lizzie asked tentatively.

The priest's sister answered right away.

"Ah, Lizzie girl, age has its privileges and its setbacks. We had a lot of ground to cover. I wanted to know everything about my brother's life in these parts and I also wanted to know everything about you. From the time I saw you and heard you call me Aunt Megan at the airport, I knew I would want to hear those words over and over again. I needed to know more about you."

Father O'Hara stepped forward. "What about me? Don't you want to hear it from the horse's mouth?"

Megan said, "Don't worry; tonight is our date to talk. I understand there will be a full moon. We'll talk like we used to do in the hills when we were kids."

"All right, I can wait. By the way, Maggie, we left the fish to be curried. That's your specialty."

A sumptuous lunch was later followed by a special seafood

dinner of shark fin soup, baked fish, Creole shrimp, crabs and squids. Those delicacies were washed down with "Congo Pump" tea, long touted by the locals as the antidote for high blood pressure and kidney troubles.

Afterwards, Maggie and Lizzie sang along with music from a portable, battery-operated tape deck while big sister and brother strolled along the river's edge and mounted a hillock where they sat and talked.

"Does Maggie remind you of your Patricia of long ago?»

"Yes, she does."

"Is that why you pour so much of your love into her daughter?"

"Is it that obvious"

"Yes. And the mother, did you ever have feelings for her?"

"Strange question, Megan. You know priests are not supposed to have those kinds of feelings. But you have always been perceptive, and you know we have never kept secrets from each other,"

Father O'Hara paused reflectively then continued, "For the first six months, she drove me crazy. Not flirting. Just throwing off the shackles she had put on herself when her parents drowned. She was fresh; lively and exceptionally bright. She challenged me in every way and I responded by channeling her energies in the right direction. She, in turn, blossomed to her full potential."

"Do you have any idea who Lizzie's father is?"

"None whatsoever. After I left here for a six-month retreat, Margaret went to work at Omai Gold Mines. It seems she got pregnant right away because Lizzie was born approximately nine months later. She refuses to discuss the matter even with her daughter. I have spoken to her many times, but to no avail. Maybe you can talk to her. Lizzie deserves to know."

"Does it affect the girl?"

"Not really. I believe the time we spend together, the lessons and the ongoing teachings fill the void. Don't forget, she is essentially my goddaughter, and we work well together."

Megan switched the line of questioning and was soon reassured that her brother was as firmly committed to his church and God as any other priest.

She looked intently at him. It was a look gravid with concern. This holy man, who had saved so many souls with his natural charismatic fervor, had to be himself saved. His life could not be ripped away from convention, nor his purpose altered.

In Ireland, the wise old ones held the belief that "what a person does not know does not hurt him/her." This was as good an example as any. Maggie had carried a weighty baton for so many years, and now, it was Megan's turn to continue the relay.

As the moon emerged from behind a slow-moving cloud, Megan mentally put herself into the correct lane, figuratively stretched her arm behind her body to prepare for the baton pass. It went smoothly.

A few minutes later, when she and her brother walked hand in hand back to Maggie's house, the die had been cast.

Mora Mission was wide awake with the shrill sounds of colorful birds chattering noisily as they hopped from tree to tree. But all three persons in the house overslept into the bright morning.

Lizzie was the first to open her eyes, and immediately, she began to rouse the others with pillow thumps and some tickling. She stood directly in front of Megan, saying, with a smile, "Time for our talk. Let's go down to the creek. Many stories have been told while enjoying an invigorating bath."

The advantage of rapping with Maggie and her brother made it easy for her discourse with Lizzie, as uncomplicated a human being as she had ever met.

The parochial and less-sophisticated aspects of rural upbringing hung heavy in the air as they splashed each other like others sharing the creek at that time of the day.

Megan marveled at the forces of nature that could pluck two women among the socially disadvantaged and catapult them beyond the pale of ordinariness. The mother, Margaret, had been an instant magnet because she reminded the priest of his exiguous sweetheart. He had accepted the challenge to remould her aimless life and point her in a positive direction. His love for Patricia was actually enacted through Maggie, and the brilliant academic results were just reward for perseverance.

Lizzie began to sing a Creole song and she encouraged Megan to join in. It was titled "Fowl Cock Ah Crow 'Fore Day Morning," and though the Irish woman did not know the suggestive lyrics, she joined in the refrain.

Megan devoured Lizzie with her eyes. She saw how her birth had fulfilled the only void in her brother's life. She was the child he could never have and so he claimed her as a surrogate. When Maggie failed to object to his overt influence, he shaped her as he would have shaped his own daughter.

The picture was complete for Megan. There was no need to tread on further dangerous ground. So she threw out a few inane questions and took note of the intelligent answers.

Right then, she knew for sure that she had to prevent any crossfire of moral conflict from affecting the lives of the entangled trio. If not, the snowball effect would cause irreparable damage to many people and the church.

For a full month, Megan inhaled the invigorating purity of the Essequibo region, with its wide expanse of water and land. At first, she saw the idyllic rural setting as "fantastic," but as the days moved on, the word seemed inadequate to describe the area's magnificence. For her, such a common description fell woefully short of expressing the essence of nature's generosity.

By the time she was ready to return home, the grandeur of Guyana had claimed her soul, and the word she settled on was "divine."

Chapter 27

Searching for Answer

Lizzie was drowning in a whirlpool of murky waters, the sound of a nearby waterfall shutting out her screams for help. On the far shore, a demon commanded the turbulence to welcome her into its vortex:. She had swallowed what seemed like a gallon of water, and her lungs were stretched to the max.

The lungs, when functioning normally, absorb oxygen from the air to pass to the blood and expel carbon dioxide, which is returned to the air. This time, however, the process seemed to be in reverse gear.

She slipped below the surface once, twice, then surrendered to the depths. Highlights of her life flashed before her. Then the camera shut with decisive finality and harp-playing angels joined in song.

"Wake up, Sister Elizabeth, wake up," an ethereal voice said through a fog of clouds.

But she was already in heaven. Would she have to wait long at the pearly gates? How would she be judged?

She shouted and struggled against pressure on her arms and body. As a fighter, she refused to lie down and die. On the other hand, she was too experienced a warrior of Amerindian heritage not to know when a tactical maneuver was in order.

She stopped struggling to search for an appropriate appeal.

And it came with lightning swiftness.

> Oh Lord, you alone are my hope;
> I've trusted you from childhood.
> -Psalm 71:5.

"Sister, sister, you're having another nightmare. Wake up."

The tone signaled a growing impatience with Lizzie's continuous heaven-earth battles, and the nun slapped her into consciousness.

"Where ... where am I?" she asked groggily.

"Don't you remember? You're in the convent."

Her face was drained of color, her now-ashen countenance frozen in uncertainty.

Clearly concerned, an elderly nun, who resembled Mother Theresa, cautiously interjected, "You came all by yourself with a letter from Father O'Hara. Are you having a change of heart?"

It took her only a second to utter "no." A beatific smile seemed to enhance the translucent halo around her pretty face, and the sisters knew that the worst had passed.

Lizzie's smile was not only because Jeremiah 29: 13 came into her head-"You shall find me when you seek me, if you search for me in earnest." It was because she remembered her wicked school friend Gabrielle warning her that if she ever became a nun, she would get "none."

She must remember to say a special prayer for such lurid ruminations. Thoughts like those were enough to endanger the ozone layer.

She had made a sudden dramatic decision to enter the Catholic convent in Georgetown to undergo training as a lay nun. She had confided in Father O'Hara, and as usual he sat her down before addressing her in his own peculiar, non-judgmental tone.

"Elizabeth, at the risk of sounding pedantic and patronizing, let me remind you of something you told me when you were just eleven years old. You said you were prepared to try every single profession until you found the one you could bond with. A vocation is also a profession, so I say continue to search for your horizon.

"It would be my dream to have you next to me preaching the word of God, but would it be your ultimate calling? I would not be true to my Lord and Savior if I attempted to influence your decision. Go with your gut feeling."

The vigorous cracking of his knuckles betrayed his acute concentration and nervousness, an annoying gesture that was yet to become a habit. It was like the awkward moments when the precocious daughter asks the father to explain what sex is all about.

Lizzie loved and respected the priest, the closest person to a father she had ever had, and so she lightened the somber mood with a playful poke in the ribs, followed by a rueful comment. "You're no help, whatsoever."

With the letter of introduction, she had gone to the convent and was immediately accepted. She was advised that she would have to go through a mentally rigorous three-month period of training to "test the commitment of the applicant."

It was at her new home that she seemed to succumb to a triad of ills that sparked anxiety and concern. An uncontrollable desire for sleep, which seemed to prompt demons to stalk her in her dreams, took control of a body pushed to its limit and a mind distorted. She tossed, turned, and talked in her sleep, and the sisters were forced to intervene whenever the periods were protracted.

A week after Lizzie entered the convent, she began to have serious misgivings and, every night afterwards, was tormented by questions and doubts.

One night into her third week, she stood at a top floor window, her mind a cyclone of fractured thoughts and emotions. She gazed in the distance, absently noting the upper sections of St. George's Cathedral, the beautiful Gothic building, reputedly the tallest wooden structure in the world.

Just beyond that lay Stabroek Market, built by the Dutch, with its huge four-faced dock, and looking like they were almost touching were City Hall and the magistrate's court.

Below, traffic flowed nonstop on streets that had parapets alive with a profusion of flowering plants and imposing trees. Lizzie agreed with those who called her country's capital "the Garden City of the Caribbean."

A sharp mosquito bite gained her attention, and she immediately shook off her musings. She reminded herself that she had to make a decision quickly, whether or not she really wanted to be a nun.

During her short stay, she had keenly observed the eager sisters bustling here and there in their lusterless raiment, all bound by their oath of poverty, obedience and chastity. She had knelt with them for hours on end, gripping rosary beads and silently reciting familiar prayers. And she had taken her turn serving lunch and dinner to the destitute people who daily thronged the outdoor canteen.

Yet she kept asking herself over and over again, Is this the life you want to embrace the rest of your days? Are these the deeds you want to perform forever?

Lizzie paced the room past midnight, sorting through the dust and debris of doubts and uncertainty, dashed hopes and dreams, disaster and lies. When the alarm dock in her head went off at six in the morning, one thing had become dear and obvious—she lacked the optimal commitment to become a nun.

She would prefer to help others in a different way. She wanted to seek new avenues to assist the countless unfortunate women who were abused every day. In fact, she was going to engineer a gale force to hasten a kind of feminist movement, teaching women to fight back mentally and physically.

She had made up her mind that she didn't want to be just another "bright prospect" within the established juggernaut that was the defence force. Neither did she want to be hamstrung by the convent's conventions.

She had to be able to operate in an unfettered manner, crisscrossing delicate boundaries and making value judgments that might not stand the scrutiny of the squeamish.

She wanted to investigate cases, decipher perplexing scenarios, trace missing people, piece together human puzzles, and correct situations. To do those and more, one had to have ... She searched for a word, other than "balls" that could effectively capture the same import, but could find none. So be it! She would somehow have to develop those appendages.

Next morning, she packed and was waiting when the mother superior emerged from her quarters. Without a word, Lizzie handed her an envelope that contained a letter of withdrawal and a check-a donation of $500,000.

The senior sister read the letter quickly but took time to absorb and fully appreciate the six figures penned in perfect handwriting. Her hands shook as she replaced the two items into the envelope.

Without realizing it, she had adopted a ruminative pose, as if pondering something cataclysmic. Then after a contemplative moment, she hugged Lizzie with surprising strength.

"You're a good girl, Liz, but you're not meant for the convent. A tiger should never be tied with a piece of string. But come unto the altar. You will lead us in prayer one last time; then be on your way. And remember to keep in touch."

An hour later, Lizzie was at peace with herself. Only one task remained.

And the time to complete it had come.

She hailed a taxi and directed the driver to the Kitty Sea Wall.

The wind was strong, almost physical, as she slowly made her way along the jetty, which impudently jutted into the ocean.

Small hard pellets of rain beat against everything and everybody in the way.

With cold, trembling fingers, she slipped Roger's ring off and let it fall into the sand below her feet, mingling with the other debris that would soon be gone with the tide.

She vigorously brushed her hands together, but there was neither sand nor sweat on them. The symbolic gesture, however, seemed to lift a weight from her body; and she felt buoyant as she walked back to the cab.

The past was now forgotten.

The man she had seen as her arch-enemy was forgiven.

Her heart was now full of love for the Almighty, who had tested her and found her not wanting.

✳   ✳   ✳

Traffic was heavy; and she had to wait a few minutes to cross the roadway. She got the opportunity when a small ambulance with flashing Lights stopped and the bespectacled driver courteously gave her the go-ahead signal. As she crossed, she could distinctly hear hysterical Laughter and incoherent rambling exploding through the wafer-thin panels, and she silently uttered a prayer for the tormented soul within.

Little did she know that the patient being transported was Robert Boatswain, also known as Colonel Roger Benson.

The colonel's mental condition had grown progressively worse. Violent mood swings occurred frequently; and he was given to frightening outbursts that could be heard outside the army compound.

Two of the country's best psychiatrists had been summoned, but they remained baffled. To make matters worse, the colonel was an uncooperative patient—mute at times, then suddenly repeating a litany about the role of women in the home and society. The only consistent action was the slamming of his right hand into his left palm.

The doctors finally diagnosed a rare kind of schizophrenia and ordered seclusion and a twenty-four-hour watch. They were aware that symptoms suffered by certain people could possibly escalate in both frequency and intensity over a short period.

But they were unaware that the officer had a morbid fear of being confined for any period at all.

The resulting claustrophobia eroded whatever was left of his senses, and he slipped unerringly towards the precipice of no return.

Regretfully, the doctors signed committal papers to the only mental institution in Guyana, and for what surely looked like the last time, the colonel was driven through the gates of his beloved army headquarters strapped in a straitjacket, shouting obscenities and bewailing the conspiracy to replace him with a female colonel.

Even in his muddled state—and though there were no windows in the rear section where he lay, he knew with certainty where he was going and how long the trip to the institution in Berbice would take. After all, an intelligence officer had to know those things.

The ambulance headed up the east coast road after the driver stopped to allow the beautiful young woman to use the crosswalk and enter a taxi. He could not help admiring her military bearing and assuredness, as if she were in full control of everything around her.

Unlike the madman he was transporting.

He shook his head and wondered about the bewildering paradoxes in Life.

⋆ ⋆ ⋆

The building housing the mental hospital was in an advanced state of disrepair, but the driver noticed that the door was sturdy and made of durable greenheart wood. He pressed a buzzer, and an electronic lock opened with a muffled dick.

"Good morning. I have a new patient for you. Can I borrow a gurney? He's in a tight suit."

Nurse Delores signaled for him to follow an orderly who was lounging against a wall, obese and red-eyed, suggesting a regular diet of cholesterol-laden food and alcohol.

The driver looked around. Inside, the cracked unpainted walls offered little in the form of comfort, in essence, complementing the foreboding facade, He smiled at a tired-looking old lady. She forced a grin, but its effect barely registered on a wrinkled face that had pendulous folds of skin hanging everywhere. Her hands and arms were withered skin and prominent bone.

"Good morning," he stammered.

The woman was not in a mood for repartee. "What's good about the morning, you son of a bitch?"

The driver's pair of spectacles almost fell off.

The new patient was being wheeled in. Nurse Dolores looked at a chart handed her and casually glanced at his face. Their eyes met briefly without any sign of recognition.

Two orderlies unhooked the straitjacket and the patient immediately began rubbing his eyes. The throbbing in his head continued.

His brain was a playground of conflict with the expression on his face bouncing back and forth between acceptance and disbelief He caught himself analyzing his situation and quickly shelved the amateur psychology.

"Roger Orville Benson? He resembles somebody I knew."

He heard the nurse speaking, as if to herself, and wondered if she was another irritating busybody. But when he turned in her direction and saw the pained and incredulous expression on her face, he knew she had made some kind of connection.

"Can I have some water?" he asked politely.

"Are you Yvonne Boatswain's son, Robert?" she demanded, ignoring the request.

"I don't know any Yvonne Boatswain. I want some water now."

The lie was plainly written on his face and Nurse Delores responded with an angry retort: "Water, water. You still think you're in the army giving orders? Well, in here, we give the orders, and you'd better fall in line quickly."

The little scene had brought back the pain with intensity and he pondered how long it would be before his head imploded with all that was going on up there. He let loose a barrage of colorful expletives, advising all the nurses to copulate with themselves.

"You're a dog. You're going to pay dearly for what you did to your mother," predicted Delores.

The nurse's words hit home like a sucker punch to the solar plexus.

Racking pain followed. His jaw quivered. Lips fibrillated.

He lay down quietly.

Then suddenly, without fanfare, the room exploded into silence.

With indifference, Nurse Delores issued a curt order to the orderly.

"Take him to the same room that Yvonne occupied, and make sure it is always kept locked."

"Yes, ma'am. Right away; ma'am," said the beefy orderly, winking in a caricature of compliance and affecting an exaggerated salute.

If the colonel were in control of his mental faculties, he would surely have shouted disapproval at the improperly executed military action.

But he was no longer in control of anything, not even his mind, which had gone completely blank.

Right then, Robert/Roger was being wheeled away, locked tightly in a catatonic prison.

The irony was not lost on his soul.

Epilogue

Four women sat around an oblong purple-heart table littered with torn envelopes, sheets of typewritten paper, facsimiles, and e-mail printouts. All the envelopes were addressed to The Committee, Women Against Abuse, P.O. Box 289742, Georgetown, Guyana.

The group was essentially the embryo of a new movement committed to the altruistic goals of helping to alleviate the suffering of women.

"This is an emergency meeting. Let's cut to the chase," said the woman at the head of the table. The measured, authoritative instruction swept across the room almost as if she had shouted.

At the other end, a buxom woman with dimples in both cheeks, shuffled a sheaf of papers. She was the secretary, and she spoke in an unhurried monotone.

"The most urgent letter is from a mother in Berbice. She says her daughter died under mysterious circumstances and she suspects her son-in-law had something to do with it. She sent a check for $200,000 and wants us to start discreet investigations, pronto. Two other letters demand attention also. One concerns the persistent sexual abuse of a ten-year-old schoolgirl by her stepfather. The other is the deliberate scalding of a woman's hand by her reputed husband, who accused her of stealing money from his pants' pockets."

The treasurer, an amiable, large woman in army fatigues, interjected, "We can put three teams in the field right away. We have the investigative force, and finance is not a problem. On a more personal note, Rainbow says the family has moved out of Yvonne's house and a carpenter and painter are already at work. We will soon be able use the premises as our Berbice headquarters."

The woman at the head of the table took off her dark glasses.

Emerald green eyes surveyed the room and its occupants. Without preamble, she said, "We begin work tomorrow. I'll take the murder case. Yolande, you handle the scalding issue, and Yvonne the sex assault is yours. Mother Turpin will coordinate all activities and approve all spending. All three cars are serviced. and ready for use."

*   *   *

Lizzie sat at the bar of a nightclub on Sheriff Street—the boulevard that never sleeps—sipping a glass of ginger ale. She was dressed in a tight leather two-piece outfit that left little to the imagination. She had been sitting there less than twenty minutes, and she had had to refuse six offers of "a drink" and numerous entreaties to dance.

It was not that she didn't like dancing. She loved the waltz and the foxtrot, and recently; she had picked up on the electric slide. Father O'Hara had taught her to dance, as he had everything else.

She, however, frowned on the provocative gyrations and suggestive movements accompanying some reggae and soca, especially the lewd "back ball," where a woman proffered her butt, and a man, sometimes a complete stranger, gleefully prodded his crotch to enjoin.

It was a similar kind of display she was forced to watch as the man she had been following for three days pranced and flounced with wild abandon on a wooden stage. His companion, a saucy "Dougla," perfectly blending the African and Indian diasporas, gave as good as she got, animated face shiny with beads of perspiration. She was attractive, petite and lithe. Even when she was motionless, she exuded a sensual aura, an animal magnetism.

When the disc jockey effected a change in pace, the two dancers were wrapped together for a dozen consecutive slow tunes. As the saying went, "Not even a breeze could pass between them."

Lizzie studied the face of Kiskadee Latchman, a supposedly grieving husband who had tearfully buried his wife of four years just a mere few weeks ago. Larchman had inherited an estate worth more than $50 million, and he stood to benefit from a lucrative insurance policy.

She had seen enough for that night. His callousness and lust for the eager young university student fitted the profile of someone who would quickly tire of a plain, boring housewife when there were so many appealing alternatives out there. Whether he would go as far as poisoning his wife was another matter.

Tomorrow, she would don the nun's habit that remained among her belongings. A trip to the University of Guyana campus, where

Latchman had studied chemistry and biology; might provide some answers.

She smiled as she remembered Father O'Hara once saying that even a beast would listen to a priest once he wore his collar. And he had added confidentially, "Especially if it were a Catholic cleric."

She eased off the stool and finished her drink, her eyes drawn to the vacant seat, the flattened vinyl cushion struggling to resile, The eerie sound was barely audible, yet it seemed like an ominous lamentation.

She bubbled with confidence. Latchman would not know what hit him when irrefutable evidence was presented. As for the stepfather and the husband, they would both get a taste of their own medicine before being handed over for due process. Quid pro quo.

It was her dream to create a special women's order—ambiguous in nature and efficient in execution. Men had all kinds of societies and lodges, and their secret ways were never questioned. Why not women?

Life was full of deadbeats, the majority of them men who did not have an iota of compassion for their victims, mostly women. It was so unfair.

Soon, lessons would be taught, and women would be respected. And although it was going to take time, it was the one thing that wasn't in short supply.

The sparkle and gas in the ginger ale had her on a high. She was looking forward to the case files piling up as mysteries beckoned to be solved.

She would immerse herself in them. It was what she would live for.

Look out for Godfrey Wray's next novel:

ISIS TERROR